THE TOWER ROOM

The dust lay over everything, undisturbed for countless years. By the flickering candlelight Susan saw her fingers blacken with grime as she lifted the trunk lid. She pulled out a crumbling piece of paper and peered at it, trying to comprehend its strange message.

Engrossed, she barely heard the creaking of the door—then heard it too late as the door slammed shut. There followed the clicking of the lock, and the muffled sound of mocking laughter swiftly fading.

Even as Susan pounded with desperate fists at the massive oaken door, she knew it was futile . . . as everything was futile now. There was no one to come to her aid . . . no means she could find to escape . . . nothing to do but wait for her candle to burn out and for darkness and dust to claim her as their own. . . .

Further Titles by Jennifer Wilde from Severn House

STRANGER BY THE LAKE

Jennifer Wilde

This title first published in Great Britain 1993 by
SEVERN HOUSE PUBLISHERS LTD of
9–15 High Street, Sutton, Surrey SM1 1DF.
First published in hardcover format in the U.S.A. 1993 by
SEVERN HOUSE PUBLISHERS INC., of
475 Fifth Avenue, New York, NY 10017.
Originally published in paperback format in the USA only
under the pseudonym Beatrice Parker.

British Library Cataloguing in Publication Data
Wilde, Jennifer
  Stranger by the Lake
  I. Title
  813.54 [F]

  ISBN 0-7278-4526-8

Typeset by Hewer Text Composition Services, Edinburgh.
Printed and bound in Great Britain by
Redwood Books, Trowbridge, Wiltshire.

CHAPTER ONE

It was pouring down rain when I got off the train, and there was no one to meet me at the station. I wasn't at all surprised. Aunt Agatha was always vague about time-tables and dates, and she had probably forgotten that I was to arrive in Gordonville this evening. It was just as well, as I was drenched, my clothes soaked and my hair a mass of limp wet tendrils. It had been over three years since I had seen my aunt, and I didn't relish the idea of our reunion taking place when I looked like a drowned cat. I would stay at the inn tonight and take a taxi to Gordonwood in the morning.

The station was deserted. It was never bustling, even on the busiest days. Gordonville was a small village over two hundred miles from London, one of those quaint, rustic little communities full of eccentrics and very little industry. Historians revered it as the birthplace of Sir Robert Gordon, the explorer and linguist who had been one of the most flamboyant and fascinating men of the Victorian age. Aunt Agatha had married his grandson. A widow now, she lived in the vast old house the first Sir Robert had purchased in 1790. Although I had been there only once before, I remembered the house vividly. It reeked of the history of those colorful individuals who had lived there in the past and was filled with curios and bizarre artifacts Sir Robert had brought back from his many explorations. I was eager to explore it again, but that could wait till morning. At the moment I was far more eager to get into some dry clothes.

Remembering that the local inn was just down the street from the train station, I hurried toward it, gripping a suitcase in each hand and holding my head down. The rain poured mercilessly, splattering noisily on the side-

walks. I kicked open the door of the inn and rushed into
the lobby, dropping my luggage and shaking myself briskly. The young man behind the desk jumped up in alarm,
his face pale. He looked as though he expected me to
pull a gun and start firing away. I smiled reassuringly,
but that didn't seem to help much.

"Where did *you* come from?" he asked shakily.

"The train station."

"In *this* downpour?"

"There was no one to meet me," I explained, "and
no taxis were available. You *do* have taxis in Gordonville, don't you? I'm going to need one in the morning."

"There's no regular taxi service, if that's what you
mean. I have an old Chevrolet parked out back. Anyone
needs a lift, they give me a call."

"Marvelous. Now, about a room—"

"How long were you planning to stay?"

"Just the night. If it's not too much trouble," I added,
somewhat irritably.

He grinned and cocked his head to one side. He was a
handsome lad in his early twenties with shaggy dark
blond hair and marvelous brown eyes. I regretted my
peevishness immediately. He handed me a pen and asked
me to sign the register, and after I had done so he picked
up my bags and led the way up a flight of broad wooden
stairs. I smoothed my hair back, wondering just how
much damage the rain had done.

"Don't get many visitors this time of year," he said
over his shoulder. "In fact, we don't get many visitors at
all. Gordonville isn't exactly a blooming metropolis."

"I've noticed that."

"Come here often?"

"I've only been here once, and I was twelve years old
at the time. My aunt lives here. She's Lady Agatha Gordon.
I'm going to be staying at Gordonwood."

We were walking down the hall. He stopped to turn
and look at me, a curious expression on his face. His
dark brown eyes were filled with suspicion and something
almost like fear. I was puzzled.

"Is something wrong?" I asked.

"No—uh—here's your room. It's the nicest we've got."

He led me inside and set the bags down beside the

door. He was studying me now as though I were some exotic creature from another land. All his cheerfulness was gone, and his mouth was tight. He looked resentful, and worried. I shook my head, certain that my imagination was working overtime. I took a few coins from my purse and offered them to him.

"No tips," he said gruffly.

"I see. Do you have room service? I'm going to want something to eat after I've changed."

"We've got a restaurant downstairs," he said. "It's the best in town. Keeps us going when the rooms remain empty." He paused, giving me a long, searching stare. "My name's Charlie Grayson," he said abruptly. "I own this inn. My folks left it to me. I don't like trouble."

"Few of us do," I said, more puzzled than ever. "Thank you, Charlie. The room's divine."

He left, closing the door behind him. I didn't know whether to go into shock or burst into laughter. Charlie Grayson was a most peculiar fellow, I thought, but then peculiar fellows were not uncommon in towns like Gordonville. Isolated, inbred, out of step with the more modern communities, places like this bred eccentrics. People were less involved with the major issues of the day, and they had more time to develop their idiosyncrasies. I thought it was charming, far more interesting than the mass conformity found in the major cities.

I put these thoughts out of my mind and surveyed the room. It was delightful, if somewhat shabby. The wallpaper was ivory with a border of blue and green flowers, and the carpet was green, the nap worn with age. There was a massive brass bed with a quilted blue counterpane, and a white milkglass vase on the dresser held a bouquet of white and yellow roses, their petals drooping sadly. Most pleasing of all was the gray marble fireplace with logs and paper fan all ready to be lighted. I took a match from the container on the mantel and had a pleasant fire glowing in a matter of minutes.

The bathroom adjoining was done in ancient jade green tiles, and the plumbing was prehistoric, but that didn't matter. It worked, although there were some rather ominous noises in the pipes. I took a long soaking bath, reveling in the hot water and the fragrant soap lather, and when I stepped back into the room half an hour later I felt like a new person. The fatigue of the long day's train ride was gone, and I felt gloriously indolent. It was nice to be away from London for a while, nice to have no more deadlines to meet, no more galley proofs to correct.

The new book was finished, and my publisher was satisfied. In a few months my fans would have another Susan Marlow novel to read, and my critics would have yet another excuse to exercise their wits and denounce such insubstantial fare. My books were light mysteries, with an emphasis on romance. They were great fun to write and, evidently, great fun to read, for they sold nicely, if not quite as briskly as I would have preferred. While they didn't bring great wealth, they enabled me to lead a comfortable life, and in between books I could travel and feel wonderfully independent. There had been several years of secretarial work before the first book sold, and I was blissfully thankful to be free of that form of slavery at last.

The fire was crackling merrily now, tiny orange flames licking at the charred logs, and the room was snug and warm and very inviting. I could hear the rain clattering on the roof, but it was a pleasant sound now that I was no longer out in it. I felt unreasonably happy as I took a dress out of my suitcase and laid it out. I was twenty-five years old and on my own. I was going to spend a week or so with my aunt and then I intended to throw caution to the winds and have two outrageously expensive weeks in Majorca. My ever-tottering budget could scarcely tolerate such extravagance, yet I was going to indulge myself just the same. Perhaps I could persuade Aunt Agatha to join me on the trip. She was a vivacious creature, full of fun and frolic, with the ability to make even the most tiresome task seem like a lark. She would be a marvelous traveling companion, and it would do her good to get away from Gordonwood for a spell.

I hummed to myself as I put on the dress. It was blue, with a snugly fitting waist and a short, full-gathered skirt that swirled about my knees. It showed my healthy figure off to advantage, and as I tugged at the waistband I wondered if that figure was growing a bit too healthy. I frequently despaired at my robust, well-rounded body. Not that I was plump, mind you, but this was the day of thin, wraithlike models, and I would always have a full-blown figure, no matter how I starved myself. I stepped over to the mirror for the first time, bracing myself to see just how much damage the rain had done to my hair.

It was an unnerving sight. No wonder Charlie Grayson had acted in such a peculiar manner. My hair looked as though I spent the majority of my time on the moors, stirring a cauldron. It was dry now, fortunately, but tangled and matted in a coiffure that would have done justice to Medusa in her heyday. Grabbing a brush from my bag, I launched an attack on the dark brown mats, brushing furiously for a good ten minutes. It finally fell in long lustrous waves to my shoulders and gleamed with golden chestnut highlights. I sighed, satisfied at last with the reflection.

My face was attractive, if not remarkably so. I had a clear complexion, high cheekbones, and a straight nose. My lips were full, naturally pink, and my eyes were large, a deep violet-blue. I would never win any beauty awards, true, but my features were pleasant and friends said I had a clean-scrubbed, wholesome look. I didn't know whether to take that as a compliment or not. At least I wasn't plain, and I had enough natural coloring to keep the use of cosmetics to a bare minimum.

I left the room and went downstairs, feeling quite contented and wondering if I should call Aunt Agatha. If I did, she would insist I come on out to Gordonwood, and I wasn't going to go out in that rain again for anyone. I would simply wait until morning and surprise her. She had probably forgotten that I intended to come at all. Aunt Agatha was always bubbling over with enthusiasms, always involved with some madly improbable project, and she had little interest in mundane matters. That was part of her charm. I was enough like her to appreciate her distressing lack of concern for the boring realities of day-to-day existence.

Charlie Grayson was behind his desk, resting his chin in the palm of his hand. The light from the desk lamp burnished his dark blond hair and cast soft shadows over his handsome young face. He looked up when he heard

me coming down the stairs, and at first he didn't seem
to recognize me. He looked bewildered, and then he must
have realized that I was the same woman who had been
so wet and bedraggled an hour ago.

"You said there was a restaurant," I remarked pleasantly.

He nodded. "In back," he said, pointing to the archway that led off the main foyer.

"Thank you, Charlie."

"You're Susan Marlow?" he asked, glancing down at
the register I had signed earlier.

"That's right."

"Would you be the same Susan Marlow who writes
all those mysteries?"

"Right again. Don't tell me you *read* them?"

"Of course not," he said irritably, as though such a
thing would be unthinkable. "I just—wondered. You, uh,
you know a lot about mysteries, don't you? A lot about
plots?"

"Not really," I replied. "I have what the critics call a
fertile imagination, whatever that means."

Charlie looked up at me, his dark brown eyes intense. He seemed worried, and he seemed to be holding
something back. It was almost as though there was something he desperately wanted to tell me but didn't quite
dare to. Although he was only a couple of years my jun-
ior, he seemed painfully young and strangely vulnerable,
a little boy plagued with some major problem. He stirred
maternal instincts I hadn't even realized I had. I wanted
to stroke his cheek and tell him everything was all right,
he could confide in me.

"Still," he said hesitantly, "it'd be hard to fool you,
wouldn't it?"

"I shouldn't think so," I said lightly. "What do you
plan to do, pad my bill?"

He didn't deign to answer. He gave me a sullen look
and turned away to examine some papers on the desk,
quite plainly dismissing me. I stared at him, deeply puzzled, and then went on into the restaurant. Charlie Grayson had probably had a bad fall on his head as a child, I
decided, or perhaps he was just mildly insane. In any
event, I certainly didn't intend to let it bother me. I was

on holiday and strongly resolved to let nothing interfere
with my hard-earned days of lazy relaxation.

The restaurant was charming but, like my room,
shabby and a bit worn at the edges. The walls were
paneled in varnished golden oak, the ceiling had sturdy,
soot-blackened beams, and the floor was covered with
dark red linoleum. A fire burned lustily in the large
rough-stone fireplace, flames reflecting in bright copper
utensils that hung on the opposite wall behind the long
counter. Baskets of ivy and pots of rubber tree plants
added a vivid green touch. I sat down at one of the golden
oak tables, ignoring the snug, intimate brown leather
booths that ran along one wall.

The waiter was a thin teen-age boy with neatly
combed black hair, his white jacket crisp, his manner extremely polite. He took my order and vanished into the
kitchen through a swinging door behind the counter. It
was still pouring down rain outside, and that probably
explained the lack of customers. I was alone in the room,
and I enjoyed the sense of seclusion. After the hubbub
and uproar of London this morning and the rattling dis-
comfort of the train during the day, it was nice to hear
only the crackle of wood burning and the muted sound of
rain. I was glad now that I hadn't gone immediately to
Gordonwood. I would be relaxed and refreshed in the
morning and in much better shape to meet my aunt.

After a delicious meal of hot roast beef, gravy, tiny
new potatoes, and buttery green peas, I hesitated over
ordering dessert. The waiter brought a tray of glorious
little iced cakes and asked if I would like some with my
coffee. The temptation was too strong: I told him to put
two on my plate. I lingered over my coffee, reluctant to
leave the pleasant room. When the waiter finally brought
my bill, I paid it and left a generous tip, hoping he
wouldn't be as offended as Charlie had been when I tried
to tip him for lugging my bags up to the room.

It was nine thirty when I stepped back into the lobby.
That was early for me. In fact, midnight was merely the
shank of the evening as far as I was concerned. Ever since
my first book had sold and I no longer had to be in an
office bright and early in the morning, I had taken to
staying up until all hours and then sleeping wonderfully

late the next day. It wasn't really wicked indulgence. I did my writing at night, frequently working until two or three in the morning. It was quiet then, with no blaring noises to distract me. I had never been able to understand those people who leaped out of bed at the crack of dawn and then bustled about with frightening industry. The mere thought made me shudder.

Charlie wasn't behind his desk. The lobby was deserted and dim, the desk lamp and a light over the stairs offering the only illumination, dark shadows spreading over the walls. Restless and not quite ready to go back up to my room just yet, I decided to sit on the sofa for a while. It was in one corner, half hidden by rubber tree plants, and I could sit and watch the rain streaking down the front windows in slippery silver-gray patterns. I leaned back against the cushions, curling one leg under me and ignoring the smell of mothballs and worn velvet.

I don't know how long I had been sitting there when the front door was thrown open and the man came rushing in. A great gust of wind and rain blew in before he could slam it behind him. He stamped his feet and shook himself, water running in rivulets off his long black plastic raincoat. He was quite tall, with enormous shoulders, and I got an impression of strength and determination as he glanced around the lobby, obviously expecting someone to be waiting for him. A black hat slanting down over his forehead obscured most of his features, but I could see a strong jaw and a wide mouth. He scowled, the mouth turning down at the corners, then walked toward the staircase, emitting a curse under his breath.

He wasn't aware of my presence. I could tell that. The room was dimly lighted, and I was half hidden behind the rubber tree plants. He stood at the foot of the staircase, his back to me. In a moment there was a sound of footsteps and a woman came down, her high heels tapping lightly on the bare wooden stairs.

She was young and stunningly beautiful. That was two points against her to begin with. She was the kind of woman who makes other women turn into vicious cats, a lush brunette with dark blue eyes and sultry red mouth. The ebony hair was clipped stylishly short, and she had a fragile, petite body ideally designed for a man's arms.

Her dress was an exquisitely simple leaf-green shift that left her arms and most of her legs bare. Needless to say, I hated her on sight.

"I see you finally got here," she said petulantly.

"What the hell is the idea of this?" he asked in a harsh, heavy voice. "Have you any idea the risk we're taking? What if someone were to see us? What if someone were to miss you—"

"Don't fret, baby," she said in honeyed tones. "This is my day off. And no one's going to see us. Who'd be out on a night like this? That's why I phoned you. I knew we could meet without any danger—"

"What about your friend?" he said, stressing the last word with sarcasm. "He owns this place. He's bound to—"

"Don't worry about Charlie," she purred. "I can handle him."

"He knows too much already—"

"Don't fret, baby. How often do I have to keep telling you that?"

"Listen, luv," he said angrily, "I spent weeks planning this, and I don't intend for you to wreck everything with this damned cavalier attitude of yours. This isn't a lark, it's for real. It could mean—"

"I know what it could mean," she retorted icily. "I also know that *I* am the one who's taking all the chances. You don't realize how hard it is! The constant deception—" She paused, frowning. "There've been some new developments. I had to see you. I have to tell you about them. Come on up to my room. We can't stand *here* all night."

They went on upstairs, much to my disappointment. I felt cheated, as though I'd seen a brief preview of an absolutely fascinating movie and knew I'd never be able to see the whole film. I adored eavesdropping on strangers, justifying this admittedly impolite predilection by telling myself that, as a writer, I needed to find out all I could about my fellow beings. I had heard some absorbing conversations on buses, in restaurants and department stores, but none of them had been quite as intriguing as the one I had just listened to. It had a flavor of mystery, of romantic conspiracy. Wondering what the two of them were planning that required such secrecy, I gave full play to my writer's imagination.

The drama wasn't quite finished. I discovered that I hadn't been the only one who had been eavesdropping on the pair. A door near the desk had been open all this time. It was recessed and half obscured by shadows, and I presumed it led to an office. I was suddenly aware that a dark form was lurking there in the doorway, and then Charlie stepped out of the shadows. He was looking toward the staircase, his expression pained, and I knew at once that he had heard everything. His cheeks were ashen, his dark brown eyes filled with conflicting emotions.

He turned to the desk and saw me sitting on the sofa. I blushed furiously.

Charlie didn't say anything. He glared at me as I got up and strolled toward the stairs. I was horribly embarrassed, yet I managed to effect an air of casual unconcern. I could feel his eyes on my back as I went up the stairs, moving with deliberate slowness. By the time I reached my room I was beginning to see the humorous aspects of the situation, and I smiled wryly as I closed the door behind me and locked it.

The logs had burned down to a heap of smoldering orange-pink ashes, snapping pleasantly and sending up little showers of sparks. The room was delightfully warm and cozy as I undressed and slipped into a pair of ruffled pink cotton pajamas. I turned out the overhead light but left the bedside lamp glowing. It was much too early to think of sleep, but fortunately I had brought along a thick historical novel all about dashing cavaliers and buxom maids, my favorite kind of reading. Crawling between the crisp linen sheets and pulling the feathery soft covers around me, I opened the book and was soon lost to the world of flamboyant romance and deeds of bold bravado.

Three hours and two hundred pages later I was finally drowsy enough to put the book aside and turn out the lamp. The room was suddenly thick with velvety black darkness that gradually lightened as moonlight seeped in through the parted drapes. It was no longer raining, but rain dripped from the eaves with a soft splashing sound, and my traveling alarm clock ticked quietly on the bedside table. I had set it for eight, and it was after one now. Closing my eyes, I nestled under the covers and let the gentle noises lull me to sleep.

"She's in there," the voice said. It was a dream voice, muffled and far away. "She's going to Gordonwood, I tell you! She overheard——" The voice drifted away, followed by the sound of footsteps moving down the hall outside my door.

I sat up in bed, abruptly awake, completely alert, with no lingering traces of drowsiness. The room was filled with silvery-gray light, long black shadows sliding along the walls, a dim pink-orange glow flickering in the fireplace. The luminous hands of the clock showed three in the morning. Something had awakened me with a sudden start, and whatever it was had been real, not a creation of my subconscious. My nerves were taut, and I was leaning forward, straining to hear.

There was a faint rattle, as though someone were turning the doorknob, then a few seconds of silence followed by a crisp, rustling sound like dry leaves. I had the acute sensation that someone was standing just outside the door, but there was no sound now. My heart pounding, I turned on the lamp. Dazzling yellow-white light flooded the room, banishing the shadows and bringing a sharp sense of reality. I got out of bed and threw open the door. The hallway was empty, although I had the strange feeling that someone had just left it. I shook my head, frowning. It must have been my imagination after all, I decided, and it was only after I had closed the door and locked it that I noticed the scrap of paper on the floor.

Someone had evidently slipped it under the door, which would explain the rustling sound I had heard. The paper had been torn off a cheap tablet, and it contained four words in a childish block print: *Go away. Don't interfere.* I held the message in my hand, staring down at it in total bewilderment. Go away from where? Don't interfere with what? It made no sense, no sense whatsoever.

I crumpled it up and tossed it into the wastebasket, convinced it was nothing more than a rather wicked prank. Checking to be sure the door was securely locked, I climbed back into bed, thoroughly irritated by the whole affair. Mysterious conversations, cryptic messages —what a preposterous way to be starting a holiday. Thank goodness I would be going on to Gordonwood in the morning. Aunt Agatha would undoubtedly find my little adventure quite amusing, and perhaps I would too. It would be absurd to let it worry me, and yet . . . I sighed deeply and closed my eyes, determined to banish the vague uneasiness I felt stealing over me.

CHAPTER TWO

Charlie Grayson agreed to drive me to Gordonwood the next morning. His manner was politely indifferent as he carried my bags out to the old Chevrolet he had brought around front. Putting my bags in the trunk, he opened the back door for me. Never once did he look directly into my eyes, and I fancied there was something rather furtive about him, as though he had indeed slipped the note under my door last night and was afraid I might make mention of it. There was a meter up front, as in a regular taxi, and he pulled the flag down and drove away from the inn as it began its monotonous click. I settled back in the seat, staring out the window at the quaint old shopfronts of Gordonville.

Gordonville proper looked much as it must have looked fifty years ago, I thought. The cobblestone street was worn smooth with age, and giant oak trees spread soft shadows over the uneven sidewalks, their leaves making a rustling brown-green canopy through which flecks of sunlight danced. With the exception of a somewhat garish cinema advertising the new Dirk Bogarde film, the buildings were of mellowed old brick, tan or beige, several of them adorned with white wooden filigree. The tea shop was pink brick, soft and subdued, while the town hall, across the village green, was of ponderous brownstone, its Victorian cupola green-tarnished copper. Were it not for the cars parked along the curbs and the unquestionably modern citizens ambling along the sidewalks, one could have sworn it was still the turn of the century.

I had been here only once before, thirteen years ago, when my mother had brought me for a lengthy visit after my father's death. I had been too young then to make any deep observations, but I remembered the bright yellow daffodils that bloomed in neat beds in the square, around the statue of the first Robert Gordon who had established the village in the late 1700's. Aunt Agatha had frequently come to London to visit my mother and me, each time begging us to come back to Gordonwood. Three years ago my mother had met and married a rather dashing middle-aged banker from Sydney and moved to Australia, where she was gloriously happy. Aunt Agatha had come up for the wedding, but I had not seen her since, although she constantly wrote witty and vivacious letters. As I had spent my last vacation in Sydney, and as Aunt Agatha constantly urged me to come for a visit, I had decided to accept her invitation at last. Majorca could wait a couple of weeks, and I really was eager to see my aunt again.

Gordonwood was a mile from the village, surrounded by woods and set on the edge of a small private lake. Charlie drove through the outskirts of Gordonville, passing small houses and cottages with neatly trimmed gardens, then turned down a country road with woods on either side. An occasional dogwood bloomed near the edge of the road, pink and white blossoms making a delicate mist of color against the darker trees, and there were wild yellow daisies and golden-orange poppies and small, purple-blue flowers I couldn't identify. Sunlight sparkled with a brilliant dazzle, and the day was one of those rare spring days unequaled in any other part of the world. I completely forgot last night's uneasiness, content to sit back and enjoy the scenery. I was beginning to see why Aunt Agatha chose to remain at Gordonwood. It would be hard to give all this up for the bustling congestion of London, no matter how exciting that city might be.

Charlie drove through two tall, precariously leaning graystone portals and we were on a wide crushed-shell drive winding through rolling lawns and untidy gardens shaded by giant oak trees that grew on the property. I could see glimpses of the lake through the trees in back, a brooding, blue-black body of water I had been warned against on my other visit, and then we came around a curve and I could see the house itself.

Gordonwood was immense, and immensely old, two stories of heavy gray stone with dormer windows and a multileveled roof of dark green slate. Ivy half-covered one side of the house, and there was a great portico in front with six round white marble columns. Pink rose trees grew in black pots on the front porch, and the great golden oak entrance doors had darkened with age. The house was undeniably ugly, too large, too ponderous, but it had an aura of history and the fascination of all houses so steeped in years. A small gray carriage house on one side had been converted into a garage, and there was a comfortable-looking terrace under the boughs of an ancient oak, white marble steps leading down into the formal gardens.

Charlie set my bags on the front porch near the door as I struggled to pull some bills out of my purse. Sitting behind the wheel again, he glanced up at the huge old house, then turned to look into my eyes. He seemed about to say something, I thought, about to impart some urgent message. Instead, he merely frowned and drove away, circling around the drive and speeding on back toward the portals. I was still holding the bills in my hand. He had been in such a hurry to leave he hadn't waited to be paid. I shook my head, bewildered by his strange conduct but relieved to be here at last. I went up the flat marble steps and lifted the large brass knocker, rapping it on the hardened wood.

I was totally unprepared for the man who opened the door. I could only stand and stare, completely at a loss for words.

He was tall, with the strong solid body of an athlete, and he wore a pair of tight faded jeans and a bulky-knit sweater that emphasized powerful shoulders and slender waist. His hair was dark brown, curling at the back of his neck and tumbling in disorderly waves over his forehead, while his eyes were a deep, magnetic blue, the lids heavy, sleepy-looking, the dark brows arched. There were slight hollows under his high cheekbones, and his nose was Roman, his mouth generously wide, lips full and pink. I had seen such men in movies, of course, but this one was undeniably real.

"I'm afraid I have bad news for you," he said in a

rich, deep voice. He folded his arms across his chest and looked down at me, head tilted at an angle.

"Oh?"

"Lady Gordon is seeing no one today," he said. "Tell *me* what you're selling. Perhaps I'll buy some."

"I'm not selling anything," I replied.

"You're not? Pity." He put a lot into that last word. I tried not to blush as he studied me, clearly liking what he saw. He was devilishly good-looking, exuding virility and rakish charm. I tried to compose myself as his mouth curled into a casual smile geared to demolish the strongest feminine heart.

"Would you mind telling me who you are?" I asked, my voice crisp and businesslike.

"The name's Craig Stanton."

"You work here?"

"You might say that, though I've been doing very little work the past few weeks."

"You're Lady Gordon's employee?"

"I'm her guest. I'm writing a biography of Sir Robert Gordon, the Victorian Sir Robert. Lady Gordon was kind enough to let me come here for research."

"Charming," I said. "Then you'll be staying here too. Would you mind bringing my bags in, Mr. Stanton."

"Your bags? I don't understand—"

"I'm Susan Marlow, Lady Agatha's niece."

He looked startled. "But you're not supposed to arrive until sometime next week. We're not ready—"

"Sorry to disappoint you."

"I'm not disappointed, believe me," he said, picking up the bags and leading me into the hall. "Agatha will be, though. She intended to have the whole house aired and cleaned from top to bottom. She's hardly talked about anything besides your visit for the past week. You've taken us by surprise, I'm afraid."

"My letter clearly stated—" I sighed, letting the matter drop. Aunt Agatha never paid attention to dates, and it was really of no importance. I was here, back at Gordonwood again, and that was all that mattered. I ignored Craig Stanton, too captivated by the grandeur of the hall to pay attention to anything else at the moment.

It was vast in proportion. There was dark mahogany

wainscoting on the lower part of the walls, the upper part done in rich light-blue paper embossed with darker blue fleurs-de-lis. A heavy chandelier dangled from the high ceiling, dripping crystal pendants that gleamed with blue and violet facets, and plush Persian carpets were scattered over the darkly varnished parquet floor. At the end of the hall a stately staircase rose halfway up to a landing, where it branched off into two flights of stairs that went on up to the second floor in either direction. The furniture was ornate, every piece an antique, and there was a profusion of plants about, their leaves of every shade from lightest jade to darkest green.

"It's breathtaking," I whispered, awed.

Craig Stanton nodded in assent. "But frightfully impractical to live in," he added. "It's impossible to heat this place, and you couldn't hire enough servants nowadays to keep it clean. Don't look too closely at anything, or you're bound to see a layer of dust."

He seemed to know quite a lot about the house, I thought. "How long have you been staying here, Mr. Stanton?" I inquired.

"Three months," he replied. "A rugged three months."

"You don't like Gordonwood?"

"On the contrary, I find it fascinating, and your aunt, of course, is an incredible hostess, but you'll have to admit the place is pretty well isolated. There's nothing much for a healthy young buck to do, once he's tired of books and examining old documents. I—uh—suddenly find the old place much more interesting," he drawled lazily, "now that you're here. I had no idea Agatha's niece was such a stunning bird."

"I'm not a bird," I said irritably. "I'm a writer."

"So I've been told. Intellect doesn't hurt, though I must say I prefer my girls to be a bit featherbrained. That sort's much easier to handle."

"Mr. Stanton—" I began.

"Craig, please. May as well start off on an informal basis. We're going to be great chums."

"I'm not so sure of that," I said stiffly.

"I am," he replied, smiling broadly.

I gave Craig Stanton a long, cool look. I knew his type all too well. He had great charm, charm it was almost impossible not to respond to, and therein lay the greatest danger. I knew from past experience that such immediate warmth often concealed an overconfident arrogance. A great many women found it impossible not to capitulate to men like Craig Stanton, and in his case stunning good looks would make it all the easier. I knew that I would have to be on guard constantly with him. He leaned casually against the wall, hands thrust in pockets, and there was a gleam of amusement in his dark blue eyes, almost as though he could read my thoughts and found my reservations laughable.

"Where is my aunt?" I inquired.

"She's at Dower House."

"Dower House?" I said, and then I remembered the small gray house with its green roof that stood under the oak trees on the other side of the gardens. Many old estates had such houses, built to accommodate newlyweds and give them a certain amount of privacy away from the rest of the family.

"She's visiting Althea," he said.

The name was vaguely familiar. Of course, I thought. Aunt Agatha had mentioned the woman in several of her letters. Althea Dawson was an artist of sorts and a permanent guest at Gordonwood. She was in her middle fifties like my aunt and also a widow. The two of them had been schoolgirls together, it seemed, and Althea had come to Gordonwood two years ago after her husband's final illness. Althea was supposed to have been quite talented in her youth, but that talent had eventually been lost due to an overfondness for gin.

"Would you like me to show you to your room?" Craig Stanton inquired. "Then I'll dash over to Dower House and inform Lady Agatha of your arrival. It'll give you a chance to freshen up a bit."

"You know which room my aunt intends me to have?"

He nodded. "Don't worry," he said, "it's not anywhere near mine. I'm on the other side of the house. Pity."

"You're rather fresh, Mr. Stanton," I said icily.

"And you're rather serious, pet. Most women like a bit of teasing. I promise to be on my best behavior."

He picked up the bags, grinning at me. "Come along now, I'll take you to your room."

I followed him up the staircase. We turned left at the landing, proceeding on up to the second floor. There was a vast hall running the length of the house, with two smaller halls at either end, each of them ending in narrow stairs in back that led down to the kitchen area and the unused servants' quarters. At present my aunt employed only two servants, a cook and a maid, both of whom lived in Gordonville, driving in every morning. There were over thirty rooms here, Craig Stanton explained, almost as though I were a tourist and he a guide. Only a dozen or so rooms were open, the rest closed up and filled with dust-sheeted furniture.

"I've been here before, you know," I said, disliking his proprietary tone.

"Of course," he retorted. "Just thought I'd bring you up to date. It's a monster of a place, isn't it? A person could easily get lost trying to find his way around."

"I know," I replied. "When I stayed here before I decided to go find a book to read. It was late at night, and I was twelve years old. I went down the wrong hall, certain I knew how to get down to the library, and I ended up in the pantry. Terrifying experience—I couldn't find the light switch, and there were so many spooky noises—"

"Still are," he said. "These old houses are full of 'em. Incidentally, pet, there's no electricity."

"What? But I distinctly remember—"

"Storm last week blew down all the lines, and they haven't got around to repairing them yet. No need to worry, though. There are dozens of old lamps and candelabra about. Gives the place a rather romantic atmosphere at night, though it's damned inconvenient when you're trying to work. They expect to have the lines back up in a few days."

"Lovely," I said.

We had made a turn and were moving down another hallway. Though not as wide as the main one, it had the same deep garnet carpeting, and the walls had the same dark golden oak wainscoting, the upper half covered with old ivory paper printed with tiny brown leaves. At various intervals there were tall green plants in heavy white pots, lending a homey touch to the formal hallway. Craig Stanton walked on ahead, carrying the heavy bags as though they had no weight at all. He moved with a graceful stride, arms swinging, shoulders rolling. An athlete's walk, I thought, wondering if he played soccer in college. He certainly had the body for it.

"That's the east wing," he said, nodding toward yet another hallway branching off the one we were in. "It's completely closed up. You can smell the dust and cobwebs."

I peered down the hall. It was long and dark, no light whatsoever penetrating the gloom. Shadows seemed to dance along the walls, and the air was cold and clammy, thoroughly unpleasant. I shuddered, glad we did not have to pass through that section of the house. Craig Stanton led the way past various closed doors, and I realized we were now in the back part of Gordonwood. He stopped in front of a corner room. Directly across the hall was a small staircase, one flight of stairs leading up to the attics, one leading back downstairs.

"Here's your room," he said, opening the door. "I'm afraid it's a bit removed from the other rooms—off by itself, so to speak. You don't mind, do you?"

"Why ever should I mind?"

"Old house, dark halls, spooky noises—"

"Nonsense," I said.

He smiled and set the bags down near the closet.

"Guess I've performed my duties," he said. "Today's Mary's day off, or else she would have answered the door. Mary's the maid, a rather flighty creature, terribly lax when it comes to dusting."

"Thank you, Mr. Stanton," I said, my voice frigid.

He lounged against the door frame, arms folded across his chest. There was an amused expression on his face, as though he found my stiff politeness devastating. I frowned, disturbed by my own reactions. I was a carefree person, ordinarily quite relaxed, but this man brought out my worst. It was hard to relax in his presence, hard not to be fretful and uneasy. At the moment I was wishing I had worn a prettier dress, and this bit of frivolity on my part made me all the more irritable. Once again I had the impression that Craig Stanton was reading my thoughts and finding them terribly funny.

"Now that you're here," he said, "perhaps you can help us look for the Gordon manuscripts."

"I have no idea what you're talking about."

"Your aunt didn't write to you about them? You didn't read the article in the newspaper?"

"My aunt never mentioned any manuscripts," I said, "and I never read the newspapers. I work the crossword puzzles and look at the ads. The rest is much too distressing—"

"Then you know nothing about it. Remarkable!"

"What *are* you talking about, Mr. Stranton?"

"The Gordon manuscripts," he said. "We have reason to believe some of them are still in existence, hidden away somewhere in the house. Sir Robert published over forty volumes during his lifetime—travel accounts, translations, anthropological studies, even a novel or two—but he left his most important works to be published after his death."

"Everyone knows that," I said dryly. "His widow was a prim Victorian matron, horrified by the highly improper contents of the manuscripts. She built a great bonfire in the backyard and hurled them all into the flames. It was one of the most notorious burnings in the history of literature."

"Right," he said. "Historians and literary scholars have never forgiven her for it. I'm writing a biography of Sir Robert, as I told you earlier, and your aunt has allowed me full access to all the family papers. I found Lady Arabella Gordon's diary. She was a fascinating creature, almost as colorful as her husband, but the diary was deadly dull, full of the most inane trivia. However, there was a most intriguing entry about that famous bonfire—"

"Yes?" I prompted.

"She did indeed burn most of the papers, but it seems she had reservations about a couple of the manuscripts. She couldn't bring herself to consign his autobiography to the flames, and there was a study of tribal customs among the African natives that, she felt, the world might someday be ready for. If she *did* save these two manuscripts, and we were to locate them, it would be the greatest literary discovery since the Boswell papers were found in Malahide Castle."

"You think they might be here?" I asked, intrigued in spite of myself.

He nodded slowly. "There was the diary entry, of course, and then I discovered a few loose pages in the bottom of an old trunk. Sir Hubert Ashcrofton came down from London to examine them. He's a fellow of the Royal Geographical Society and an expert on old manuscripts. He claims the pages are in Sir Robert's own handwriting, part of an introduction to one of his supposedly burned manuscripts. He was quite excited—"

"And?"

"And that's all. Your aunt let Sir Hubert take the pages back to London to show to his colleagues, and we haven't turned up anything else. The newspapers carried the story. It caused quite a lot of excitement in scholarly circles, needless to say, and your aunt's been besieged with requests from people wanting to come to Gordonwood and search for the papers. Some were from men quite prominent in the field of historical research, and some from mere curiosity seekers."

"Incredible," I said.

"She turned down all requests, although one or two of the more adventuresome fellows tried to slip into the house on their own. I caught them, luckily, and there've been no more such attempts since Lady Agatha got the watchdogs."

"Watchdogs?"

"Prince and Earl. They're Great Danes. Belong to Dr. Paul Matthews, actually, but he brought them to Gordonwood soon after the last attempt was made."

Dr. Matthews, I knew from my aunt's letters, was her personal physician and a great friend. He was in his early forties and, according to my aunt, an absolute dream.

"To think I knew nothing about any of this," I said.

"You should read the newspapers," Craig Stanton replied, curling his lips in a slightly mocking smile.

"These manuscripts," I said, "if they *do* exist, they must be utterly priceless—"

"Any number of private collectors would pay a king's

ransom for them," he said. "A publisher would pay even more. However, their greatest value wouldn't be monetary. Think what it would mean if we could read Sir Robert Gordon's autobiography. He was one of the greatest explorers the world has ever known, one of the most daring and courageous men—" He paused, giving his head a shake. "I get carried away," he apologized.

"I can easily see why."

"Your aunt has been wonderful to me," he continued. "Since I discovered the diary, she said I should have first crack at the papers, which is why she would allow no one else to come to Gordonwood. She's quite excited about all this herself, like a child on a treasure hunt. We've gone through every room in the house, searching from top to bottom. It's been a futile search," he added with an elegant shrug of his shoulders. "I'm beginning to believe the manuscripts were destroyed after all, but even if they were it's been great fun just the same. Your aunt's had a ball—"

"I can see how it would capture her imagination."

"She's a remarkable woman. I've never known anyone with such incredible vitality—"

I could tell from the tone of his voice that Craig Stanton had a genuine affection for my aunt. I liked him for that, some of my earlier reservations about him vanishing. He smiled a little as he spoke of her. His lips curled lightly at the corners, and his dark blue eyes were filled with admiration. Perhaps I'd misjudged him earlier, I thought. He heaved a deep sigh and brushed a lock of dark brown hair from his forehead, hunching his shoulders and cramming his hands back into the pockets of his jeans.

"She'll be delighted to know you're here," he said. "I'll run over to Dower House and tell her the good news. Do you want to meet her downstairs in the drawing room in, say, about twenty minutes? It's right off the main entrance hall, to your left as you come down."

"Fine," I said.

"I'm glad you're here, too," he added. "For purely selfish reasons."

"Indeed?"

"We'll discuss it later," he replied.

He gave me a boyish grin and then sauntered away, leaving me alone. I stood by the door a moment, thinking about what he'd said. I wished I were one of those svelte, sophisticated women who could take such things with casual disdain. I wasn't, and I could still feel the man's charm after he had gone, even though I had done my best to ignore it. Watch it, ducky, I told myself. You may not be a *femme fatale,* but neither are you a gushing schoolgirl. Craig Stanton was decidedly disturbing, and I was far too happy with my hard-won independence and well-ordered life to want to be disturbed by any man, no matter how charming he might be. I forced these thoughts out of my mind and turned to examine the room.

It was lovely, a room designed for a Victorian maiden, with green and beige striped Chinese silk wallpaper and dark beige carpet, both faded with age. The antique furniture was dark ivory, heavily carved, and there was a chaise longue upholstered in emerald green velvet, the nap silvery and worn. The bedspread was heavy tan satin embroidered with tiny green leaves, and a huge green, gold, and black Chinese vase in one corner held old dried peacock feathers. Plush jade green draperies hung at a pair of French windows that opened out onto a small balcony. The windows were open, a slight breeze making the draperies rustle stiffly.

Stepping out onto the balcony, I rested my hands on the sun-warmed railing and looked out over the shrub-cluttered back lawns that led down to the lake, barely visible through the oak trees. Lady Arabella Gordon had built her bonfire down there near the privet hedge, I knew, and she and Sir Robert were both buried in the sinister mausoleum down by the lake. It was of black marble, in the shape of an Arab tent, and I remembered seeing it one morning when the mists were heavy and a chill wind blew across the lake with the sound of whispers. It was said that one could still hear the tinkling of a camel's bell when the wind was right, but I believed that no more than I believed any of the ghost stories associated with old English houses like Gordonwood.

What fabulous originals they had been, I mused, thinking about Sir Robert and his wife. He had been tall and brawny with sun-bronzed skin and piercing black eyes,

so much like an Arab that he had been able to journey
to Mecca in disguise, the first white man to penetrate
that most sacred of cities. He had traveled all over Arabia, living with Bedouin tribes, speaking their dialects
like a native, and Lady Arabella had been right beside
him, her job to pay, pack, and follow. Throughout it all
she had remained a prim, proper Victorian in high-but-
toned boots and half a dozen stiff petticoats under her
dress, her wide-brimmed hats swathed in veils to protect
her porcelain-white English complexion.

I thought about the Gordon manuscripts, wondering
if they really did exist. Sir Robert had been a gamy
character, an expert in erotica, and even today a few of
his books were in the restricted stacks of libraries. He
had been fascinated by the sexual customs of the East
and had written of them with clinical precision. Many
of his books had been privately printed, and although I
had read none of them, I had read about all of them in
a biography of Gordon Aunt Agatha had sent me years
ago. The book had been written at the turn of the century, without the family's authorization, and was delightfully florid in style. I remembered the account of the
burning: Lady Arabella in white muslin dress and laven-
der shawl, face pale with horror as she threw page after
page into the crackling orange flames. Judging from the
books that had actually been published during his lifetime, those that had remained unpublished must really
have been shockers, I thought. How exciting it would be
if the manuscripts were still here in the house, turning to
dust in some hidden nook or cranny. Very unlikely, I
reasoned. Despite the evidence Craig Stanton had found,
the manuscripts would surely have been discovered long
before now, had they actually escaped the flames. Cold
reason told one that.

The merry warble of a robin broke my chain of
thought, and I hurried back into my room. Opening my
bags on the bed, I began to put my clothes in the chest
drawers, taking the dresses over to the closet on wooden
hangers. I had been wise to bring my own hangers, I
saw, for there were none in the closet. As I intended to
go directly on to Majorca, I had brought a variety of
things, formal and informal, and I was glad now. I would

have someone to wear the dresses for. I stroked the folds of the violet-blue silk cocktail dress, wondering what Craig Stanton's reactions would be when he saw me in it. It was frightfully sexy, with no back at all, the swirling skirt several inches above my knees. I could visualize his expression, one dark brow arching in thoroughly male approval. . . .

Stop it! I admonished myself. I had no intentions of wearing the dress for him. It didn't matter what I wore around him. I had come to visit my aunt, not to try and captivate an arrogant young biographer who was far too sure of himself and far too cheeky for my taste.

I was putting the empty suitcases on the closet shelf when I heard the footsteps on the back stairs across the hall. I couldn't tell if they were coming up or going down, and I wondered who in the world it could be. Craig hadn't had time to come back from Dower House yet, and he had told me this was the maid's day off. Stepping out of the closet, I glanced toward the hall through the opened bedroom door. There was no one there, and the footsteps had been silenced, yet I had the peculiar sensation that someone had passed down the hall, pausing to glance into my room. I couldn't have said why, yet the sensation was very strong. It was almost as though the air still bore the invisible impression of a presence there at the door. I went to the door and peered out. The hall was empty.

Perhaps I had imagined the footsteps, I told myself. I had been making so much racket trying to heave the suitcases in place that I might easily have heard my own echoes. These old walls did strange things to noises, picking them up, magnifying them, throwing them back with unusual reverberations. I remembered how, on my earlier visit, I had lain awake for hours, listening to the night noises in the house and imagining all sorts of gruesome things. I had been a child then, with a child's delight in ghost stories and tales of bloody horror, but I was a big girl now. I managed to laugh at my moment of uneasiness, stepping over to the great gilt mirror to brush my hair and apply a touch of pale pink lipstick.

I left the room, closing the door behind me, and hoped I would be able to find my way down to the drawing room. The hall seemed inordinately long, and not nearly so well lighted as I would have preferred now that I had to walk down it by myself. Even though the sunshine was dazzling outside, the hall was undeniably gloomy, misty gray shadows thronging along the walls. I proceeded down it at a brisk pace, curbing a foolish impulse to whistle. I loathed that type of nervous female always eager to grow faint or go into hysterics at the first opportunity. Though perhaps not made of steel, my own nerves were reasonably healthy. I smiled wryly, amused at my earlier apprehension, and turned the corner.

I had gone several paces before the cold, clammy air engulfed me. The walls on either side were dark, and I was moving down a long black passage swathed in dense shadows. I stopped, startled, and the fetid air swirled around me, stroking my bare arms like ghostly fingers. There was a horrible sour odor, an odor of mildew and dust and decay, and I realized that I had turned into the east wing. My heart began to beat rapidly, and my throat went dry, just after I had been complimenting myself on my strong set of nerves. My first impulse was to turn and run, but something held me there. Perhaps it was my own chilling fear.

I had the undeniable impression that I was not alone in this dark corridor. I could feel someone watching me, and the feeling was as strong and unnerving as it would have been had someone reached out to touch me. A pair of eyes stared at me from somewhere down the hall. The sensation was too strong, too real to be my imagination. I peered into the gloom, trying to adjust my eyes to the darkness, but there was nothing but shadow, rippling black shadow that seemed to stir in the air, caressing the walls with sable darkness. At the very end of the hall, far away, heavy draperies were drawn over windows, and they billowed, making a raspy, rustling sound like the sound of hoarse whispers. As my eyes grew accustomed to the dark, I could see the recessed doorways on either side, and then I saw the dark form in one of the doorways halfway down the corridor, an immobile black shape outlined by the lighter darkness around it.

"Who's there?" I called.

There was no reply, just the heavy silence emphasized by the rustle of the drapes. Minutes passed, each second punctuated by the beating of my heart, and I was paralyzed, unable to move away from the evil that I felt like a living substance around me. I stared at the dark form hovering there in the doorway, my eyes straining to see distinct details, and then everything blurred together and I heard a loud click followed by a soft creaking sound that echoed along the walls. The dark form had vanished. It was no longer in the doorway. Shadows blurred and blended and there was only the fetid air, the sharp, sour odor. I was alone in the deserted corridor, left with only my own fear.

That, too, vanished, and I felt incredibly foolish as reason returned and I realized how preposterous the fear had been in the first place. I had reacted in precisely the same way the heroine of one of my books would have reacted. Had someone glided down the hall, pausing at the door of my room and then turning into the east wing, and then waited there in the doorway? I doubted it now. The dark form had been merely a mass of shadows, and the click, the creaking had been perfectly normal noises. I tried to convince myself that someone hadn't opened the door and gone into one of the rooms. There was one sure way of finding out. I could march down the hall, open the door and look inside. I wasn't about to. Not that I was *afraid*, I told myself. The idea simply didn't *appeal* to me.

Leaving the east wing, I returned to the other hall and hurried down it, turning left and going down the wide main hall, relieved to see sunlight spilling through the west windows and dappling the garnet carpet with flecks of gold. I paused at the head of the stairs, smoothing the skirt of my green linen dress and brushing a curl away from my temple. Aunt Agatha would be waiting for me, and I wanted to be composed. I took a deep breath, ridding myself of the last traces of uneasiness, and then moved down the stairs, a bit too briskly to be really dignified. I told myself that it was merely my eagerness to see Aunt Agatha that made me move so quickly.

CHAPTER THREE

I was rather surprised to find the drawing room empty. Aunt Agatha hadn't come in yet, which gave me further time to compose myself and examine the beautifully appointed room. Victorian in style, with ornate furniture, it was nevertheless light and airy, done in shades of brown, beige, yellow, and golden wheat color. A pair of French windows stood open, leading out onto the terrace, and sunlight came pouring through in shimmering rays that brought out golden tones in the waxed parquet floor and touched the edge of a brown, orange, and beige Persian carpet. A portrait of Lady Arabella Gordon hung over the white marble fireplace.

I studied the painting. Done in the florid, overly dramatic style of the period, it showed a plump, rather self-satisfied matron posed against a backdrop of rocky gray hills with yellow flowers growing in the crevices. She wore a flowing white dress with a bold green sash, and held a green parasol over her shoulder. Dark ebony hair was pulled away from the oval face in a severe bun, and the features were patrician, the eyes dark brown, the mouth quite smug. Certainly not a beautiful woman, I thought, but a strong one. I could easily imagine her trouping through the deserts and giving the Arab bearers hell.

There was a noisy patter on the terrace outside, and I gave a little cry of alarm as a great silver-gray creature came bounding in through the French windows. He stopped, staring at me with startled yellow-brown eyes, evidently as surprised as I was. He was a magnificent animal, his body lean and sleek, his short fur like glossy velvet, and he looked bewildered at finding me here, not knowing whether to growl or whine with pleasure.

"Friends?" I said, my voice a bit shaky. "You're a lovely thing, you are, but do you *bite?*"

The animal lunged toward me, placing two padded paws on my shoulders and giving me a great slurpy kiss with a long pink tongue. I almost lost my balance.

"Easy, fellow!" I protested. "Let's not carry this friendship thing too far!"

"He *likes* you," Aunt Agatha exclaimed, striding briskly into the room from the terrace. "Great clumsy beast, isn't he? Down, Earl! Sit! You see, he has a frightfully affectionate temperament, completely unlike his brother. Prince is another matter altogether. Surly as can be, and quite disrespectful—not on the *carpet*, Earl. On the hearth. There, that's a love."

Earl curled up on the marble hearth, head resting on his front paws, and his eyes devoured me with excessive affection. I felt sure he was going to pounce over for another kiss at any moment.

"My dear Susan!" Aunt Agatha cried, throwing her arms wide to embrace me. "This is outrageous! You weren't supposed to get here till next week and everything's disastrously disordered. We don't even have electricity! Can you imagine?" She gave me a vigorous hug and then held me back at arm's length to examine me. "Nevertheless, I'm elated. Simply elated! It's such fun having you here."

Aunt Agatha was tall and large-boned, a big woman with the red-blooded vitality of a female athlete. Her short-clipped hair was sandy, liberally streaked with gray, and her long face was undeniably plain, weatherworn, lined with age, yet her large blue eyes were radiantly clear and sparkled with youthful enthusiasm. She wore sensible brown shoes and a pinkish-brown tweed suit, the skirt several inches below the knees. She was a striking figure, exuding strength and character that would have made beauty superfluous.

"Sorry I didn't meet you when you came in," she said, her voice rich and hearty, "but Althea was having one of her spells this morning and I had to scold her out of it. She keeps *imagining* things—I'm quite worried. Of course we have had a lot of excitement recently, but I'm afraid she's going off the deep end——" She shook her head, a crease between her brows.

"I'm eager to meet Althea," I said.

"You will, dear. She's divine, actually, though hardly a day passes that we don't go at it like a couple of cats. But then our quarrels are so *stim*ulating. Poor thing's been a bit under the weather lately what with all that's been going on. Susan, dear, do sit down. Don't hover!"

Aunt Agatha sprawled out on the Victorian sofa, crossing her legs and resting her elbow on the arm, her long body completely relaxed. I sat in one of the yellow chairs, and Earl padded over to lay his heavy head in my lap, his eyes looking up at me with slavish devotion. I scratched his ears, still a little perturbed by this sudden outpouring of affection.

"Tell me, dear," Aunt Agatha said. "Did you have a nice journey down?"

"The train ride was uneventful," I replied, "though I had a dandy time at the inn last night."

"You spent the night at the inn?"

I nodded. "There was no one to meet me," I said, "and it was pouring rain. The room was quite pleasant, but the innkeeper——"

"Charlie Grayson's tetched," she interrupted. "Poor thing's always been a bit *slow*, though he's a fine, responsible lad, quite capable of running the inn. He's an amiable sort—though distracted! What happened?"

I related my experiences at the inn, telling her about Charlie's curious attitude, the mysterious conversation I had overheard, and the message someone had slipped under my door. Aunt Agatha laughed uproariously, shaking her head.

"You blundered into the middle of one of our famous illicit affairs," she said. "They're rampant in Gordonville. You see, we get very poor reception on the telly, dear. What else is one to *do*? Gordonville's a veritable—what's that place in America? There was a book about it, I believe, and a television series——"

"Peyton Place?"

"Gordonville's a veritable Peyton Place, though you wouldn't guess it on first sight. So quaint and serene on the surface, but *sub rosa*——"

"What about the note?" I protested. "Surely that——"

"Oh, I have no doubt Charlie slipped the note under your door, afraid you'd talk about what you'd overheard and give the inn a bad name. He tries to run a respectable inn, though I must say *his* conduct hasn't always been blameless. Involved in a rather delicious scandal himself, he was, a few months ago——"

Her eyes danced with glee as she told me about Charlie's affair with a young actress who had come down from London to stay at the inn. According to Aunt Agatha, the girl had been stunning, a rather mysterious figure in Gordonville. No one knew who she was or why she had come, but Charlie had been fascinated by her. She had her bit of fun, leading him on, no doubt finding it amusing to toy with the affections of a boy much younger and obviously smitten.

"Shameless hussy!" my aunt exclaimed. "Probably couldn't pay for her room. People were outraged, I don't mind telling you. Charlie may be a bit peculiar, but he *is* a strikingly handsome lad, quite virile. Several local girls would like nothing better than to snare him. He's dependable, and he owns the inn, and there's plenty who'd consider themselves lucky to marry his likes. Good husband material isn't all that common in these parts."

"What happened to the actress?" I inquired.

"No one knows. She just—vanished, I guess you might say. No one saw her leave town. She just suddenly wasn't there. Some say Charlie strangled her in a fit of anger and buried her in the basement of the inn. Nonsense, of course! People love to imagine such horrors, love to talk about 'em even more."

"Strange," I said quietly, thinking about the tormented expression I had seen in Charlie's handsome brown eyes.

"Speaking of horrors, dear, your last book——"

"You didn't like it?"

"I adored it! But those last few chapters—chilling! So wonderfully scary. When the girl was trapped in the ruins and the murderer was prowling the moors—absolutely unnerving. I didn't sleep a wink after I finished it. Is the new one scary, too?"

"Very," I said.

"Be sure you send me a copy when it comes out. I read so much, over a dozen books a week. Now that I no longer gad about there's nothing else to do. Incidentally, dear, how's your mother?" she asked, changing the subject abruptly. "I want to hear all about her. She's so wrapped up in that rich Australian of hers that she never writes. It's been ages since I've even received a *post*card! Fancy your mother catching a banker. At *her* age, I might add. But then she always was a captivating creature, even as a girl. I remember how she used to fascinate all the boys——"

Having asked me to tell her all about my mother, she proceeded to tell *me* all about my mother, relating a whole series of splendidly funny anecdotes about the days when they had both been daughters of a country parson, wildly unconventional lasses eager to leave the parsonage and kick up their heels in the city. No one could talk like Aunt Agatha, and I sat back in my chair, smiling at her phrases and relishing her bawdy humor. She was quite earthy in a hearty, rollicking way that was sheer delight.

"What do you think of *him*, dear?" she asked. I saw that I was going to have to get used to these sudden changes of subject.

"Who?" I asked, not very convincingly I must add.

"Craig Stanton, idiot. Don't tell me you didn't *notice?*"

"I noticed, all right," I said.

"You couldn't help but, what? If I were thirty years younger I'd give him a run for his money, and that's no joke! As is, I find it enchanting to have him about. Such charm, and such manners! Fancy a man who looks like that being a scholar. I could easily imagine him stamping through the Amazon jungles on some dangerous expedition or stealing diamond bracelets from dissolute countesses on the French Riviera, for that matter, but he's actually quite dedicated to his work. Frightfully intelligent chap, and very respected in academic circles."

"Aunt Agatha, who *is* he? I must say I was startled to find him here, and all this talk about the Gordon papers——"

"He told you about that? I was rather hoping to save it for later on, as a surprise. I'm so excited about it! And you can help us search! But in answer to your question:

Craig Stanton is thirty-three years old and a graduate of Oxford. Graduated with several honors, as a matter of fact. He wrote a book about the Koh-i-noor diamond and the intrigue surrounding it—a colorful, exotic book, full of strange lore and bloody deeds, absolutely fascinating. You must read it, dear. I have a copy upstairs."

"I will," I said. "And?"

"And he went to India to do research, and while he was there he became interested in Sir Robert Gordon. Gordon was a lieutenant in the dragoons, you know, in his youth before he started his explorations. He was an aide to Sir Charles Napier, that crusty old commander. Gordon was the only man in India who could speak all the dialects, and he could also pass himself off as a native. He was invaluable to Napier, acting as a sort of secret service agent, living with the natives, finding out things no other white man could hope to learn——"

"You're wandering," I said.

"Be patient, Susan! It was while he was in India that Gordon conducted his famous experiment with apes. He knew all the *other* languages, and to pass the time he decided to learn ape-talk too. He had several apes living in his quarters, and he actually recorded over eighty distinct sounds. If he could have continued with it, I'm sure he would ultimately have learned to communicate, but of course the infamous brothel report put an end to his career in India. Napier wanted to know all about the notorious houses full of painted men his officers were said to visit. Gordon's report was a little too clinical. He was just being thorough, of course, but guilt by association—all that sort of thing. His fellow officers were jealous of him and used the report to drum him out of the service. Just as well. He went on to do much more exciting things——"

"Marvelous," I said. "I've learned all about Sir Robert Gordon's early career, but absolutely nothing about Craig Stanton."

"It's all relevant, dear," Aunt Agatha said a bit testily. "You see, Craig learned all this while he was in India and decided that his next book would be about Gordon. Naturally, he came to Gordonwood. He'd already done reams of preliminary research, but of course he couldn't write the book he *wanted* to write without access to the family documents. I gave him my permission, although I did have my doubts about it. Why dig up all those old Victorian scandals? Why let a perfect stranger prowl through the trunks and boxes and read all those intimate letters and journals? It had never been done before. My husband's ancestors refused to let anyone see the material, and even my husband, may he rest in peace, refused to grant permission to any would-be biographers."

"Then why did you?" I inquired.

"I thought, what the hell? So many books have been written about Gordon, why not let someone write the *real* story? And I must say Craig was very persuasive."

"So he moved in."

"Not at first, dear. He stayed at the inn and came out every day, but I thought that was terribly impractical. Why spend all that money to rent a room at the inn when Gordonwood had so many rooms? I asked him to come, and I must say I haven't regretted it. It's been divine to have a man around again, and I don't know when I've had so much fun."

"I see," I said, rather primly.

"You don't approve?"

"It's not my place to approve or disapprove either one."

Aunt Agatha narrowed her eyes and gave me a wicked little smile. "So," she said, "you two have already had differences?"

"Hardly that," I retorted. "He just seems terribly cheeky, and——"

"Wonderful!" she cried. "The chemistry's already beginning to work! You two were made for each other. You both write, and you have so much in common. *He's* a marvelous catch, and he couldn't do better than you, even if you *are* my niece. What fun! He's ripe for the right woman, and——"

"Nonsense!" I said.

"——and," she continued, "you aren't getting any younger, dear. Being a writer, being independent is all very well and good, but a woman needs a man, and this one's perfect. Grab him!"

"I'm not the least bit interested in Mr. Craig Stanton," I told her in a cool reserved voice. "Simply because a man has a magnificent build and sexy blue eyes doesn't mean I'm going to lose my head. You may find him irresistible, but I can assure you my own reactions——"

"Fiddlesticks!" she exclaimed, interrupting me. "You modern girls are so clever in so many ways. You make your own careers, support yourselves, take karate lessons, and learn to fly airplanes, but when it comes to the fundamentals you're sadly lacking. *I* knew how to get my man—once I laid eyes on him he didn't have a chance —and look at your *mother!* She snapped up a banker and shipped off to Australia when she was old enough to take up knitting and forget the whole thing."

"There are more important things in life," I retorted.

She smiled, fiddling with the string of pearls around her neck. She was a lusty, indomitable old girl with marvelous traits, but she could sometimes be quite irritating. She went right to the heart of the matter, stripping away all pretense and nonessentials, and I had the impression she knew more about my emotional makeup then I knew myself. It was an infuriating feeling, and I frowned, rubbing Earl's head vigorously. He looked up at me with such soulful eyes that I had to laugh.

"How much did Craig tell you about the Gordon papers?" she asked.

"He told me about the diary entry," I replied, "and the loose pages he found in an old trunk. He said Sir Hubert Ashcrofton came down to examine them and verified their authenticity. Do you really believe the manuscripts exist, Aunt Agatha?"

She nodded briskly. "I'm certain of it. They're here— somewhere in the house."

"I find it hard to believe," I said. "Such things just don't happen in real life. If the manuscripts did exist, surely they'd have been discovered years ago. It's—it's too incredible to think they'd still be here after all this time."

"Humph! I suppose you would have said the same thing if you had been at Malahide Castle fifty years ago. *That* was pretty incredible, too, and the Boswell papers were much older than the Gordon manuscripts would be."

I had to agree with her there. The discovery of the Boswell papers had been one of the most amazing and romantic episodes in the history of literature. Malahide Castle was in Ireland, a rambling old place with battlements and turrets and even a moat. It had been crammed full of letters and journals that James Boswell had written during the eighteenth century. They had turned up, over a hundred and fifty years later, in garrets and attics, in cupboards and ancient chests, in an old box that was supposed to contain a croquet set. As late as 1940, when the government was looking for a place to store food during wartime, two chests of valuable papers had been discovered in an outhouse at Malahide. It was a remarkable story, undeniably true. The papers were still being sorted out and published by Yale University.

"Still," I protested, "Lady Arabella burned all her husband's unpublished papers, and if one or two of the manuscripts *did* escape the flames, I could hardly believe they'd still be here——"

Aunt Agatha sighed heavily, giving me an exasperated look. She clearly enjoyed believing in the manuscripts, and I could easily see why. She was old, and alone most of the time, and this had undoubtedly brought a great deal of excitement into her life. She had always been given to enthusiasms: raising snails, gardening, collecting books on Victorian crimes, studying ancient Egyptian mystic cults. This was merely another enthusiasm, and she must have great fun looking through old boxes and prowling in the attic for such unusual plunder.

"I'm not the *only* one who believes in the manuscripts," she said, almost as though she had been reading my mind. "After the story came out in the papers, I was besieged by people who wanted to come to Gordonwood and hunt. A couple of chaps even tried to break into the house."

"Mr. Stanton told me about that," I said. "I find it rather alarming. If they did exist, the manuscripts would be more valuable than a cache of precious gems. That could easily attract the criminal element——"

"Bosh!" she cried. "You've been writing far too many thrillers. These chaps were perfectly harmless. But there's no need to worry about that sort of thing now that we've got the dogs. They'll keep out any unwelcome visitors. Still," she reflected, "I'm glad we've got a big strong man about the place. Makes one sleep easier."

I couldn't help but think of my experience in the east wing. It still bothered me, even though I knew deep down that it had been nothing more than a combination of nerves and over-active imagination. Suppose someone else, someone outside Gordonwood, was as interested in the manuscripts as my aunt? Suppose they were determined to find them on their own and had, somehow or other, managed to slip into the house? What if . . . I shook myself mentally, refusing to give way to my novelist's imagination. There was no sinister stranger lurking among the shadows at Gordonwood, and there were probably no manuscripts either, though my aunt enjoyed thinking there might be.

Sunshine streamed into the room in long yellow rays, and I could see a clump of daffodils and part of a dark green hedge through the windows. It was absurd to imagine anything amiss on such a glorious day. The room was cozy, faded and worn and full of character, and I was delighted to be with Aunt Agatha again. Most women her age were putting up strawberry preserves or knitting woolen sweaters, but my aunt was original. I could hardly visualize her doing anything domestic. She would read about horrendous crimes instead of dusting, collect enamel snuffboxes and grow exotic herbs instead of sweeping. That was part of her charm, part of what made me love her so dearly. Aunt Agatha might be madly impractical at times, but she was never dull, never commonplace.

"I'm a wretched hostess," she said, getting to her feet and smoothing down her pinkish-brown tweed skirt. "Keeping you here all this time, talking like a garrulous old fool. It's almost noon, and you must be starved. Lunch is quite informal. Cook just puts sandwiches and tea on the table in the breakfast nook. Come along, dear. Not you, Earl! Out you go. Find Prince."

Earl looked crestfallen, but he slumped outside, turning to give me a parting look of love. Aunt Agatha rattled her pearls and brushed a fluff of sandy hair from her forehead, linking her arm in mine and leading me out to the hall.

"Craig's book is going to be smashing," she said as we moved down the hall. "He's finished several chapters already, and they're vastly readable, quite racy. I'm sure it'll be a best seller. I may be a selfish old woman, but I adore having him here. He's pure sterling."

"I'm sure it's been jolly for you."

"So grand having young people around—first him, now you. I hope you didn't take offense at my remarks, Susan dear. I'm an incurable matchmaker. I have this wild compulsion to pair people off, particularly when they're two such gorgeous people." She threw back her head, laughing gleefully. "I'm sure I won't have to do any matchmaking in this case. Craig's bound to fall for you, and he's a very determined young man."

"I can be very determined myself," I replied, "particularly when it comes to preserving my——"

"Virtue?" she asked merrily.

"——my independence," I said firmly.

"You're such a *stick*, Susan!" She scolded. "But that'll change. You're your mother's daughter and *my* niece. Blood is bound to tell!"

I laughed in spite of myself. It was impossible to be irritated with Aunt Agatha for long. Life itself was a miracle to her, and she celebrated it every day with vivacious zest. Her gaiety was infectious, and I felt myself loosening up, forgetting my qualms. She was chatting about her collection of cactus plants as we turned the corner and a woman stepped out into the hall from one of the back rooms, giving both of us a start.

"My God, Mildred!" Aunt Agatha cried. "Do you have to *creep* like that? Can't you make a little noise and let people know you're about?"

"I'm sorry, ma'am," the woman sniffled.

"Don't whine, girl! I can't abide whining!"

I stared at the woman in fascination, not knowing whether to burst into laughter or draw back in horror. She was truly pathetic, almost comically so. She wore heavy white shoes, white cotton stockings, a rumpled white nurse's uniform, and a shapeless brown sweater pulled around her shoulders. Her face was round and jowly, a thick layer of pancake hiding blemishes, and her brown eyes were mournful. Her mousy brown hair was

worn in an untidy bun on the back of her neck, limp
strands spilling out of place. She could have been twenty
—or fifty-five.

"I've been looking all over for you," Mildred said in
her weak, nasal voice. "You know it's time to take your
pill. Dr. Matthews says one pill before every meal and it's
lunchtime now and——"

"Run along, Mildred," Aunt Agatha said in haughty
tones. "I have no intention of taking one of your bloody
pills, and you can tell Dr. Matthews I said so! Out of my
sight! Why I keep you on I'll never know——"

"But Lady Gordon——" she protested.

"Out, out!" my aunt cried, as though she were shooing
away a bothersome child. Mildred shuffled on down the
hall, casting mournful glances at us over her shoulder.

"What on earth——" I began.

"A creature as ugly as that should be chloroformed
at birth!" my aunt said irritably. "God knows we can't all
be attractive, but Mildred seems to glory in her drabness.
I expect her to vanish into the woodwork any day now!"

"But she was wearing a nurse's uniform——"

"She's a nurse! It stands to reason she'd be wearing a
uniform."

"But what——"

"It's very simple, dear," she said. "I was down with a
rather bad spot of flu last month and had to stay in bed
a week or so—nothing serious, I assure you. Paul insisted
on sending that wretched creature over. She drove me up
the wall, I don't mind telling you! Can you imagine being
cooped up with someone like Mildred hovering over you?
Sheer horror! I went hoarse shouting at her."

"Why is she still here?"

"Poor thing hasn't anyplace else to go, actually, and
Paul thinks she should be on hand to see that I get the
proper rest and take my pills. Nonsense, of course, but I
appreciate his concern. Paul is an old and dear friend. I
let Mildred stay just to humor him, although I spend most
of my time trying to elude the creature!"

"But if you're not still sick——"

"Do I *look* sick?" she snapped.

"Of course not, but——"

"There's absolutely *nothing* to worry about," she said

impatiently. "I have never felt better in my life. The pills are merely vitamin capsules, and I wouldn't touch 'em for the world! I have my own herb garden in back, you know, and it's kept me fit as a fiddle for thirty years. I wouldn't have caught the flu in the first place if I hadn't gone out in the rain to take Althea some broth. That was pure folly."

She gave my arm a tight squeeze and led me toward the kitchen area. I could smell bread baking, and there was the tangy aroma of apples from the pantry. Aunt Agatha stopped to brush a speck of lint from her skirt, then turned to give me a close scrutiny, an expression of deep concentration on her long, plain face.

"You know, dear," she said briskly, "you could use some of my herbs yourself. I don't know that it's *healthy* living in that crowded city with all those fumes and that nasty wet weather. I suppose you still have those dreadful habits, too. Sleeping till noon—shocking! I'll make you some of my special tea. It'll build up that tired blood."

"But I don't *have* tired blood," I protested.

"Works wonders for constipation, too," she continued, ignoring my comment. "Come along, Susan!" She nodded her head firmly and linked her arm in mine again, leading me on toward the kitchen. I felt absolutely helpless against her authoritative manner, and delighted, too. Aunt Agatha was like a force of nature, sweeping one along with her. I found it delightful to be swept along with such incredible gusto.

Although she refused to take her pills and led the poor nurse a merry chase, Aunt Agatha's one concession was to take a nap every afternoon after lunch. She wanted to make today an exception, but I insisted she go on upstairs. She did so with reluctance, first having a long consultation with Cook and then informing me we were to have a grand dinner that evening, candlelight and wine, quite formal. Dr. Matthews would be coming, and it would be super. After she had gone to her bedroom I decided to take a tour of the gardens. I hadn't seen Craig Stanton since he showed me to my room. I supposed he was working on his book or, perhaps, searching for the

manuscripts. I didn't particularly want to see him again
just yet, and touring the gardens would give me an opportunity to think about some of the remarkable things I
had learned this morning.

The terrace was charming, the cracked white tiles
washed with sun and dappled with soft purple shadows
from the trees growing around it. Earl was curled up on
a shabby chaise longue with green plastic cushions, and
an old yellow straw hat and a pair of shears rested on a
low white iron table beside the chaise longue. Pots of vivid
blue delphiniums added a friendly touch. It was a peaceful
spot, one Aunt Agatha had described in many of her
letters. I knew she liked to sit out here in the morning
sun, write her letters, and read the bloodthirsty thrillers
she devoured so ardently.

Earl looked up with sleepy eyes when he heard my
heels tapping on the tiles. He gave a formidable yawn,
shook his sleek silver body, and leaped from his bed. I allowed him one kiss, then told him in no uncertain terms
that our friendship was going to be strictly platonic. He
tilted his head to one side, listening intently, and I could
have sworn he understood every word. Nevertheless, he
gave me another slurping smack on the cheek and capered about like an overgrown puppy, following me
down the low white marble steps that led to the gardens.
Outrageous animal, I thought, rather flattered to have
inspired such immediate and abounding affection.

Although the lawns and gardens of Gordonwood were
vast and wooded, the gardens near the house were neater,
more formal in arrangement, a flagstone path winding
among them and narrow white marble steps leading down
from one level to another. There were shady arbors and
tall green shrubs and latticework trellises covered with
thick honeysuckle making fragrant tunnels, cool and
green. I wandered aimlessly, admiring the full-blown yellow and salmon-orange roses in their neat beds. Holly-
hocks and blazing red poppies grew against rough-hewn
graystone walls, and birds scolded from the leafy seclusion of the oak boughs overhead. Earl ran on ahead with
energetic leaps and bounds, looking around to see that I
was following, quite clearly showing off for my benefit.

I paused at one of the lower levels, looking back up

toward the house. Seen from this distance, it was still large and formidable, black-green ivy growing up one of the gray walls, crumbly orange chimneys and squat black smokestacks adorning the multileveled green slate roof. The leaded windows were dark, almost opaque it seemed from here, and the enormous oak trees growing so near the house made it seem even more ponderous. It looked much as it must have looked a hundred years ago, when Sir Robert Gordon stalked through the halls in one of his dark rages and Lady Arabella in cool muslin gown served tea and cakes to the ladies in her charity organizations. I could imagine the two of them dwelling within those somber walls with their son and the frail young daughter who had died from consumption, but it seemed unreasonable of Aunt Agatha to stay here when she could have a charming flat in London. She loved the place, though, and it was home to her, for all its size and inconveniences.

A squirrel chattered noisily on the shaded green lawn behind me, darting from tree to tree on nimble feet, and Earl took out after it, barking lustily and deserting me for livelier activity. I slowly wandered down a narrow path between two solid walls of tall green shrubbery that towered up a good ten feet. Sun gilded the thick rustling leaves, and insects buzzed loudly. It was pleasant here, I thought, turning a corner, still surrounded by shrubs. There was the pungent odor of soil and healthy growth, a vivid blue sky above filled with wind-torn clouds and, on either side, the thick green walls. Charming place. One could forget everything. . . . I turned another corner, only to find another aisle between the shrubs. I was curious now, wondering where all this was leading.

I turned corner after corner, only to find more aisles. The shrubs were not so neatly trimmed here, ragged limbs and leaves sticking out, the path between them more narrow. I stopped, staring about me in dismay, and then I realized what I had done. I remembered my aunt's voice from a long time ago, telling me not to wander in the maze, little girls got lost there and missed their dinners. I had completely forgotten that warning, had forgotten that the maze even existed, yet I had plunged straight into it like a prize idiot. I remembered looking

down at it from my bedroom window when I was a child
on that first visit: a great green square of shrubs that
covered the whole lower level. It looked like a pretty
geometric pattern seen from the bedroom window, but it
didn't look so pretty now.

I told myself not to panic. I was ordinarily quite calm,
unruffled by most feminine phobias. Mice didn't bother
me, and I was tolerant of spiders and wasps and assorted flying insects that caused many of my girlfriends to
go into screaming hysterics, but the one thing that
caused me to lose complete control was closed, confined
places. I'd walk up ten flights of steep stairs to avoid
riding an elevator, and closed public phone booths were
out of the question. You're not confined, I told myself,
there's a bright blue sky above and all this fresh *air*, but
nevertheless the dark leafy walls on either side seemed to
loom up with a sinister force, pressing towards me,
threatening to crush and destroy. It was absurd, absurd,
I knew, yet the panic was there and it was a very real
thing inside me.

I forced myself to turn around and walk back the
way I had come, moving at a normal pace when I wanted
to run. I knew that if I once let go, if I ran screaming
down the aisles with pounding heart, I would be utterly
demolished. Turning the corner, I strolled down the next
aisle, then turned again, quelling the panic. Yes, I was
going the right way. I remembered that shaggy tear in
the shrub and that patch of jade-green leaves among the
darker ones. In a matter of minutes I would be out of
this dreadful place, back among the roses and the sweeping lawns. I wondered what diabolic mind conceived the
maze in the first place. What *purpose* did it serve? It was
a wretched thing, designed to confuse and bewilder. I
walked slowly down the narrow pathway, branches brushing my shoulders, concentrating on the turns. I felt quite
confident now, certain I was going the right way. Then I
saw the patch of jade-green leaves again.

I wanted to cry, but I didn't dare. My face was
flushed, my cheeks a bright pink, and hair had tumbled
over my forehead. I brushed it away, trying to maintain a
degree of calm. I had made a simple mistake, turning to
the left when I should have turned to the right, and it

had brought me back to the place I started from. Hysteria began to mount inside, threatening to spill over any minute now. I could visualize hours and hours spent trying to find my way out of this hellish trap.

Use your logic, I told myself. The house was due north from the maze, but which way was north? I had absolutely no sense of direction. I remembered those awful weeks at camp when I was a child. We had worn white middy blouses and blue skirts and I had been utterly miserable when Old Hatcher with her blonde braids and stocky body had herded us out into the woods, barking commands and blowing her whistle if any of us got out of line. She had pointed out all sorts of dreary things like bark and birds' nests, and there had been lectures on survival. You could always find your way out of the woods by looking at the lichen, I remembered, and any fool could get a sense of direction by seeing where the sun was in the sky. Great, but there was no lichen on the shrubs, and I could see nothing overhead but the blue sky. The sun was up there somewhere, most assuredly, but I couldn't see it from where I stood.

I could stand here and scream until someone found me, I reasoned, or I could hold on and hope to find my way out on my own. The first alternative was far too humiliating to contemplate, so I chose the second one, squaring my shoulders and marching with brisk determination down the narrow pathway between the towering green walls. Fifteen minutes later I was in a state of nervous shock. The exit might be right around the next turn, I told myself, but I had been telling myself that every time I took another corner. Freedom was so close and yet so tormentingly out of reach.

Then I heard footsteps and the sound of someone whistling. I felt an unreasonable panic, remembering the dark form in the east wing, remembering there had been prowlers at Gordonwood. I was trapped, helpless . . . errant nonsense, of course. It was broad daylight, and surely no one with sinister motives would whistle like that. I forced my leaping pulses to be still and drew myself up with shaky composure. Rescue was at hand. Should I call out? The thought of anyone finding me in this ridiculous predicament was embarrassing, yet the thought of spending the rest of the afternoon in the maze was even more alarming. I cleared my throat, preparing to call out as casually as possible.

"You there?" a voice called before I could make my presence known. It was Craig Stanton. It *would* be him, I thought miserably, brushing back my disheveled hair and smoothing my skirt.

"I say, are you there?"

"H—here," I stammered.

"Louder. I'll have to locate you by the sound of your voice."

"Here!" I shouted.

A few minutes later Craig Stanton strolled around the corner, a look of devilish amusement in his eyes. He cocked his head and grinned boyishly. He was still wearing the tight jeans and bulky white sweater, and I tried not to marvel at his stunning good looks: those sculptured cheekbones, that strong jaw, those magnetic blue eyes, and the dark brown hair that tumbled over his forehead in such rich locks. His virile male beauty disturbed me, and I was painfully conscious of my own state of dishevelment: green linen dress rumpled, hair spilling down untidily, cheeks flushed a bright pink. He chuckled, lips still curled in that maddening grin.

"This is delightful," he said. "It isn't often one has an opportunity to rescue a maiden in distress."

"I don't need rescuing, thank you. I–I was just taking a pleasant stroll——"

"And I just happened to be on the terrace when I saw you stepping into the maze. Thought at the time it was a damned foolhardy thing to do, but I assumed you knew how to find your way about. When half an hour passed and you still hadn't come out——"

He paused. "Well," he said huskily, "here we are— alone." He lowered heavy lids over lazy blue eyes, turning it on full blast. Some women would have melted. I found it slightly ludicrous.

"Do you try to seduce every woman you meet?" I asked, my voice pure acid.

"Not all of them," he said lazily. "Once in a while I let one or two slip by."

"Your conceit knows no bounds, Mr. Stanton."

He looked at me beneath drooping lids, blue eyes lazy and seductive. "We both know there's going to be something between us," he said. "Don't fight it."

"My God! Where did you pick up *that* bit of dialogue?"

"From your last novel, as a matter of fact. Norman said it to Lauren as they were standing in the ruined temple. Agatha insisted I read the book when she found out you were coming. I must say, it was quite revealing. One can learn a great deal about the author from the book——"

"It was a work of pure fiction," I said calmly.

"The hero was very interesting, the kind of man women dream about. I gather you've done your share of dreaming."

"Nonsense. Heroes in romantic novels have to be dashing. I can assure you that if any man acted like that in real life a woman would laugh in his face."

"Indeed? You're quite sure of that?"

"Quite sure," I said icily. "Shall we leave?"

I gave him a cool, frigid stare. He frowned, lowering his brows. He looked rather angry, eyes dark, mouth turned down, as though he found it incredible that I hadn't tumbled into his arms. Turning abruptly, he strode briskly down the aisle between the shrubs. I had to trot to catch up with him. He moved up and down the aisles with complete confidence, turning left and right and left again without the least hesitation, obviously familiar with every shift and change of its intricate pattern. I stumbled, almost crashing into a leafy green wall, but Craig Stanton didn't hesitate, didn't so much as glance back. He moved quickly in that long stride, turning a corner and going out of sight. I was infuriated, but I ran like crazy, terrified at the thought of losing him. A few minutes later I stumbled out of the maze, incredibly relieved to see the open air again. Craig Stanton was waiting, arms folded across his chest.

"Took your time, pet," he said.

"I almost lost you," I snapped. "You're hardly gallant, Mr. Stanton."

"Gallant? Guess I'm not. I'm a real man, you see, not one of your romantic heroes."

He gazed at me for a moment while I tried to compose myself. I loathed the man, I told myself, yet in all honesty I had to admit I wasn't entirely immune to his charm. The charm was quite real and, combined with his good looks, quite formidable.

"You're an expert at handling fictional romance," he said, "but I wonder how much you know about the genuine article."

"I hardly think I need lessons from you," I retorted.

"No?"

He stepped over to me and laid his hands on my shoulders, looking down into my eyes. The smile curled lightly on his lips, and his eyes gleamed with intolerable amusement. I stood rigid, far too aware of his nearness, far too disturbed by those heavy hands kneading the flesh of my shoulders. His face was inches from my own, and I could see the tiny scar at the corner of his mouth where he had cut himself shaving. I felt totally helpless, hypnotized by the man. He raised one hand and curled his fingers around my chin, tilting my head back.

"We'll see," he said quietly.

He pulled me into his arms, holding me loosely, and I didn't make any attempt to struggle. He looked deep into my eyes for a moment before leaning down and fastening his mouth over mine. The kiss was casual, not at all passionate, but it was effective nevertheless.

"Lesson number one," he said.

I drew my arm back and smashed my palm against his cheek, putting all I had into the slap. He looked stunned, eyes wide, mouth parted. Then he threw back his head and burst into gales of hearty laughter.

"You've got good reflexes," he said.

Locks of dark brown hair had fallen forward, almost covering his forehead. He brushed them aside and rubbed his cheek.

"Now if I were one of your heroes," he said, "like Norman, for example, how would I react? Let me see— ah, yes——"

He took hold of my wrist and swung me into his arms again, holding me in the curve of his arm. His second kiss was as casual as the first, and as effective. I gathered his hair in my fingers, intending to jerk his head back. Instead, I slipped my hands down, placing the palms flat on his back. I could feel his muscles tense under the bulky sweater. Craig Stanton got the response he wanted, and then he released me, smiling a smug smile.

"I hope you're satisfied with yourself," I said angrily.

"Oh, I am," he replied lightly. "You're not laughing. You're supposed to laugh in my face, remember?"

He folded one arm across his waist, extending the other toward me. He leaned forward, executing a mocking bow, for all the world like an Edwardian dandy.

"Farewell, fair maiden," he teased.

"Go to hell!" I cried.

He walked away, heading for the house. I stood watching him, furious, of course, loathing his arrogance, yet disturbed by those other reactions that were as real as my rage. He was far away now, moving toward the terrace. He had an attractive walk, as though he owned the world, and the sun seemed to gild his dark hair with bronze highlights. He strolled on across the terrace and into the house through the opened French windows. I thought about the dinner party Aunt Agatha had planned for this evening. I wondered if I should wear my sexy violet-blue silk cocktail dress.

CHAPTER FOUR

As it happened, I didn't wear the dress after all. Aunt Agatha and I spent the remainder of the afternoon talking about things that had happened to us since our last meeting. I told her about my flat in London, my friends, my publisher, and she chatted volubly about the Gordon papers, describing the search she and Craig were making. By the time I finally got to my room, my whole attitude about the incident in the maze had changed. I realized that I had acted like a bloody fool and decided that cool dignity would certainly be the best policy to employ towards Craig Stanton. I fingered the sexy dress for a moment, rubbing the violet-blue silk between my fingers, then took down a dress of crushed golden-brown velvet. It would be far more appropriate.

Nevertheless, I took great pains with my appearance, spending almost half an hour on my hair. I arranged it in an elegant French roll, a string of pearls entwined in the carefully stacked waves. The result was extremely flattering. Applying subtle brown shadow on my lids and a suggestion of coral to my lips, I stood back to examine myself. The dress had a modest neckline, long sleeves and form-fitting bodice, the full skirt falling in velvety folds to my knees. I looked quite unlike the hysterical ninny who had acted such an idiot this afternoon. In the warm golden glow of the oil lamps, I looked, in fact, frightfully sophisticated. Craig Stanton wasn't going to think me an inexperienced schoolgirl tonight.

Taking one of the oil lamps, I left the room. It was after seven thirty, and we would dine at eight. The corridors were dark and gloomy, but I was prepared for that. I knew my way about now and certainly didn't intend to go traipsing into the east wing. Still, I wished I had had the foresight to leave few lamps scattered about along the way. The lack of electricity might be romantic, but it hardly helped relieve the gloom. The light of my lamp flickered on the walls, making dancing gold and black patterns, and I had to restrain a shudder as I passed the east wing. I walked rapidly, my high heels tripping along on the carpet, the dancing shadows following me as I turned down the main hall and reached the head of the staircase.

I heard someone knocking on the front door as I went downstairs, and turning down the landing I saw the nurse, Mildred, opening the door for a man. Tall white candles burned in half a dozen candelabra, illuminating the hall with a bright golden light. The man stepped inside and Mildred closed the door behind him. Poor thing, she was wearing an unfortunate dress of blue-gray velvet, the nap worn and shiny, the cut impossibly old-fashioned. Her mousy brown hair was worn in an untidy bun, a gold barrette clipped on as an afterthought. Her pathetic attempt at elegance only emphasized her ugliness, and I found it rather touching. With her slumped shoulders and clumpy black shoes she looked like something out of an old horror film.

"And how's the patient today?" the man asked.

"I don't *know*," Mildred whined. "She won't let me *do* for her. I tried to make her take her pills, but——"

"I'll talk to her," he said pleasantly, smiling warmly. "And who is this?" he added as I walked towards them.

"Susan Marlow," I said. "Agatha's niece. You must be Dr. Matthews."

I set my oil lamp down on a table. The man nodded, still smiling.

"Right," he said, extending his hand. He gave my hand a firm, hearty shake, and I could feel the energy and vitality of the man as he squeezed. Mildred shuffled away, disappearing into one of the rooms, leaving the two of us together.

"Agatha told me you were coming," he said, "although I didn't expect you so soon. I hope now that you're here you'll help us keep her in line."

"Is my aunt really ill?" I inquired.

"No, not seriously—nothing to be alarmed about.

She just needs to slow down a bit, needs to get more rest, take her vitamins. The flu left her rather weaker than she imagines, and she insists on charging about like a sergeant major on maneuvers. I hoped Mildred would be able to subdue her somewhat, but—" He shrugged his shoulders. "Maybe you'll be more successful."

"I'll certainly try," I replied.

Dr. Paul Matthews was in his early forties, one of those ruddy, robust men who was a walking advertisement for his profession. Quite tall, he was solidly built, with broad shoulders and a large frame. His features were rough-hewn: square jaw, wide, rather sensuous mouth, large nose, and heavy brows over dark brown eyes. Deeply tanned, his face was lined and stamped with character, and his hair was golden-bronze, more red than brown, very thick and wavy. He was the kind of man who immediately inspires confidence, who exudes strength and purpose. Dressed in a formal black suit with a poorly knotted black bow tie above a gleaming white shirtfront, he looked rather uncomfortable. I imagined he would feel more at home in stout boots and an old tweed jacket with leather patches at the elbows.

"I must say," he remarked, "your photographs hardly do you justice."

"You've seen photographs of me?"

"On the dust jackets of your books," he explained. "Agatha has given me copies of all of them—which I've read, incidentally, and enjoyed enormously. You're remarkably talented, Miss Marlow, as well as being quite a fetching young woman."

"I can see why your patients love you," I said, pleased by his gallantry. The man was so large, so hearty, with undeniable warmth. I wondered how he had managed to stay single. He was everything a woman could hope for in a man. He was not really handsome, I thought, but he had an overwhelming magnetism, that rare quality that show people called great presence.

"Oh, I'm quite severe with them," he replied. "Have to be firm, you know, keep the upper hand. Don't believe in coddling them. If you were one of my patients, I wouldn't dream of complimenting you. I'd treat you with the proper severity."

"I'm sure I'd love it," I said, smiling.

"Let's hope you never have occasion to find out," Paul Matthews said. His voice suited him perfectly: it was rich and deep, rather harsh, the voice of a big man full of self-confidence.

"I believe Aunt Agatha plans to meet us in the grand drawing room," I said. "Shall we go?"

Paul Matthews took my arm and led the way. The grand drawing room was much larger than the one leading onto the terrace. The walls were covered with richly embossed dark blue paper, and two tremendous chandeliers hung from a dark ivory ceiling, candles burning, crystal pendants reflecting spokes of rainbow-hued light. The carpet was rich purple, the draperies heavy beige satin embroidered with gold. There were antique white tables, chairs upholstered in blue and violet, two long white sofas. Craig Stanton stood at the enormous white marble fireplace, prodding the crackling logs with a long black poker. He looked up as we came in.

"Matthews," he said, giving a curt nod. He didn't acknowledge my presence.

"Stanton," Paul Matthews said, returning the nod. "How are you?"

"Healthy," Craig said, and I sensed immediately that the two men did not care for each other.

"Aunt Agatha hasn't come down yet?" I inquired.

"She's gone to fetch Althea. They'll be here shortly. Mildred's gone to help Cook with last-minute preparations. Any more questions?"

"I say, Stanton," Paul protested. "You needn't be so rude."

"Was I being rude?" Craig asked, lifting one eyebrow. He gave a wry smile. "Perhaps I was. I've spent the last half hour lighting all these damned candles. Somebody should set a fire under those people at the power plant. Frightfully inconvenient having no electricity."

"I think the candlelight is charming," I said.

"It certainly becomes you," he replied. He tossed the compliment out as though it were a rather shabby bone, his attitude nullifying the words. I tried not to show my anger.

"Care for a drink?" Paul inquired, moving over to a

silver cart laden with various bottles and decanters.
"Sherry?"

"Scotch," I said, "if there is any. Straight, please."

Craig Stanton smiled at this, as though I were a child
playing at being a grown-up. He was formidably handsome in his dress clothes: the black pants narrow, the
white shirt ruffled down the front, the black bow tie at
a rakish angle. His loosely cut jacket was dark maroon,
embroidered with black silk flowers. As is frequently the
case, the fancy clothes merely emphasized his virility,
pointing it up and making it all the more apparent. He
might have stepped right out of a spinster's dream.

Paul Matthews handed me my drink. I thanked him,
flirting just a little. If I had hoped to make Craig notice,
it was wasted effort. He had turned back to the fire, viciously jabbing at the logs with the poker. Paul Matthews
sipped his drink, the glass looking shockingly fragile in
his big brown hand. He was not the sort of man to be at
ease in a drawing room, I thought, too robust, too vital
to be quite comfortable among all the elegant trap-
pings.

"Are you working on another book?" he asked.

"I've just finished one," I replied. "I'll begin the next
as soon as my holiday is over."

"Another thriller?"

"Naturally," Craig Stanton interrupted. "With lots of
romance. She's an authority on romance."

"As a matter of *fact*," I said stiffly, giving him a
furious glance, "it will be primarily an historical novel
about young John Gordon's attempt to abduct Mary
Queen of Scots during the early days of her reign. He
was quite a dashing figure, and she was a beautiful young
widow at that particular time."

"Sounds like a fascinating idea," Paul replied, nodding.

"My editor likes it," I said. "It has all the elements of
good fiction: a beautiful heroine, an attractive, irrever-
ent young hero, a rowdy period of history. Of course I'll
have to include all those embellishments my fans have
come to expect—suspense, chills, narrow escapes. That
will mean taking a few liberties with the facts, but that's
a novelist's prerogative."

"Naturally," Craig said. "Facts aren't all that important."

"I suppose you've done a lot of research?" Paul inquired, deliberately ignoring Craig's remark.

"Oh yes, I've spent hours in the reading room of the British Museum, and I've collected a great many books on the subject——"

Dr. Matthews and I began to discuss historical research. Craig Stanton listened, his manner condescending, a rather smug look on his face. He was, of course, an expert on the subject, but he chose to remain silent, going over to the cart to mix a drink, prowling around the room like a graceful animal in captivity. His movements distracted me, and I found it hard to concentrate on what Paul was saying. I was relieved to hear footsteps in the hall and see my aunt come in with the much-mentioned Althea.

Aunt Agatha wore a simple black gown, long-sleeved, the skirt sweeping the floor. The rope of lustrous pearls was around her neck. Her face was radiant with excitement, and she managed to look almost beautiful. The woman at her side was another matter altogether. Almost as tall as my aunt, she was undeniably heavy, plump and round all over. Her taffeta dress was bright green, crackling stiffly with every step she took, and her face was almost clown-like with its ludicrous makeup. Her mouth was too red, her cheeks too pink, her lids coated with violet eye shadow. Her hair was an incredible shade of red, blazing red curls tumbling in shrieking profusion to frame her round face. There was a foggy look in her greenish-gray eyes, and she staggered as she came into the room, holding onto my aunt's arm for support.

"I *hate* to meet people!" she protested. "I don't know why you drug me over here, Aggie! There are so many more interesting things I could be doing."

"Hush, Althea," my aunt scolded. "Look, here's Susan. Susan, this is Althea."

"Pleased to meet you," I said.

"My, you *are* pretty," Althea said, smiling a lopsided smile. "Aggie always exaggerates so. My dear, you've got lovely bone structure. You must let me paint you!

Yes," she added, nodding briskly, "I'm going to like you. I fancy I shall. Twenty years ago, I'd have hated you on *sight* with those glorious cheekbones of yours, but now——"

"Here's Craig," Aunt Agatha interrupted, "and Dr. Matthews."

"Evenin', ducky," she said, waving gaily to Craig. "God! Such a gorgeous male! And the good doctor— don't say a word to me. I've had one or *two* drinks. Yes, I'll admit it, and I don't intend to listen to any of your stuffy old lectures. So there!"

With that, she opened her evening bag, whipped out a flask, and took a mighty swig, staring at us defiantly as she fastened the top back on the flask and put it in her bag again. Aunt Agatha raised her eyes heavenwards, Paul Matthews frowned, and Craig merely grinned wickedly. As for me, I found the old girl thoroughly enchanting. She might stagger, she might reek of gin, yet she knew exactly who she was, and she couldn't have cared less what anyone thought. She marched unsteadily over to one of the white sofas and plopped down, green skirt crackling noisily. She glared at us for a moment, then fell back against the cushions and was instantly asleep.

"She's a pet, actually," Aunt Agatha told me.

"I don't doubt it for a moment," I said.

"I felt it would do her good to get out for a while," she explained to Paul. "She didn't want to come, but I insisted. She's really been quite upset by all the excitement——"

Paul frowned, looking very much the professional doctor. "I'm afraid we're going to have to do something about Althea one day soon," he said in a sober voice. "She isn't getting any better——"

"Nonsense! Althea's the happiest creature on earth. As long as she has her daily quota of gin——"

"That's precisely what I mean," he retorted. "She's too much responsibility on you, Agatha. You can't keep on nursing her like——"

"I refuse to hear another word on the subject!" Aunt Agatha said firmly, cutting him short. "Tonight we're celebrating the arrival of my lovely niece. We're all to be merry and gay. You two gentlemen must amuse us!

Fetch me a drink, Craig, and make it a double!"

Paul Matthews lifted his heavy shoulders in a shrug, smiling in spite of himself. Aunt Agatha downed her drink like a trooper, with considerable relish. She and the doctor chatted about the citizens of Gordonville, my aunt pumping him for all the newest gossip, and I sipped my Scotch, perching on the arm of the sofa. Craig was standing across the room, apparently intrigued by a set of prints hanging on the wall, but I saw him glancing up at me every now and then.

I felt very content. I was sure I had captured his interest, and it was pleasant to contemplate. The room was lovely by candlelight, all faded elegance and old world charm. The fire burned quietly in the fireplace now, washing the hearth with a flickering orange light, and soft shadows spread over the dark blue wallpaper. Aunt Agatha reached up and squeezed my hand, and I gave her a reassuring smile. It was so grand being here, temporarily freed from the furor and routine of London. I finished the drink, alcohol enhancing my mood.

"Cook says dinner's ready," Mildred said, creeping into the room like a mournful vampire. "We can be seated now, ma'am."

"Thank you, Mildred," Aunt Agatha replied. "Craig, if you would help Althea into the dining room——"

"Come on, luv," Craig said, seizing Althea's wrists and pulling her to her feet. "Time to eat."

"What? What's happening! I was havin' the most *amazing* dream——"

"Tell us about it later," he said. Holding her firmly by the elbow, he propelled her towards the dining room. She lolled against him, a merry smile on her lips. Aunt Agatha linked her arm in mine, and Paul was left to escort Mildred out of the room.

The dining room was paneled in dark fumed oak, with colorful enameled shields and spears on the walls. Heavy brass chandeliers hung from the high beamed ceiling, spilling light over the long baronial table with its tall, heavily carved oak chairs upholstered in old red velvet. It was an impressive room, I thought, though hardly cozy. Cook started serving the meal as soon as we were seated. She was a large, heavy-set woman with a no-nonsense face and steel-gray hair, wearing a white apron over her black uniform. She was obviously in a hurry to get the meal over with so that she could clear up and drive back to Gordonville. She looked rather grumpy as she brought in the soup.

"I'm afraid she's rather put out because I asked her to stay so late," Aunt Agatha apologized. "Too, this is Mary's day off and she wasn't here to help. Oh dear, isn't the soup a bit *cold?*"

"It's fine," I protested.

"Tell me, Agatha," Paul Matthews began, "have you made any more progress in your search?"

"We haven't found anything yet," she said, "but we're still looking. We didn't search today, of course, what with Susan arriving, but yesterday we started going through all those trunks and boxes in the basement. Craig had to move ever so many. There are several more we have to go through. I'm sure we'll turn something up sooner or later——"

"You've searched the whole house?"

"Most of it. There are a few rooms we haven't got to yet."

Paul shook his head. I could tell that he had little faith in the existence of the Gordon papers. Althea had been sitting slumped back in her chair. She suddenly sat up very straight, her gray-green eyes alert.

"Nothing but trouble," she mumbled.

"What's that, Althea?" my aunt said.

"I said there's been nothing but trouble ever since you started poking around for those papers. That article in the paper, all those letters, and then those men trying to break into the house——"

"They were harmless chaps, just looking for excitement," Aunt Agatha protested. "Besides, Craig caught them. I'll never forget the way he tackled that poor chap on the terrace. You should have seen it, Susan! He ran outside and *flew* at the man, knocking him down and then getting a firm grip around the startled chap's throat. I'm quite sure he would have strangled the man if I hadn't intervened——"

"Didn't you call the police?" I inquired.

"Of course not! He was merely a rather dim-witted fellow from the village, looking for thrills. I let him off with a stern warning. The *second* intruder was another matter altogether. He was actually in the house! How he broke in I'll never know. Craig caught him, too, but the fellow fought loose and ran away before we could catch him again. Paul sent the dogs over after that, and we haven't had any more trouble."

"Humph!" Althea snorted.

"Althea, you know there haven't been any more intruders. You have a very vivid imagination, and——"

"I-know-what-I-know," she said enigmatically, pushing her soup aside and taking out the flask for another nip.

"Althea claims she has seen people on the property at night," my aunt said, raising her brows. "Dower House looks out over the back lawns, down towards the lake, and she claims——"

"I-don't-want-to-discuss-it," Althea said haughtily. "I've warned you, Aggie, but you won't listen to me. Oh no, I *imagine* things! Well, when we all wake up with our throats slit you'll sing a different tune."

"I rather fancy it would be difficult to wake up with a slit throat," Craig said, grinning at Althea, "much less sing a tune afterwards. But if anyone could do it, you'd be just the girl, Althea. I'm betting on it."

"Go ahead and mock," she said with tipsy dignity. "See if I care. I may *nip*, but I'm not blind!"

"You've been nipping far too much," Paul said sternly. "Two bottles of gin a day, more or less. It's a wonder you don't see bats——"

"Oh, I do. A whole flock of the charming little creatures hang about on the trees down by the lake. You're not so smart, you and your pills and prescriptions and fancy Latin words. I know what's-real-and-what's-not." She made a face at him and slumped back in her chair.

"I hope this isn't *alarm*ing you, Susan," Aunt Agatha said.

"I have nerves of steel," I said, not quite truthfully.

"We turn the dogs loose in the house when we get ready to retire," she explained. "They roam up and down the halls. I can assure you, if anyone tried to break in we'd know about it. Besides, Craig's a judo expert. He's won several trophies."

"Wonderful," I said.

"I'll teach you a few locks and holds," he told me.

"I'll bet you'd love that," I replied.

"So you see," Aunt Agatha continued, "there's nothing whatsoever to be alarmed about."

"Ta ta!" Althea clucked. "You'll see."

Mildred hadn't said a word during all this time. Her face was chalky pale beneath the pancake makeup, and she looked tense, as though she might bolt out of her chair at any moment and run screaming out of the room. The poor thing was undoubtedly nervous to begin with, and all this talk about intruders didn't help. She was pathetic in her worn gray velvet and untidy coiffure, completely out of place at this baronial table, and I couldn't help but be a little sorry for her. Paul Matthews evidently felt the same way. He gave her a reassuring smile, but she merely drew back in her chair and stared fixedly at her plate.

We were on the third course now. Aunt Agatha was complaining that the meat was tough, which was certainly true. The wine was slightly sour, but that didn't prevent Althea from gulping hers down with gusto. Seeing that I didn't intend to drink mine, she reached over and took my glass, giving me a sly little smile, as though we were conspirators. Craig immediately set his glass in front of her as well, and Althea looked positively elated. Dr. Matthews frowned disapprovingly. Althea actually stuck her tongue out at him.

"——an American, I think," my aunt was saying. "Anyway, he's shockingly wealthy. Over a million dollars he offered me. Over a million! Of course, I wrote back that it was out of the question. If we *were* to find the manuscripts, I certainly wouldn't sell them to some eccentric American collector. The fellow's living in London, and he wanted to come to Gordonwood to discuss the matter. What was the fellow's name, Craig?"

"Stephen Kirk, I believe. From Texas."

"That's right. Anyway, he was frightfully persistent. When I wrote back that I wouldn't see him, he phoned from London. Such a *drawl!* I told him, I said, 'Mr. Kirk, we haven't *found* the manuscripts, but if we do, they're certainly not for sale.' He upped his price, and I finally had to hang up on him."

"What *would* you do with the papers if you happened to find them?" Dr. Matthews asked.

"First of all, I'd let Craig use them for his book, and then I'd give them to Oxford, probably, for their collection, with permission to publish. I certainly wouldn't expect to make *money* from them."

Cook tromped in with dessert, bowls of starchy chocolate pudding. She plunked them down and looked at her watch rather pointedly, her stern face resembling thunderclouds. None of us found the pudding particularly appetizing, and in a few minutes Aunt Agatha told Cook she could clear the table and drive on back to Gordonville.

"I'm not intendin' to do all these dishes tonight!" Cook stated, very emphatic. She stood with hands on hips, glaring at all of us.

"Of course not," Aunt Agatha said, pacifying her. "Mary can help you with them in the morning."

"Some people expect a *lot,* and that's a fact!" Cook grumbled, her expression so fierce I wouldn't have been surprised to see her grab a butcher knife and go berserk.

We adjourned to the drawing room. Althea pranced merrily over to the liquor cart and started examining the bottles. Mildred asked to be excused, claiming she wanted to wash her hair. Aunt Agatha dismissed her promptly, with considerable relief, and Mildred shuffled out of the room, taking up an oil lamp to carry back upstairs with her. Craig stationed himself by the fireplace again, and Paul Matthews stood rather clumsily in front of the beige satin draperies, as though trapped by all this elegance.

"The meal was a disaster," Aunt Agatha said petulantly. "Cook deliberately planned it that way because I asked her to stay late. She's a *marvelous* cook—you know that, Paul. She deliberately sabotaged the meal tonight. That pudding! She makes smashing pastries, Susan. Please don't think tonight was any indication of what we usually have——"

"The meal was divine," I lied. "Even if it hadn't been, just being here with you——"

"You're so diplomatic," she said, sitting down on a padded blue chair. Althea finally selected a bottle, poured her drink, and trotted over to the sofa. The candles spluttered, burning down. I wandered over to examine some engravings on the wall on the other side of the room. Paul sat down beside Aunt Agatha and they began to discuss her refusal to take her pills. There was a loud explosion in front of the house, followed by the rumbling of a decrepit motor. I assumed it was Cook on her way back to the village.

"I see you survived this afternoon's perils," Craig Stanton said in a low voice, standing beside me. I had been concentrating on the sound of the car leaving and hadn't noticed him coming over. The others were across the room, Aunt Agatha and Paul immersed in their conversation, Althea twirling the liquor around in her glass.

"Yes, thank you," I said, my voice icily polite.

"I didn't go to hell," he told me. "I went to work instead, which is more or less the same thing. I spent the rest of the afternoon at my desk in the library, trying to finish up a rather difficult chapter. Thought I'd let you know, in case you were looking for me."

"Why on earth should I have been looking for you?"

"I can think of a lot of reasons."

"I'll bet you could at that," I said acidly.

"Do we have to be enemies?" he murmured seductively.

"We don't have to be *anything*," I hissed, glancing across the room to make sure the others couldn't overhear us. "I intend to avoid you like the plague, Mr. Stanton. I've had plenty of experience with men like you."

"You're delightful, you know," he said. "Most women throw themselves at me. You're the first one in a long time that's tried to resist me. Quite a novel experience."

"I'm sure it must be."

I was standing against the wall now. Craig glanced over his shoulder, saw that no one was paying attention to us and stepped closer, standing directly in front of me. He placed his palms on the wall, an arm on either side of me, making a prison. He leaned forward, his dark maroon jacket hanging loosely, the black silk embroidery gleaming in the candlelight. I saw the ruffles on his shirt, the rakishly knotted black bow tie, and I could smell his after-shave lotion, teakwood, a strong male scent.

"We're going to be great friends," he told me. "You enjoyed our little encounter this afternoon. Don't say you didn't."

I gave him a cool stare, not deigning to reply.

He chuckled and stepped away, strolling casually over toward the fireplace. He took up the poker and prodded the glowing orange logs, making blue and yellow sparks fly. I marched over to the liquor cart and poured a stiff Scotch. Craig laughed aloud when he observed this, the others turning to stare at him. He made a bow and grinned a cocky grin. Aunt Agatha smiled, pleased with him, and Paul looked bewildered. Althea merely nodded sharply. I had the strong impression that she had observed everything.

"Did you finish your chapter this afternoon, Craig?" Aunt Agatha inquired.

He nodded. "The first draft, at least. I'll have to check a few of my facts before I put it in final form."

"I'd like to see it later on tonight," she said.

"Feel free."

Paul Matthews stood up, heaving a sigh and taking out his watch. "It's getting late, Agatha," he said. "I imagine I should be getting back to town."

"I'm ready to leave, too," Althea said, pulling herself up with much crackling of green taffeta. "Craig, you want to escort me?"

"Certainly, luv. My pleasure."

He linked his arm in hers and took her out of the room. Aunt Agatha and I walked to the front door with Dr. Matthews. Earl and his brother were in the front hall. They leaped up happily when they saw their master. He petted both dogs, smiling at their enthusiasm. Prince was darker than his brother, his coat a sleek silvery blue.

"Down!" Paul cried. "That's enough! Run along now."

The dogs looked unhappy, slumping down on their haunches. Then Earl leaped up to give me another kiss on the cheek and both of them bounded out of the hall, their heavy paws making loud thumps.

"Earl has taken a fancy to Susan," Aunt Agatha said.

"Quite," I added.

"I'm glad to be rid of 'em for a while," Paul said, smiling broadly. "It's been a nice evening, Agatha. Thank you for asking me. I don't want to hear any more about your refusing the pills, hear? You need them, or I wouldn't have sent 'em over. It's been a pleasure meeting you," he continued, turning to me. "You keep an eye on her. Promise?"

"It's a promise," I replied.

Paul left, and Aunt Agatha squeezed my hand. "I'm going to go fetch Craig's chapter and take it on up to my bedroom," she said, brushing her long black skirt and fiddling with the rope of pearls. "Are you coming up, dear?"

"Not just yet," I replied. "I—I think I'll take a little walk in the gardens. I'm afraid I had a bit too much Scotch. The night air will do me good."

"Very well," she said, giving me a hug.

"What about the candles?" I inquired.

"Craig will put them out when he comes back. Your oil lamp is there on the table, I see. Be sure you take it up with you——"

"I wouldn't dream of going up without it," I said.

Aunt Agatha went on upstairs, and I was alone in the great hall, the candles splattering the walls with wavering golden light. I wasn't at all sleepy, and I *was* a bit giddy from the Scotch. I stepped through the small drawing room and opened the French windows, going on out onto the terrace. The moon was high, half obscured by enormous gray clouds, but pouring silvery light over their dark rims. Leaving the terrace, I strolled aimlessly toward the lake, positively determined to avoid Craig Stanton if he should by any chance see me on his return from Dower House.

CHAPTER FIVE

The gardens were drenched in moonlight, everything black and silver, sharply outlined, a misty haze in the air. It was rather like a neo-impressionist painting, I thought, pink and orange-pink roses barely showing their colors in the mellow light, tall green shrubs more black than green. Moving down the flat marble steps, I smelled the fragrant odors, a stronger odor of soil and dead leaves underlining the sweet smell of rose petals. It was rather chilly out, a breeze causing leaves to tremble. I paused, standing beside a broken marble column, staring up at the sky: moon free from clouds now, silver beams melting against the black-gray expanse overhead. It was a romantic night, I thought, a night made for lovers.

I frowned, thinking about Craig Stanton. In truth, I really hadn't stopped thinking of him. I was furious with him, and yet I wondered if the anger wasn't merely a self-imposed smoke screen to cover up deeper emotions I refused to acknowledge. The man had allure, quite plainly. I couldn't deny that. Was I really a stiff little prude, running away from him as he had suggested? Of course not, I told myself, moving on along the rows of rosebeds. I was just wary, and rightly so.

There had been other men in my life. A few years ago I had been smitten with a handsome young poet with soulful brown eyes and thick blond hair and a wide, sensuous mouth. I was still working as a secretary then, and Eric had seemed the epitome of all a young girl could dream of. He was attentive and kind, gentle and considerate but very male. He was also quite poor, living in a slum attic and scrounging for enough to live on. I gladly bought his lunches, his dinners. I even bought him a lovely brown suede jacket lined with sheepskin so he wouldn't catch cold. My secretary's wages weren't all that grand, and Eric found someone else, richer, better able to promote his poetry in the right circles. I was stung by the experience, yet I could afford to laugh at it now. I had been quite foolish, but I had learned to beware of too-tender sentiments.

Last year, while visiting my mother in Sydney, I had met a rich Australian rancher who tried to sweep me off my feet. He was robust and bursting with hormones, determined to take me into the bush and make me his bride. Quite handsome, he was, with unruly black hair and sapphire-blue eyes, and he owned half a dozen ranches. My mother was enthusiastic about my prospects and couldn't understand why I resisted. Reggie was a bit too aggressively male for my taste. He was like a force of nature, strong, obstinate, knocking aside all obstacles. He threatened to kidnap me if I didn't give him an answer soon. I booked immediate passage back to England, bidding my mother a fast farewell. Poor Reggie was probably still prowling the streets of Sydney, trying to abduct a suitable bride.

So I wasn't completely without experience. I had certainly had enough experience to be wary of a man like Craig Stanton. Actually, Paul Matthews was more my type: solid, strong, dependable, attractive with his craggy face and big, healthy build. A man like that would wear, with none of the mercurial, quicksilver qualities that were so dazzling and, ultimately, so elusive. But I wasn't ready for any kind of man. I was too content with my life the way it was. I had my career, my freedom, my cozy little habits. I wasn't about to cast all that aside because some man decided to give me a break and take over. I had resisted Reggie, who had wanted to marry me, and I could certainly resist Craig Stanton, whose intentions were hardly that honorable.

Forcing all these thoughts aside, I concentrated on the gardens and the beauty of the night. Crickets chirped raspily, and there was the rustle of leaves and, from down near the lake, the solitary song of a bird hidden among the trees. I walked under a trellis of honeysuckle and found myself at the edge of the gardens, the lawns sloping down toward the wooded area that surrounded the lake. I

remembered the black marble mausoleum there on the
edge of the water and decided to go and look at it.

The lawns were spongy, already damp with night
moisture, and my high heels were hardly the appropriate
shoes for such activity, but I walked on nevertheless, the
grounds gilded with silver and spread with long shadows
that moved slowly as clouds drifted across the face of the
moon. The woods were very dark, and I hesitated just a
moment, not really from fear. I remembered what Althea
had said about bats, and I didn't relish the idea of any
of the furry creatures swooping down on me. I moved on
into the trees, curious to see the black marble tent again,
wondering if it were as bizarre and sinister as I remembered.

I could smell the water now, smell moss and rotten
logs and mud, and in the distance, through the trees, I
could see the lake itself, its surface half obscured by veils
of mist that swirled over it like ghostly white wraiths. I
stumbled over a root and had to grab a low-hanging limb
to keep from falling. What nonsense, I told myself, I
should have waited until I was properly dressed to go exploring. I knew I should have turned back but I went on,
trees thick on either side, only a few rays of moonlight
seeping through the canopy of branches overhead. I could
hear birds stirring in the boughs, and I kept thinking of
bats, peering at every limb that might possibly harbor
them.

Stepping out of the woods at last, I found myself on
the shore of the lake. The mists were really heavier than
I had imagined at first, a blanket of thick white vapor
spreading, growing thicker. The water lapped at the
shore, stirred by the evening breeze, and there was the
sound of whispers. I stopped, momentarily paralyzed,
and then I realized that it was only the combination of
wind and water and rustling leaves that caused that curious sound. It was not unpleasant, rather like crooning,
voices crooning to the night, whispering voices that lifted
and blended together. There was nothing sinister about
the sound, yet I felt a chill creeping over me. I fervently
wished I had waited till daylight to come down here. This
was sheer folly. . . .

My thoughts had been all about romance before, but

now, naturally, I thought of the dinner conversation
about intruders, remembering that Althea insisted she
had seen prowlers on the grounds even after Paul had
sent over the dogs. Pleasant thoughts, very cheerful at
this particular moment. I remembered turning into the
east wing, remembered the cold, clammy air and the dark
form hovering in the doorway. I scolded myself mentally,
trying to get hold of myself, but the sinister thoughts per-
sisted as the mists spread and the water slapped gently at
the muddy shoreline.

Fear welled up inside me, rising quickly, forcefully,
and I stared at the lake, wondering what on earth had
possessed me to leave the gardens and come down here.
It was almost as though something had summoned me, I
thought, and now I was surrounded by darkness and water and trees, at the mercy of the night. There was a moment of sheer panic, and then I managed to laugh at myself. I was acting exactly like one of my own heroines.
This was Gordonwood, not a spooky estate, and I was a
level-headed young woman taking an evening stroll, not a
damsel in jeopardy. I had come to see the mausoleum of
my own volition. I certainly hadn't been summoned by
some sinister force outside my control. I wandered along
the shore, the earlier apprehension gone now.

It was lovely, really. The water was black, a vast expanse of inky wetness undulating with tiny waves, the
mist hanging over it in gently waving white veils. There
was enough moonlight to guide my way, wavering beams
pointing out the smooth, narrow curve of land between
trees and water, an occasional log blocking the way. A
frog croaked nearby, startling me, and there was a loud
splash as it hopped off a log and plunged into the water.
I wasn't exactly sure where the mausoleum stood, but I
was sure to find it if I followed the shoreline. The mists
were spreading, obscuring part of the land now, visible
white vapors waving in front of me. Perhaps I should go
back, I thought calmly. It really wasn't so important that
I see the place tonight. Perhaps . . . .

I saw it ahead of me, sitting at the edge of the water,
shrouded by mist. It was a vast black marble tent, but it

looked like black silk, and the sides seemed to billow in
the breeze. I stopped, staring at it from the distance. Sir
Robert and Arabella were resting there, as they had
rested so many nights in so many distant lands, and it
was almost as though they were merely sleeping and in
the morning would fold up the tent and move on to another place. I listened to the whispers, and there was a
faint tinkling sound. The tinkling of a camel's bell, I
thought, my flesh suddenly cold. I actually hear it, but
it's a legend, a ghost story. . . . I closed my eyes, listening,
straining to hear the sound again, but it was gone. Romantic nonsense, I told myself, still a bit shaky. For a
moment I had actually believed I had heard the sound. I
hadn't, of course. It had been the product of an over-
active imagination.

I moved toward the black marble tent, amazed at the
way it seemed to billow. The marble gleamed darkly in
the moonlight, like the purest silk, and the sculpture was
so realistic. There were even black marble ropes and
stakes to hold the poles in place. I stood before it, peering at the words engraved on the plaque: HERE LIES SIR
ROBERT GORDON, with the dates of his birth and death,
and, below that, AND HIS WIFE, no further legend given,
not even her name. She had been submissive, even in
death. The front flaps of the tent were slightly parted,
permitting entry into the mausoleum, but no force on
earth could have induced me to step inside. The mists
rose up, wrapping the tent in trailing white vapors even
as I stood there. I turned to go back, musing on the
couple resting in that bizarre tomb.

I had taken several steps before I heard the wood
cracking. It made a loud popping noise, as though someone had stepped on a fallen branch, snapping it with his
foot. I stopped, standing very still, my body seemingly
frozen in place. There was a shuffling sound at the edge
of the woods, the sound of someone pushing aside a
branch of shrubbery. My heart pounded violently, and I
caught my breath, every nerve jangling. I wasn't imagining anything this time. Someone was there, at the edge of
the woods, watching me. I was standing in a pool of
moonlight, clearly visible, my shoulders trembling. Eyes

peered at me from out of the darkness, and I heard a cough. I closed my eyes, wondering if I were going to pass out, and my body swayed a little.

"Miss Marlow?" The voice was a whisper, blending with the whispers from the lake. At first I wasn't sure that someone had actually spoken my name.

"Is—is someone there?" I stammered.

"Over here———"

I peered in the direction of the sound. I could see the man standing just in front of the trees, his form clearly outlined against their darker shapes. The features weren't visible, but I could see the gleam of blond hair and a pale, oval face. He stepped toward me, and I clenched my hands tightly at my sides, preparing to scream.

"Don't be afraid," he said, moving closer. "I won't hurt you."

He stepped into the shaft of moonlight, and I saw him clearly for the first time. He was wearing tennis shoes, tight beige denim trousers, and a soft brown turtleneck sweater. He looked young and vulnerable, as he had looked last night at the inn, but I no longer felt maternal. I remembered what Aunt Agatha had said: "Poor Charlie is tetched." Tetched was merely a quaint word for mad. This handsome boy might be a maniac, I thought, my pulses leaping, and I recalled my aunt saying that some villagers believed he had strangled the mysterious woman and buried her in the basement of the inn.

"It's me," he said, "Charlie Grayson."

"I—I know," I said, striving to control myself. "Don't —come any closer. I'll scream."

"Why should you do that?" he inquired. "I wouldn't want you to scream, Miss Marlow. Someone might hear."

He moved very quickly, darting toward me, seizing my wrist, whirling me around and clamping his hand over my mouth. Holding my wrist in an iron vise, the other hand gripping my chin and covering my mouth, he pulled me out of the moonlight, toward the trees. He was quite strong, despite his slender build, and my feeble efforts to escape were futile. This is it, I thought, my mind racing. He intends to rape me, and then . . . we were at the edge of the woods now, in darkness, and Charlie stopped, holding me against him.

"I don't intend to hurt you," he whispered softly.

He released my wrist and slowly removed some of the pressure of the hand clamped over my mouth.

"Promise not to scream?" he said. "If you promise, I'll let you go, Miss Marlow."

He moved his hand away, holding it cupped inches from my lips, ready to clamp back in place should I cry out.

"Promise?" he whispered.

"I—yes," I mumbled. "You—you won't get away with this. There are dogs loose, and——"

"The dogs are in the house," he said quietly. "They roam the halls at night."

"How do you know?" I asked, still fighting to control myself. He was far too strong for me to hope to break away. My only hope was to outwit him.

"Everyone in the village knows about the dogs," Charlie replied. "Dr. Matthews made sure everyone knew, to discourage intruders."

"What—what do you want of me?" I said, and my voice was at last under control, no longer quavering.

"I've got to talk to you," he said. "I came here—I didn't know how I was going to reach you. I thought maybe I could slip into the house. The dogs know me—I kept them in a kennel in back of the inn one time when Dr. Matthews went to London. They wouldn't hurt me. I was on my way up to the house when I saw you moving through the woods. I followed you——"

"You were in the woods?"

"I was waiting till later, when everyone was asleep. It was a great stroke of luck, your coming down here like this. It saved me ever so much trouble——"

"You want to—talk?"

"I wouldn't hurt you, Miss Marlow. I wouldn't hurt anyone. I'm sorry I had to grab you like that, but if you'd screamed——" He stepped from behind me, moving around until he was a few feet in front of me.

I could have fled then, but in my high heels I hadn't a prayer of outrunning him. He would have caught me in no time, and I would have incurred his wrath. Angry, he might resort to violence, those strong hands flying to my throat. His voice was gentle, almost caressing, but I knew from extensive reading that some of the maddest madmen had been gentle, apparently lovable creatures, kind and affectionate one moment, raging lunatics the next. Reason and superior intellect were my only weapons, and I had to employ them carefully.

"Did you slip the note under my door last night, Charlie?" I asked.

He nodded. Although we were in darkness, my eyes were accustomed to the night by now and I could see him clearly. His face was sculptured in shadow, the planes of his cheekbones light, eyes and jaw dark. His blond hair was silken, curling about his temples and spilling forward in shaggy locks over his forehead. The corners of his mouth quivered, and I suddenly realized that Charlie was as frightened as I was, if not more so. His shoulders were hunched forward, his arms folded tightly across his chest. He was shivering visibly, and in the brown sweater he couldn't possibly have been cold.

"It was a warning," he said. "They——"

He cut himself short, staring at the ground. My own fear had vanished now. I knew Charlie didn't intend to do me harm. He was like a frightened child. All around us the night noises rustled, leaves stirring as birds flitted from branch to branch, frogs croaking hoarsely, waves lapping, and there was the constant crooning as wind skimmed over water with the sound of whispers. The mausoleum was almost completely shrouded in mist now, only the base of the tent visible, and the mist was reaching long white fingers towards where we stood.

Charlie was alert to every sound. He seemed poised for flight. I wondered why he was so frightened.

"The note," I prompted. "Why did you write it?"

"I told you. It was a warning."

"A warning? What are you trying to tell me, Charlie?"

"It's a plot. You overheard. They—I didn't want you to get hurt. I slipped the note under your door to warn you. I hoped you'd go away. They know——"

"You're not making sense," I said. "Who are 'they'? What are they planning to do?"

"I begged her not to," he said urgently. "I knew he was a bad 'un. I told her, but she wouldn't listen. He has her under a spell. She's fallen for him. She'll do anything he says——"

His incoherent urgency was maddening. He was trying to tell me something vastly important, I knew, but he was so frightened that the words came tumbling out in cryptic patterns, making no sense at all. I laid a hand on his arm, trying to calm him.

"Charlie," I said, "what is it? Take your time. No one can hear us. There's no reason to be frightened."

"You don't *know*——" he whispered.

"What don't I know?"

"The old lady trusts him," he replied, attempting to speak in a level voice. "She doesn't suspect—and now you're in danger, too."

"Please try to control yourself," I said, thoroughly irritated now. "What are you *talking* about? Are you accusing someone of——"

"They plan——"

We both heard the noise at the same time. Charlie jumped, backing up against a tree trunk, his face stark white. I gave a little cry, as disturbed by his reactions as by the noise. Someone was coming towards us, walking along the shore. The footsteps were loud, shoes treading heavily on the earth. Whoever it was made no attempt at silence. Charlie seized my wrist, looking up at me with frantic eyes.

"Tomorrow," he whispered, "at the inn."

He let go of my wrist and hurried away, disappearing into the woods with remarkable agility. One moment he was there, the next he was gone, the noise of his movements no louder than the rustling leaves. He might truly have been swallowed up by the woods. I was incredibly frustrated, completely bewildered by his hysterical words, and at the same time I was furious that he had run away, leaving me to face the intruder alone. I was too numbed to be frightened now. I stood silently, listening to the footsteps draw nearer and nearer. I could see the figure approaching, his upper body shrouded in mist, only his feet and legs visible as he came towards me. I seemed to be in a trance, unable to move.

"Susan!" Craig Stanton cried.

"I'm over here," I said. My voice was quite calm.

The mists parted and he stepped forward, stopping a few feet away from where I stood. The moonlight gleamed on his ruffled shirt and silk embroidered jacket. He tilted his head to one side, thrusting his hands in his pants pockets, the tail of his jacket bunching up. There was something quite unreal about all of this: the lake, the black marble tent, the mist, the panic-stricken boy, and now this handsome stranger standing in the moonlight in his absurd formal clothes. I took a deep breath. It was just too unbelievable, all of it.

"Fancy meeting you here," Craig Stanton said.

"Quite a coincidence," I replied.

"Not really. I was coming back from Dower House when I saw you plunging into the woods. At first I couldn't believe my eyes, but on second look I saw that it really was you and that you were, indeed, going straight into the woods."

"So?"

"I figured I might better stroll down and make sure you didn't blunder into the water or something like that."

"Thoughtful of you."

"Wasn't it? I'm a very thoughtful fellow."

I was almost certain that he hadn't seen Charlie, but there was something curious about his manner. He was casual, relaxed, amiable in a cocky sort of way, yet he seemed a bit tense, as though he really had been worried about my safety. That was one explanation. There could have been several others. He sighed, heaving his chest, and shook his head slowly, as though thoroughly disgusted.

"You said at dinner you've got nerves of steel. You weren't kidding at all, were you?"

"What has that got to do with it?"

"Heading out here all alone, after all that talk about intruders and people prowling about the property—I assume you really do have nerves of steel or else you're a damn fool. I'm rather partial to the latter assumption."

"Why should I be afraid to come down to the lake?"

"Why, indeed," he said, rather irritably. "Suppose there *had* been someone lurking about down here—"

"But there wasn't," I said hastily.

Craig shook his head and stepped over to me, standing very close. He was frowning, his brows lowered, his mouth turned down at the corners. I could see the look of irritation in his eyes.

"You should be kept under lock and key," he said. "First you get lost in the maze, now this—I'm beginning to think you're an absolute idiot."

"Thanks a lot."

"Why *did* you come down here?"

"I wanted to see the mausoleum."

"Perfectly logical explanation," he said sarcastically. "It's almost midnight, you're wearing high heels and velvet and you suddenly feel an uncontrollable impulse to come traipsing down to the lake. Jesus! Come along, I'll take you back to the house."

"I can find my way back on my own," I retorted.

Craig Stanton shook his head, giving me the disgusted look one gives a tiresome child.

"Come along," he said impatiently.

I drew myself up, mustering all the dignity at my command, and started to walk through an opening in the trees. "This way!" he snapped, jerking his head. He walked back down the shore, turning to make sure I was following. I could barely see him in the mists. He turned into the woods, and I saw that there was a wide pathway leading back up to the lawns, a path I hadn't been aware of before. I had come through the trees, not knowing of this far simpler method of reaching the lake. I trudged through patches of moonlight and shadow, keeping an eye on Craig's back. I was really quite relieved that he was there, although I would have gone to the stake before admitting it to him.

He stepped out of the woods, waiting for me to catch up with him, and we walked up the lawn toward the gardens, Craig beside me, still silent and irritated. I could see Gordonwood, an immense dark shape against the night, the windows of the downstairs rooms glowing like warm golden squares. Craig walked on ahead of me through the gardens, passing the fragrant rosebeds and the broken white marble column where I had stood musing earlier. Craig moved up the flat marble steps to the terrace, and I followed, stumbling on the second step. There was a loud crack, and the heel of my shoe gave way, snapping completely off and flying away.

"Damn!" I cried, almost falling.

"What is it now?" he asked angrily.

"I've lost my heel!" I snapped.

"Pity," he replied. "Life is full of these little trage-dies."

"Damn you," I muttered. "I could have fallen and broken my neck. You might at least help me look for the heel."

"It'll be there in the morning."

I hobbled onto the terrace and sat down on the chaise longue, pulling off both my shoes. He stood with hands in pockets, watching me. Candlelight poured out through the opened French windows, staining the tiles with soft yellow light. I stood up in my stocking feet, holding both shoes in my hand and glaring at Craig Stanton.

"These shoes happen to have cost a small fortune," I said nastily. "Not that it would matter in the least to you."

"Not in the least," he replied pleasantly. "You ready to come inside now?"

I followed him into the drawing room and walked on into the hall while he paused to close the windows and lock them. Setting the shoes down on the table, I picked up my oil lamp, the flame still burning under its round glass shade. Moving briskly up the stairs, I reached the landing before he caught up with me. He took the lamp out of my hand, shoved me aside, and led the way on up to the main hall above. I was furious at his rude-ness, too furious to speak. He strolled down the hall, holding the lamp aloft, and turned the corner and moved on down the narrow hall leading to my room. My stock-inged feet rustled on the carpets, making a crisp, scratchy sound as I hurried to keep up with him.

We passed the east wing, cold air eddying out into the hall, and Craig opened the door to my room and stepped inside, setting the lamp down on the dressing table.

"Here you are," he said, "safe and sound. I hope you have enough sense to stay put for the rest of the night."

"Thank you ever so much," I replied sweetly. "You've

been kind and considerate and frightfully gallant."

Craig smiled. It was a warm smile, dazzling in its impact. His good looks were overwhelming in these close quarters, and I felt a little apprehensive. He glanced at me and glanced at the bed and then glanced back at me again. The smile grew broader, playing merrily on his lips, and his dark blue eyes had a mischievous twinkle.

"Don't I get a reward?" he asked.

"I'm not asking you in for a nightcap," I said, "if that's what you're thinking."

"I'm already in," he said lightly.

"And I suggest you get *out*."

He chuckled to himself, his eyes dancing. The room seemed so small, and he was so close. I stood rigidly with my arms folded across my waist, trying not to show my nervousness. Craig leaned over and touched my cheek, his fingers stroking the flesh with a gentle rub. I drew back, disturbed. He clicked his tongue and shook his head, moving away from me.

"You really *are* nervous," he said. "Exactly like one of the girls in your books."

"I wish you'd stop referring to my books."

"They're charming, and so are you. Exasperating—but charming nevertheless. Good night, Susan. I'll look forward to seeing you in the morning."

He left, and I had a wild impulse to call him back. I didn't want him to go, I realized, even though I had been in a nervous panic all the while he stood here in the room. I had been so sure about my indifference to the man, and yet . . . he wasn't at all like Eric, not at all like Reggie. He was infuriating, rude, insufferable, but so devastatingly handsome. I touched my cheek where his fingers had stroked it, and there was a rich elation inside me, as though someone had just given me a beautifully wrapped present. It was a long time before I closed the bedroom door and started preparing for bed.

Later, in my melon-pink cotton clown pajamas and a quilted pink robe, I set the lamp on the bedside table and took out the historical novel I had been reading the night before. Sleep would be impossible for a long time, and I decided I might as well finish the book. Crawling

under the covers, I took up the book and sat up against
the pillows, but I couldn't concentrate on the print before me. Too much had happened. I closeJ the book and
watched the warm yellow light that danced on the wall
as the lamp spluttered.

Craig Stanton had such a forceful personality that my
encounter with him had almost driven the earlier encounter with Charlie from my mind. The man had
aroused emotions so strong that they eclipsed anything
else, overshadowing the panic and frustration I had felt
with Charlie. Now, for the first time, I put aside all
thoughts about Craig and considered what had occurred
before he arrived on the scene.

I thought about Charlie. Surely he was insane. I
couldn't make heads or tails out of his incoherent bab-
bling. Something about a plot, something about not wanting me to get hurt. Charlie must live in a fantasy world
full of mad delusions, I told myself, thinking of his
frightened expression. He probably had a persecution
complex, probably believed the whole world was in
league against him, yet he had seemed so *sincere* in his
efforts to tell me whatever it was. I shuddered as I recalled my fright when he first came toward me. Charlie
might not be so harmless after all, I reasoned, remembering his remarkable strength and the way he had seized
me. If Craig hadn't come along when he did . . . the
incident confused me. Toward the last I had been certain
that Charlie meant no harm, but I couldn't be sure he
wouldn't have turned on me after he spilled out the rest
of his mad babblings.

I frowned. No, Charlie hadn't meant to harm me. He
had looked so vulnerable, so young. He had come to
Gordonwood to tell me something, and he had been
frightened out of his wits. I tried to remember his exact
words, but I couldn't. They had been spoken too quickly,
too incoherently. There was a puzzle in my mind, but I
couldn't put the pieces together. The conversation I had
overheard at the inn, the mysterious actress who had been
Charlie's friend, the note he had slipped under my door,
Gordonwood, the manuscripts, Althea's remarks at dinner
—they were all pieces of the puzzle, and I tried to as-
semble them into a clear picture. It was a futile effort.

Something seemed to gnaw at the back of my mind, and there was a vague alarm, an uneasiness, as though I were overlooking something frightfully obvious.

I blew out the lamp and snuggled down under the covers, still trying to put my finger on what it was that bothered me. Charlie had been so intense, and I had covered up for him. I hadn't let Craig know I had seen the boy. I had pretended to be all alone there by the mausoleum. Something had warned me not to mention the incident, and I had followed my instincts. I thoroughly intended to go to the inn tomorrow, even if it was a fool's errand. I had to know what it was Charlie had been trying to tell me. Perhaps then I could solve the puzzle.

I closed my eyes, but sleep eluded me. I found myself listening for noises in the house. Absurd, I told myself, and yet I gripped the covers tightly and strained to hear any unusual sounds. Naturally I thought about the east wing, so near by, and the shadowy form in the doorway. I kept telling myself that I wasn't afraid, of course not, a grown woman isn't afraid of the dark, yet I gave a start at every creak and groan of the old house. I thought I heard footsteps moving down the stairs outside my room, just as I had heard them in the morning when I was hanging up my dresses. Nonsense, it was merely my imagination. I must stop this. . . .

Eventually, I slipped into a state of semiconsciousness, not really awake, not quite asleep, and I seemed to hear Charlie say, "Now you're in danger, too," and the words seemed to echo over and over. Tossing restlessly on the pillows, I finally went to sleep, only to be awakened by a loud thumping noise in the hall. I sat up, shivering, and heard the scratching at my door, followed by a low whine that sent cold chills up my spine. It took me a full minute to realize what the noise was, and then I got out of bed and threw open the door. Earl came bounding into the room with joyful yelps. He wasn't half as glad to see me as I was to see him. I scolded him and made him settle down and finally persuaded him to lie down on the floor at the foot of my bed. He minded beautifully, content just to be with me. I climbed back under the covers, terribly pleased that he had come. I would sleep much better now.

CHAPTER SIX

I awoke at the crack of eleven thirty, outrageously late, admittedly, but I had forgotten to set the alarm and Aunt Agatha had kindly permitted me this one morning of wicked indulgence. Earl was gone, but a saucy young blonde in short black uniform and frilly white apron stood at the foot of the bed, balancing a tray on one hand, the other resting on her hip. The rattle of dishes had awakened me. I sat up, rubbing my eyes. There was the rich, heavenly fragrance of coffee, a glorious smell at this time of day.

"I'm Mary, ma'am," the girl said pertly. "The old girl—I mean, Lady Agatha says this isn't going to become a *habit*, but I should take up some coffee just this once and see that you get up."

She tossed her head, short, corkscrew blonde curls bouncing. She was a pleasant-looking girl, just chubby enough to fill out the uniform with a decided aplomb. Her bright pink mouth was small and sassy, her large blue eyes surrounded by long, sooty-black lashes. She was the kind of girl men liked to reach out and pinch, I decided, and the kind of girl who would undoubtedly adore such bawdy treatment.

"Hello, Mary," I said, yawning.

"She says I should tell you it's *sinful* to sleep this late. *She's* been up since six."

"Bless her heart," I replied, rather grumpily.

Mary set the tray on the bedside table, making an unnecessary amount of racket I thought, cringing. The sound of dishes clattering isn't exactly pleasant when one has just struggled into consciousness. Mary marched over to the French windows and jerked open the jade-green draperies. Shatteringly bright sunshine poured into the room. That didn't help either. I glared at the girl, wishing I had something to throw at her. She was definitely a menace.

"I've read *all* your books," she said, hand on hip. "You're my very favorite writer."

I had misjudged her, of course. She was an enchanting creature. Not only did she have remarkably good taste, but she was intelligent as well. I would gladly have hopped out of bed to kiss her hand, but Mary merely gave an indifferent shrug and marched out of the room, leaving me with the firm conviction that life was beautiful and all merits justly rewarded. I poured steaming hot coffee into a thick blue cup and lifted a silver lid to find a flaky, buttery sweet roll.

After this decidedly luxurious breakfast, I took a long time dressing. I was never able to hustle after getting up, but this morning I was deliberately slow, carefully selecting what I should wear. I finally decided on a pair of slender brown and burnt-orange checked slacks and a burnt orange turtleneck sweater. I might not be able to wear the wraithlike garments that hung on the fashion models, but I could certainly wear a sweater, and wear it well. Standing before the mirror, I turned this way and that, admiring the way the soft wool clung in all the appropriate places. I brushed my hair back, fastening it into a ponytail with a dull gold ribbon, then left the room, quite satisfied with my appearance.

My shoes were still on the table in the main hall downstairs, the broken heel beside them. Craig must have found it earlier this morning and put it there, I thought, rather touched. I was glad now that I had broken the heel. Having it repaired would give me a perfect excuse to drive into Gordonville today. Mary came into the hall with feathery dustmop in hand, informing me that Craig and my aunt were in the basement, had been all morning long.

"Looking for them—those papers," she said irritably, "raising great clouds of dust, stirring everything up. This whole house is already *buried* in dust, and they stir up more! Some people have no consideration whatsoever for a girl's feelings."

She left, pouting prettily, and I went down the hall to

the door under the staircase that led down to the basement. It stood open, and there were, indeed, flurries of
dust in the air, eddying up the stairs and into the hall.
Mary's complaints had been justly expressed, I thought,
moving down the steep, narrow stone steps.

The basement was a great labyrinth of connecting
rooms, some holding racks of wine and kegs of whisky,
others lined with shelves filled with my aunt's jellies and
preserves and boxes of herbs. Still others were littered
with trunks and boxes and assorted junk, all layered with
dust, spread with silky cobwebs. There was no natural
light here, but oil lamps had been set at various intervals,
their wavering yellow light revealing the low ceiling and
brown walls stained with moisture. It was quite chilly, the
air cold like cold water, and I was glad I had chosen the
sweater. Hearing activity in one of the distant rooms, I
moved down a narrow hallway toward the sound.

I discovered my aunt in an enormous room with a
low beamed ceiling and hard earthen floor. It was filled
with piles of boxes and old, discarded furniture and huge
old brassbound leather trunks. Aunt Agatha looked up
when I came in, waving merrily. She perched on top of a
trunk, her sandy hair disheveled, her cheeks streaked with
dust. She wore a long black smock and, incongruously,
several strands of gorgeous coral beads that gleamed in
the lamplight. There was a pile of books on the trunk beside her, and they tumbled off as she got up to greet me.

"Well, it's about time!" she cried, giving me a robust
hug. "We've found some most interesting things—not any
important papers, alas, but something almost as good.
Look!"

She picked up the books, handing them to me. "First
editions of *Pickwick Papers* and *Dombey and Son,* hidden
away in one of the trunks. Imagine! They're rather battered, of course, but then they've been well read by my
husband's ancestors. Look, the original Seymour and Phiz
illustrations! I must say I'm rather pleased."

I examined the books, holding them reverently. Dick-
ens was my favorite Victorian novelist, and it was thrilling to think that these worn, rather musty volumes had
been published during his lifetime. Aunt Agatha rattled
her coral beads, her long, plain face as enthusiastic as a

child's. She put the books back on the trunk when I returned them.

"You never know what you'll turn up," she said, brushing a speck of lint from the front of her floppy black smock. "This is such fun! Almost like a treasure hunt."

"Are you down here alone?" I asked. "Mary said Craig was——"

"I'm over here," he said, stepping into the lamplight with a large battered box. "This is the last one, Agatha. If they're not in here, we can check the basement off our list."

He set the box down and threw his shoulders back, stretching his arms out and heaving a sigh. He wore tennis shoes, tight gray sweat pants, and a loosely fitting gray sweat shirt, sleeves pushed up over his forearms. It was a rugged outfit, quite a contrast to the one he had worn last night, yet he looked even more appealing. There was a smudge of dirt on his jaw, and his hair tumbled forward in rich brown profusion. He gave me a grin and nodded toward the box.

"Come down to help us search?" he inquired.

"Not exactly," I said, turning back to Aunt Agatha. "I broke a heel off one of my shoes last night," I explained, "my best pair. I want to take it into town and have it repaired. I wonder if I could borrow your car?"

"You want to go now? But it's almost time for lunch!"

"I just ate breakfast," I admitted, somewhat sheepishly.

"Hump! Two cups of coffee, I presume."

"Three, and a perfectly marvelous sweet roll. Does your old Bentley still run?"

"What do you mean, does it still run! It outruns any of these souped-up tin traps they make nowadays, I can tell you that. In perfect condition, it is, and——"

"I'd be glad to drive you in to Gordonville after lunch," Craig said, interrupting. "I need to pick up a few items from the stationer's myself." He lowered his heavy eyelids, one corner of his mouth curling up.

"That would be lovely," Aunt Agatha agreed. "The two of you could go when I take my nap."

I smiled rather stiffly. "I—I'd rather go now," I said,

"and alone. I thought I might do a little sightseeing——"

"In Gordonville! You must be out of your mind. There's nothing whatsoever to see besides the statue of——"

"Aunt Agatha," I said firmly.

She shrugged her shoulders. "Very well. The keys to the Bentley are in that little bronze chest on the hall table. But, really, Susan—why, if I didn't know you better I'd think you were going to meet some *man.*"

"Perhaps she is," Craig said.

"Perhaps I am," I retorted.

Aunt Agatha looked thoroughly perplexed, and Craig looked suspicious. Legs wide apart, arms folded over his chest, he stood staring at me with a dark look, brows lowered. I had the curious feeling that he knew all about my meeting Charlie by the lake and the real purpose of my wanting to go into Gordonville. I felt sure that he would have tried to stop me had we been alone. He seemed about to say something very stern, restrained only by my aunt's presence. Curious, I thought, uncomfortable under his steady gaze. There was no way he could possibly know about Charlie, unless . . . no, of course he didn't know.

"I'll see you later, Aunt Agatha," I said.

"Of course, dear. I hope you *enjoy* yourself."

Mildred was standing in the hall when I came back up. She was wearing the same rumpled white uniform and shapeless brown sweater she had worn the day before, and she drew back a little when she saw me, as though she expected me to kick her. Poor dismal creature, I thought, smiling brightly and bidding her good morning. Mildred shook a bottle of pills and looked at her wristwatch. I took the car keys out of the bronze chest, picked up the shoes, and started to leave. Mildred crept up behind me, reaching out to touch my shoulder. I almost let out a bloodcurdling scream.

"My, you *do* move quietly, don't you?" I said, shaken.

"Miss Marlow," she sniffled, speaking very low. "I wonder if—maybe I shouldn't ask this." She glanced around the hall as though to detect a possible eavesdropper, her mournful brown eyes finally coming back to me. "I wonder if you—if you *heard* anything last night," she

finally said. "My room is right down the hall from yours,
and——" She broke off, clasping her hands together. Her
hands were surprisingly lovely.

"*Did* you?" she asked.

"Nothing out of the ordinary," I replied. The woman
looked unusually nervous, and I saw no point in men-
tioning the footsteps I had imagined coming up the stairs
outside my door.

"You—you're sure?" she asked.

"Did *you* hear something?"

"I thought so," Mildred said, frowning. "Maybe—maybe it was just all that talk at the dinner table."

"Or maybe you heard Earl," I told her. "He came
tromping down the hall in the middle of the night,
scratching on my door. Perhaps that's what you heard."

"The dog came to your room?"

I nodded, and Mildred looked vastly relieved. She
pulled the old brown sweater closer around her and
moved away, gliding silently down the hall in her heavy
white shoes. It was very hard not to laugh at the pathetic
creature. I smiled to myself and went on outside, pulling
the dark golden oak door shut behind me.

The great portico was shady, the six marble columns
casting long blue-gray shadows. I walked the length of it,
pausing to examine the pink rose trees in their round
black pots, and went on down the three short steps to
the flagstone path leading to the small gray carriage
house that had been converted into a garage. The sunlight was blinding after the dimness of the portico; silvery
rays sparkled on the crushed-shell drive and gilded the
dark green grass. The air was fresh and clear, a slight
chill making it all the more invigorating.

"You!"

I was standing in front of the garage with my hand
on the door handle when I heard the voice calling. At
first I couldn't locate its source, but then I saw Althea
leaning precariously out the window on the second floor
of Dower House. She called again, waving at me. Dower
House was some distance away, sitting under the boughs
of a great oak tree beyond the gardens on this side of the
main house. Althea leaned out even further, her shrieking red curls tossing in the breeze.

"Come here!" she cried. I could barely make out the words from this distance.

I gave an exasperated sigh and moved rapidly through the gardens. They were smaller, less extensive than the ones I had explored yesterday. There was a charming pond with cracked white marble fountain and beds of glorious yellow daffodils. Leaving the gardens, I followed the worn path leading to the house. When she saw that I was coming, Althea disappeared from the window. She was unbolting the door as I stepped onto the tiny porch.

"Hurry up!" she cried. "Come on in before someone sees you."

She took my hand and pulled me inside and then slammed the door behind us, sliding the bolt back in place and fastening a chain lock as well. She nodded emphatically, pulling the doorknob to make sure the door was securely locked, then led the way into the living room, giving me no explanation for her curious conduct. I felt that, like Alice, I had stepped through the looking glass and entered a whole new world. The living room was littered with empty gin bottles and painting materials, canvases leaning against the wall, tables strewn with pots of paint and brushes and sketchbooks. There was an easel near the window, sunlight streaming in to reveal a half-finished portrait of my aunt. Althea saw me looking at it.

"Quite a mess, isn't it?" she said briskly.

"It—it's remarkable," I replied, stepping closer to examine the canvas.

Aunt Agatha's plain face had been captured in exact detail, every line precise and, even more impressive, the personality shining clear. The zest, the wit, the warmth: all were there on the canvas. She was wearing a ruby velvet gown, and the texture of the cloth was glossy, nap gleaming darkly. I knew without question that I was looking at the work of a master.

"I used to have something," Althea said impatiently. "My portraits used to hang in all the best galleries. That was—God, that was at least twenty years ago. Agatha insisted I paint her—I've spent three months on this thing, haven't had the guts to try and finish it——"

"You're incredibly gifted, Althea. I don't know when I've seen——"

"I still fool around a bit, in between binges. I don't have the touch anymore. But I didn't get you over here to talk about my painting."

She marched over to one of the tables, poking around to find a bottle that still contained a little gin. She poured a glass half full and leaned back, downing the drink in one great gulp. Her cheeks were flushed, her gray-green eyes shining brightly. I couldn't tell if she was drunk or not, but there was an intensity about her quick, jerky movements. She was wearing floppy brown slippers and a loose, billowing orange robe printed with enormous brown and purple flowers, the garment old and tattered. She looked wildly improbable as she plunked her glass down and stood among the litter, a caricature, not real at all.

"What are you doing with those *shoes?*" she asked.

"I'm taking them into town. One of the heels is broken, and——"

"Spare me the details," she said, waving a chubby hand. "I want to talk to you, Susan. Everyone thinks I'm a harmless old lush, muttering in my cups, and no one *listens* to me. Perhaps you'll be the exception." She pursed her bright red mouth and frowned. "I certainly hope so," she continued. "The others're hopeless."

"What did you want to tell me?"

"Things are going on, dear."

"Things?"

"*Suspicious* things."

"I see," I replied, humoring her.

"Ah, yes, you've got that look in your eyes, just like the others. She's a dotty old lush, you're tellin' yourself, she's mad. Well, I *see* things. You think I'm lying? I saw *you* last night, coming out of the woods with that handsome fool. No, no, don't blush. I don't *blame* you. I just wanted to prove that I'm not imaginin' things."

"I walked down by the lake," I said defensively. "I wanted to see the mausoleum. Craig came to find me——"

"Ta ta! Great good luck, what?" She clicked her tongue, giving me a bawdy wink.

"Nothing happened, I can assure you."

"Really? You have my deepest sympathy, dear, but don't be discouraged. Perhaps he had a *head*ache."

"You're outrageous," I said, smiling in spite of myself.

"That's right, I'm outrageous—that's why people don't pay any attention to what I say. I have this *image*." She gave an exasperated sigh. "I suppose that's the price I have to pay for lovin' to nip!"

She stood with hands on hips, round and plump, red curls falling about her chubby face. She was absurd in her bizarre clothes, and she reeked of gin, but I found myself reevaluating Althea. There was a certain shrewdness in her eyes, a look of undeniable intelligence. The woman who had painted that portrait of my aunt had to have great powers of observation, and I was sure a lot of Althea's mannerisms were put-on, sheer camp. She was a lonely old woman who had found a way of getting attention, and she played it to the hilt.

"Would *you* care for a nip, dear?" she asked abruptly.

"I don't believe so."

"Think I'll have another. Then we'll get down to business."

She prowled around, examining empty bottles, opening drawers to peer inside, finally pulling open the doors of a small, lacquered chest to find a brand new bottle sitting inside. She gave a little cry of triumph, taking the bottle out as though it were a priceless treasure, and after pouring a brimming glassful she went over and plopped down on the shabby brown velvet sofa, first pushing aside a stack of old magazines.

"I've told Agatha about this prowler," she began summarily. "She's convinced I imagined him. The others think I'm mad. So much for that. My bedroom upstairs commands a terrific view of the grounds. I can see the big house and the back lawns and the woods, even part of the lake. I have a pair of powerful binoculars."

"And you've seen someone?"

"A man," she said, "always at night, always lurking about in the shadows, moving surreptitiously—my, that's a fine word, isn't it? One night he was standing by the lake in a raincoat—there was bright moonlight, and I could see him through a clearing in the trees. Couldn't

make out any details, of course, but there was a stranger
by the lake. He stood there for a while and then walked
away, out of range.

"This was after Craig caught the other intruders?"

"This was no more than two weeks ago," she retorted.
"I've seen him several times since. Once he was sneaking
towards the house." She looked up sharply. "Do you believe me?"

"Yes," I said. "Yes, I do." And I did. "Were—were
you ever able to identify him?" I asked.

She shook her head. "Never saw 'im that close, just a
dark form prowling about."

Her choice of words caused me to shudder. Dark form
. . . an apt description of what I had seen in the east
wing. I had passed that off in my mind as a trick of the
imagination, but now I began to wonder if I hadn't really
seen someone after all. The experience, in retrospect,
made my flesh turn cold. Althea was watching me closely,
and she noticed my reactions. She bobbed her head up
and down, nodding.

"At least *someone* takes me seriously," she said.

"You've seen him recently?" I asked. "In the past
few days?"

"Four or five nights ago. He was with the girl then."

"The girl?"

"I saw *her* good and close. I saw her *first,* in fact, before I ever saw the man. About three weeks ago I was
strolling around the grounds. It was right after sundown,
not quite dark, the air all hazy with purple haze. She
was standing at the edge of the woods, preoccupied like,
like a statue. She seemed to be *waiting* for someone."

"She didn't see you?"

"I don't think so. I was in the grove of oak trees, in
the shadows. She just stood there for ever so long—not
twenty feet away from me. She finally went on down towards the lake. I waited and waited, expecting her to
come back. She never did."

"And you saw her with the man?"

"Just that once. They were standing in back of the
house. I was up in the bedroom, lookin' through my binoculars. It was around midnight, very dark, but I saw
them all right! He was wearing his raincoat, and she was

clinging to him—a regular mantrap, small and delicate but pouting."

Something registered in the back of my mind. Her description reminded me of someone I had seen, but I couldn't for the life of me think who it might be. Althea got up and stepped over to one of the tables, shuffling through a stack of papers, her brows pressed together. She finally found what she wanted and handed it to me.

"I made a sketch from memory," she said, "made it as soon as I came in after seeing her standing by the woods that first time. It isn't a very good sketch, I'm afraid, but she looked something like this."

I recognized her immediately. Althea had done a marvelous job. The girl had a pouting expression, the eyes dark and sexy, the mouth as sultry as it had been two nights ago, when she had come downstairs at the inn to meet the man in the raincoat. The face was stunningly beautiful, framed by the short-clipped hair. I studied the sketch, and my hands trembled a little, causing the paper to rattle.

"You look pale," Althea said. "Do you *know* her?"

"N–no," I replied. "I just thought—she reminded me of someone I used to know." I was lying, but I didn't want to tell Althea about that mysterious conversation I had overheard at the inn. I gave the sketch back to her.

"Have you shown this to anyone else?" I asked.

"You're the first one who's seen it. I *told* Aggie I'd seen a girl by the woods, but she merely laughed and said it's a wonder I hadn't seen a pink elephant. Aggie is such a *trusting* soul. She doesn't seem to realize that—" She broke off, frowning. "This all started after that article came out about the Gordon papers, sayin' they might exist, sayin' how *valuable* they'd be. Do you follow me?"

"I–I believe I do."

"I think someone *else* is lookin' for those papers," she said bluntly. "Gordonwood is such a big, rambling place, full of dark halls and staircases and nooks and corners— I think someone is slipping into the house." She paused dramatically, her gray-green eyes very wide.

"But what about the dogs?" I replied. "Surely——"

"Those damn dogs!" she snapped. "They're so *corruptible!* Toss 'em a bone and they're your friends for

life. I gave them some scraps one afternoon, and they
followed me around for days!"

She narrowed her eyes. "Something's *afoot*," she said.

I agreed with her silently. Something was definitely
afoot, and I had a pretty good idea what it was.

Althea finished her gin and poured another. It was beginning to tell on her now. She was weaving just a little,
her eyes slightly out of focus. Her cheeks were bright
pink, her eyelids coated with violet, and she made a face,
taking a gigantic swallow of gin. "I wanted someone else,
to *know*," she said, voice slurring now for the first time.
"As for me, I'm keepin' my doors locked. Agatha can get
herself murdered if she wants to, but no one's sneakin' up
on me!"

"I'm glad you told me, Althea," I replied. "I–I don't
know just what I'll do, but—I'll keep my eyes open."

"You do that, ducks. Come back and see me again—
don't forget those shoes."

I picked up the shoes, having almost forgotten them.

"And be *care*ful," Althea said. "I wouldn't stay in
that house, I can tell you that. Not for a million."

She led me to the door, orange robe billowing. I
stood nervously as she slid back the bolt and unfastened
the chain. I was eager to be gone, eager to sort everything out in my mind and think things over. Althea made
a clucking noise and squeezed my hand and gave me a
gentle push, slamming the door behind me. I heard her
ramming the bolt back in place as I walked away.

The day was still gloriously bright, sky pale blue,
sunshine splattering, but everything looked gray now,
clouded by my own suspicions. Pieces of the puzzle were
beginning to fit together, and the picture taking place
was a frightening one. I hurried toward the garage, glad
that I was driving into Gordonville immediately. There
were a great many questions I wanted to ask, and I was
almost positive that Charlie Grayson could provide an-
swers to all of them.

CHAPTER SEVEN

The Bentley handled beautifully, and it was a pleasure to drive such an expensive, powerful car. The big body was dark brown, trimmed with glistening chrome, the interior dark yellow leather, the top down. The car roared over the country roads with scarcely a bump, and I had the feeling I was in control of a magnificent metallic animal, every spring, every coil, every intricate part created to do my bidding. The breeze stung my cheeks, and the sunlight poured down, making sunbursts on the hood and warming the leather. Approaching Gordonville, I slowed down, the motor purring now. I had been driving too fast, but it had been a release.

I found a parking place across from the village green, in front of the ponderous brownstone town hall with its grotesque Victorian architecture, and walked across the square, pausing to admire the tarnished bronze statue of the Robert Gordon who had established the village. He was a solemn-looking chap, stern bronze features made slightly ludicrous by the pearl-gray pigeon perched irreverently on his shoulder. The daffodils growing around the statue in a neat circular bed nodded bright yellow heads in the breeze, and sunlight washed the ancient blue-gray marble bench across from it.

With shoes in hand, I strolled on across the square toward the cobbler's shop, passing the pink brick tea shop and the beige brick bookstore with stacks of books behind the murky blue plate glass windows. It was difficult for me to walk past a bookstore without going inside to explore, but there was no time for it now. Perhaps I would come back after I had talked with Charlie.

I had been eager to come into town, eager to see Charlie, but now I found myself dreading that talk. I stepped into the cobbler's shop, glad I had a legitimate reason to delay a bit. Shoes hung from the ceiling. Racks of shoes stood against the wall, all of them tagged with squares of yellow paper. The cobbler was working at a table littered with tools and scraps of leather, punching tiny holes in a thick tan sole. He finished the job before acknowledging my presence. He was small and stooped, with dark-gray hair, grumpy-looking tanned face and steel-rimmed spectacles, and he wore an apron of thin black leather, the sleeves of his old white shirt rolled up over muscular biceps.

"Want a pair of shoes?" he inquired. "I can make you a smashing pair, quite stylish. I make 'em, I repair 'em. You won't find better shoes anywhere in England, and that's a fact. Here, take a look at this."

He pulled out a stack of hides and slapped them on the counter. They were beautifully dyed: red, green, dark blue, tan, soft and pliable. "Take your pick," he said eagerly. "You want a pair of red shoes? I'll whip one up. Factories! The curse of our times. No factory can produce a work of art. Look at those shoes over there." He pointed to a pair of black patent leather pumps. "Every stitch hand sewn. Look at the craftsmanship."

"Actually," I said, "I'm not in the market for a new pair. I'd like to have this pair mended. The heel's broken off this one, and I think the other heel may be a bit loose."

He looked disappointed, then disgruntled. He took the shoes from me and examined them, shaking his head. "Shoddy work," he grumbled. "Sure, I recognize the name stitched inside. You paid a lot for these shoes, but they're shoddy. That actress woman, she brought in a pair almost exactly like these, with the same label."

"Oh?" I said, trying not to show my interest.

"Instep was cracked on one of *hers*. I had to practically rebuild the shoe. Lotta good it did me—I've still got 'em. She never came to pick 'em up. Something funny going on there. All right, ma'am, I'll mend these for you. You want to leave 'em, or you want to wait? It won't take me more'n twenty minutes or so."

"I'll wait," I told him. He took the shoes over to his table, handling them as though they were contaminated.

Clearing a space on his table, he assembled his tools and began to prise off the tiny nails that stuck out on the broken shoe. I was eager to learn more about the actress and wondered how I could bring the subject up again without arousing his suspicion. He tapped and tampered, mending the shoe, while I wandered about the shop examining the shoes and hides and machines. There was a strong smell of oil and sawdust and wax. Although I affected an air of casual curiosity, there was a purpose behind my survey.

I finally found the shoes similar to mine. They were smaller, I noted, and dark gray instead of brown, but the label was the same: chic, expensive. I was more interested in the square yellow tag the cobbler had tied on. It identified the owner as Vanessa Shaw and gave the date the shoes had been brought in, almost a month ago. The name meant nothing to me. If Miss Shaw was an actress, she was an obscure one.

"Are these the shoes you were talking about?" I asked casually.

He looked up from his work. He had secured the heel back on the shoe now and was tightening the heel of the second shoe. He nodded with an expression of disgust.

"Those are them all right," he informed me. "Tacky things, not fit for a human foot, no matter how much they cost."

"I find it strange that she wouldn't have come back for them," I remarked, holding one of the sleek gray slippers in my hand. "Did she leave Gordonville abruptly?"

"Some folks think so," he said brusquely.

"Vanessa Shaw——" I said, stretching the words out. "I wonder—you said she was an actress. I saw a Vanessa Shaw in a play a year or so ago. I wonder if it could possibly be the same woman? Small, delicate, quite beautiful, actually, with short black hair and dark blue eyes——"

I had captured his interest now. I had banked on that. Almost everyone in small towns like Gordonville thrived on gossip. The cobbler was no exception. He gave the shoe a final tap, tugged the heel to see that it was securely fastened, and then brought both shoes over to the counter. He wore that eager expression that all good gossips employ: eyes narrowed a little, mouth a bit pursed.

"Ah, she was pretty all right," he said. "I'll hand 'er that. Pretty as a picture, but sly looking. I knew her sort right away. Carrying on with Charlie Grayson, she was, and making no bones about it. I don't blame Charlie, just felt sorry for 'im. Knew right away she was a fickle thing. A woman like that wouldn't be satisfied with the likes of Charlie, not for long. He's a good-lookin' lad, strong as a horse, makes a good livin' from the inn. Lotta girls'd be happy to have him, but this one—it was only a matter of time before she ditched him for someone else. Them city girls are a bad lot."

He muttered something unintelligible and glanced up suspiciously, suddenly realizing that I was a city girl myself. For a moment he glared at me as though I had designs on his virtue or, at the very least, planned to snatch the shoes and dash out without paying. He actually pulled the shoes away from the counter, frowning. I smiled reassuringly and tried to look very sweet and innocent. It wasn't until I took some bills out of my purse that the look of suspicion left his eyes.

"You do beautiful work," I said, handing him the bills.

He rang the amount up on the battered old cash register and started to return the change. I shook my head, smiling for all I was worth.

"Oh, no," I said, shameless. "You keep the change. You did such a good job, and so quickly. I really should give you *more*."

My ploy was quite obvious, but it worked beautifully. The grumpy old man rubbed the front of his leather apron and grinned. I could tell that I had made his day. "Take pride in my work," he said. "Not everyone appreciates a good job nowadays. Some people think a *label*'s all that counts."

"What happened to the girl?" I asked, interrupting him before he had a chance to launch into another tirade about factory-made shoes.

"The actress? She vanished. Lotta people thought Charlie had something to do with it. Some even said he'd murdered her. You know how people talk. Long-tongued gossips—a bunch-a old women wagging their tongues. This town is full of 'em. If you want to know what I think, I think she ran off with that man she was seeing."

"She was seeing someone else?"

"Oh, she was sly about it, all right, but she was seeing him. I was working late one night, went out to the alley in back of the shop to throw some scraps away, and I saw her with him. They were standing just inside the alley, talking real intensely. Both of 'em looked startled when they heard me rattling the lid of the trash bin."

"Did you know the man?" I inquired, ever so casual.

"Couldn't rightly say. His back was to me, and he was wearing a heavy overcoat and a black hat, brim pulled down. Could've been anyone, though there're not many men in this town who'd be brainless enough to fool around with a piece of goods like her. No, I figure it was some stranger passing through. I figure she ran off with him."

He started wrapping the shoes up in brown paper, and I didn't want to press him further. I had already learned a great deal, and it wouldn't be wise to ask any more questions. He handed me the neat brown parcel, and I thanked him again.

"You ever want a new pair of shoes, you let me know. I'll make you a smashing pair. Red shoes, or even boots. I make smashing boots."

"I'll do that," I replied. "You've been very kind."

I stepped back outside, very pleased with what I had learned. Gordonville was such a quaint, peaceful little town with its mellowed brick shopfronts and shady sidewalks and turn-of-the-century atmosphere, yet my aunt had compared it to Peyton Place. I was beginning to see why. I strolled toward the inn, immersed in my thoughts, and at first I paid no attention to the man peering into a shop window halfway down the block. He was wearing a pair of hand-tooled leather boots. They were unusual boots, and I wondered vaguely if the cobbler had made them. A bell seemed to ring in my mind, and I stopped abruptly, staring at those boots.

They were cowboy boots, the kind a Texan would wear.

The man was tall and lanky, loosely built, wearing an

expensive pearl-gray raw silk suit elegantly tailored to fit his rangy frame. His face was deeply tanned, the features broad and open, and his hair was sandy blond, cut much shorter than was currently the fashion in England. Despite his expensive attire, there was something essentially rugged about the man. I had no doubt that he was American, and the boots indicated that he was probably from one of the Western states.

I frowned, wondering why I should be so interested.

It seemed someone had mentioned a Texan. Who? Where had I heard something about a man from Texas? I pressed my brows together, concentrating, and then I remembered. Last night at the dinner table Aunt Agatha had told us about a Texan named Stephen Kirk who had been pestering her about the Gordon papers. He had phoned her from London. He had wanted to drive down to Gordonwood to discuss a sale. He had offered her over a million dollars in American money for the manuscripts. I was willing to bet twice that amount that the man peering into the shop window was the same Stephen Kirk.

I had to find out. It took me only a moment to decide my approach, and then I removed the ribbon that held my ponytail in place and shook my hair loose and tugged at my sweater until it fit outrageously tight. I took a deep breath and got into character and walked towards him, stopping a few paces from where he stood.

"Why—Stephen *Kirk*," I cried. "As I live and breathe —what are *you* doing in Gordonville?"

The man whirled around, startled. He stared at me, clearly not recognizing me but intrigued just the same. His eyes were very blue, and they lingered on the sweater for a few seconds. His wide, thin mouth spread into a pleasant grin and he nodded.

"Howdy, ma'am," he drawled. It was quite a drawl.

"Do Texans actually say 'Howdy'?" I inquired, batting my eyelashes. "It's such a charming word—"

"We're pretty charmin' fellows," he replied, quick on the uptake. "Do I know you?"

"Don't tell me you've forgotten," I said, pouting. Think sexy, I told myself.

"Uh—let's see, was it that party in Mayfair last month? Lady Somebody-or-other——"

"Lady Florence Whitelaw," I said.

"That's right. I'm not very good at names. Swell party——"

"*You* seemed to enjoy it. You were drinking quite a lot, as I recall, and all the women found you absolutely fascinating. They simply flocked around you, and you were telling the most interesting stories."

He smiled sheepishly and shuffled his feet. Stephen Kirk was a tall, good-looking man with a considerable amount of boyish charm. He reminded me of one of the Western heroes in the American television series that were so popular over here. He looked like he could rope a steer or knock a man down without blinking an eye, yet at the same time he could blush and stammer in the presence of a pretty girl. There wasn't a sophisticated bone in his body, and that made him all the more appealing. I felt rather guilty at my deception, but he was buying it.

"Nice to see you again—uh——"

"Winifred," I said, "but all my friends call me Winnie."

"Nice seein' you, Winnie," he said. His blue eyes were full of boyish pleasure. As though he'd suddenly been handed a brand new slingshot, I thought. He tried not to stare at the sweater, but it was a losing battle. There was an honesty about the man. Honesty, not innocence. He knew his way around where women were concerned. I sensed that immediately, playing upon it without the least shame.

"Look," he said, "is—uh—is there anyplace 'round here where a fellow could buy a girl a drink?"

"It's rather *early*," I replied, "but the tea shop is right down the street. They serve tea and cakes——"

"I'd be mighty pleased to treat you," he said, that wonderful grin still lingering on his lips.

"I'd be mighty pleased to accept," I replied.

Stephen Kirk threw back his head and roared with laughter. It was a rich, lusty sound, thoroughly enchanting. Hooking his arm in mine, he led me down the sidewalk, taking great, manly strides, the heels of his boots clicking loudly. I had to trot a little to keep up with him. People stared at us, undoubtedly amazed to see such an unusual couple in their midst. I was elated with my success. I was really rather good at this sort of thing, I thought, wondering if Mata Hari had found it as easy. When we reached the tea shop, he held the door open for me, executing a curt little bow as I passed in front of him.

The tea shop was charming, with soft beige walls and lace curtains and small marble-topped tables. On each table there were vivid blue larkspurs and yellow daffodils, freshly cut, arranged haphazardly in white vases. The proprietor was a tall, thin woman with fluffy gray hair and wrinkled face. She wore a long-sleeved mauve dress and a white organdy apron, and she was obviously startled to see us come in.

"Howdy, ma'am," Stephen Kirk greeted her as she approached us. "Can you fix us up with some goodies?"

She raised her eyebrows, alarmed, not understanding a word he said.

"Tea and cakes," I said, "and some sandwiches if you have them."

"Cucumber or watercress?"

"Ham," he said. She stared at him in bewilderment.

"Watercress," I told her, smiling.

Stephen pulled out a chair for me, helped me get seated, and then sat down across from me, spreading his long legs out awkwardly. I noticed his hands: long and slender, very tan, quite strong. He stared at me, his blue eyes open and honest, and I wondered just how I was going to go about getting the information I needed. Everything had worked well so far, but I was suddenly at a loss. I would have to be extremely careful. Stephen Kirk was no fool.

"Tell me about yourself," he said. I loved his drawl. He drew each word out slowly, slurring it just a little. "What's a pretty lass like you doin'———"

"In a place like this? I'm visiting relatives, actually. My aunt lives in Gordonville and I came to see her. I simply had to get away from London for a while. Frightful drag, all that rush. Gordonville's a bit of a drag, too. No interesting men around."

"What do you do? For a livin' I mean."

"Well, as a matter of fact I—I'm a writer."

"A writer?" He looked suddenly suspicious, thrusting his jaw out. "Are you a reporter?" he asked gruffly.

"A reporter? Gracious no! I write—poetry. Nothing elaborate, just free verse. A reporter? Do I look like one of *those* dreadful people?"

"I guess not," he said, relaxing. "They're all the time botherin' me. Wanna know what I'm doin' in England, wanna know if I'm plannin' some kind of deal. One of th' rascals slipped into my hotel room in London a few days ago, snoopin' around, tryin' to find something he could use."

"You don't *mean* it?" I said. "Why, I've never heard of such a thing. You must be very important——"

"Not important, just rich. You see, I've got all these oil wells——"

It went very smoothly after that. I knew from past experience that men liked nothing so much as talking about themselves, and Stephen Kirk was a case in point. His eyes lighted up and he grew very enthusiastic as he told me about his business ventures—terribly complicated, having to do with oil and stocks and bonds and private corporations—and in his zeal he forgot all about me and my sweater. The woman in mauve brought over a tray of food: tiny frosted cakes, delicate sandwiches with the crust trimmed off, a thick blue pot of tea with matching cups. The Texan continued to talk as I poured the tea.

"My, that's terribly impressive," I said when he finally paused for breath. "All that money——"

"That's just the problem," he replied. "All that money —how to spend it. We've established this foundation, you see, and we give grants, scholarships, all that sort of thing, but there's still too much money left. I'm over here lookin' for a way to unload some of those dollars."

"Oh?" I reached for one of the small sandwiches, politely interested, rather vague. In truth, I wanted to bombard him with questions, but that would have spoiled everything.

"Something big," he continued, "something we can write off on the tax returns. You see, I went to this small

Methodist college, and I've already built 'em a library
and a science building and a couple of new dormitories.
I was thinkin', we've got this great new library, but there's
nothing special about it, nothin' to distinguish it from
hundreds of other libraries in colleges all over the states.
I decided to start a collection. You know, private letters
and journals and manuscripts of famous writers and
painters and poets, that sort of thing. The University of
Texas has one of the best collections in the states, and at
Baylor they've got the Browning Library. Waco's the Mecca of Browning scholars. They have the largest collection
of Browning papers in the world. That's the kind of thing
I'd like to get started at my old alma mater."

"Fascinating," I said. "Here, have some more tea.
These cakes are delicious. And so you came over to England to try and find things for your collection?"

He nodded. "I heard about some Shelley items. There
were some letters he'd written to Claire Clairmont and
the original drafts of some of his minor poems, privately
owned. The fellow was plannin' to sell 'em, and I was
ready to buy, but then I got wind of something much
more exciting."

"Indeed?"

He nodded. This is it, I thought. He's going to tell me
about the Gordon papers. I waited, but Stephen Kirk
sipped his tea and lounged back in his chair, silent for the
first time. It was terribly frustrating, but I knew I
couldn't prod him. He gave the impression of an innocent
abroad, a simple, genial fellow with hayseed in his hair,
but that impression was vastly deceiving. He was extremely intelligent, extremely capable, but these traits were
worn like a loose garment. His brash charm and boyish
mannerisms could be terribly misleading to the unwary.

"And did your business bring you to Gordonville?" I
inquired, my voice light and airy.

"You might say that," he replied. "Uh——surely
you've read about the Gordon manuscripts?"

"It seems like I remember something in the papers——"

"They haven't been located yet," he continued, "but
there's a strong possibility they exist."

"You hope to buy them?"

"That's right. It'd be a coup, a real coup."

"What if they're not for sale?" I asked.

"They will be," he said firmly. "This fellow——" He paused, frowning. "I can't really discuss it yet. All very hush-hush, you know, but I've been in touch with someone who promises me he can deliver the papers when and if they're found."

It was pure hell, not being able to ask him the name of the man he was in touch with. I finished my tea and ate one of the tiny cakes. I didn't really need to ask the name. I felt sure I knew who it was, and I wondered how he planned to work it. Stephen Kirk was a genial philanthropist, colorful in his way but, I was sure, scrupulously honest. Aunt Agatha had made it clear that she wouldn't sell the papers, but . . . Aunt Agatha could be dealt with. A horrifying thought entered my mind. My face must have turned pale, for Stephen Kirk leaned forward, a look of concern in his eyes.

"Somethin' wrong?" he inquired.

"No. I—I just remembered an appointment."

Stephen Kirk smiled, relieved. "Glad you said that," he told me. "I have an appointment myself." He glanced at his watch. "Guess we'd better break up this little party. Shame I'm driving back to London tonight. I'd like to see you again."

"Maybe we'll run into each other at Lady Whitelaw's next party," I replied, in control now.

He paid for the tea, leaving an outrageous tip, and escorted me out of the shop. I saw a gleaming white Cadillac parked across the street, the interior tan rawhide, a Stetson hat sitting on the dashboard. It was precisely the kind of car the Texan would drive. We stood in front of the shop, exchanging polite remarks. He grinned amiably, tall and handsome in his pearl-gray suit and hand-tooled boots. He was reluctant to leave me, his eyes back on the sweater now. I gave him a false address in London and told him to look me up when I returned to the city.

"It's a promise," he drawled.

I started back towards the inn. Half a block away I paused, turning to watch Stephen Kirk cross the street. He looked larger than life, bizarre and incongruous in this quaint, very British town. He climbed in the Cadillac and drove off, maneuvering the big car around a corner and disappearing down a side street.

The inn looked strangely solemn as I opened the front door and stepped inside. No lights were burning, and only a few rays of pale yellow sunlight managed to seep in through the dirty glass windows in front. The lobby was deserted, curiously tomblike. I stared at the desk, littered with papers, and the shabby old sofa in a corner half hidden by rubber tree plants. Had it been only two nights ago that I had been sitting there, listening to the mysterious conversation between Vanessa Shaw and the man in the raincoat? It seemed that it had been weeks ago, so much had happened since. I thought about that conversation as I waited for someone to come to the desk. What I had overheard no longer seemed so mysterious.

I remembered the man in the long black plastic raincoat and the black hat with the brim pulled down over his forehead. I hadn't really been able to discern anything definite, but he had been tall, with broad shoulders. I had seen a strong jaw and a wide mouth. I was almost certain who he was, and Charlie would confirm it. It was a plot, all right, and it was extremely clever, but it wasn't going to work. As soon as I had proof, I intended to contact Scotland Yard. Sergeant Jacobs was a friend of mine, and he would take over. I fumed, thinking of the bold audacity of what they were attempting to do. They might have succeeded, had I not decided to pay a belated visit to Gordonwood, had Althea not owned a pair of powerful binoculars. . . .

Where was Charlie? I stepped over to the desk and rang the bell, impatient. He would tell me everything, I was sure, even though he was still infatuated with Vanessa Shaw. I remembered how frightened he had been last night down by the lake when he had heard Craig Stanton approaching. He had been terrified, poor lad, but it would be different here at the inn. We would go into the office and close the door, and he would be calmer today. He would tell me everything, and then I would phone Sergeant Jacobs. Where *was* Charlie? I rang the bell again, slamming my palm down on the tiny silver button.

I don't know how long I had been standing there before I noticed the silence. It hung heavy in the air, unnatural. There was no sound whatsoever in the inn. There should have been the sounds of activity from all over the place: electricity humming, dishes rattling, people moving about, however muted they might be here in the lobby. There was nothing but silence, like a pall in the air. I stepped through the archway that led into the restaurant. The huge room was very dark, deserted, walls spread with shadows, fireplace filled with cold ashes. Something was wrong, very wrong. I could sense it. There was an atmosphere, heavy, brooding. I had the feeling I was in a ship at sea, completely alone, adrift. I went back into the lobby, disturbed. I rang the bell again.

There was no response.

"Charlie!" I called.

Charlie, Charlie, Charlie . . . the sound echoed up the stairwell. I was trembling now, although I didn't rightly know why I should be.

There were footsteps outside, and I saw the doorknob turning slowly, stealthily. I backed up against the desk, my heart beating rapidly. The fear was a live thing, there in the room with me, as real and tangible as the walls themselves. The door creaked loudly as someone pushed it open. I gasped, wanting to scream, but no sound would come. I saw the shadowy figure step inside, closing the door behind him. It was so dark in here, the only light coming feebly through the murky glass windows.

My throat was dry, and my wrists felt limp. I was still clutching the neatly wrapped shoes, and I raised the bundle in one hand, prepared to hurl it at the intruder.

The boy jumped when he saw me standing by the desk, as startled as I was. His thin face was quite pale, and he stood poised for flight before he finally recognized me. His thick black hair was combed back neatly, and he was wearing street clothes instead of the crisp white jacket he had worn two nights ago when he served me in the restaurant.

"I've just aged ten years," I said, attempting levity. "Tell me, is my hair still the right color? I have the strangest feeling that it's just turned white."

He didn't answer. He simply stared at me, his face

still the color of ashes. Poor boy, I thought, amused. He had come in to start opening up the restaurant, only to find a stranger lurking in the lobby, ready to hurl a package at his head. I smiled wryly, stepping towards him.

"I'm Susan Marlow," I said. "I stayed here two nights ago. Remember? I have an appointment with Charlie."

"You—had an appointment?" he stammered.

"I've been ringing the bell, but apparently no one's around. Business really *must* be slow. Do you happen to know where Charlie is?"

The boy nodded slowly. He was acting very peculiar, I thought, beginning to grow just a little irritated.

"I came to get my things," he said. "I don't know what I'll do now. I guess maybe I'll find another job somewhere."

"What——?" I saw his expression. His eyes were red-rimmed. He had been crying.

"He was such a good person. He never harmed any-one——"

"Where is Charlie?" I whispered.

"In the morgue. He tripped on the stairs in the middle of the night. He tumbled all the way down. He—his neck was broken. It was a terrible thing, terrible——"

"Charlie had an—accident?"

"We found him this morning. He—he was wearing slippers, one slipper. The other one was at the top of the stairs."

I stared at the boy, and I was surprised at how calm I was. I should have been stunned, I should have been terrified, but I had none of the reactions I should have had. It was as though I were standing in ice cold water. Perhaps I wasn't calm after all. Perhaps I was merely numb.

"Did anyone see it happen?" I asked. My voice was level.

The boy shook his head. "Charlie was all alone here last night. No one was staying in any of the rooms. There hasn't been anyone here since you checked out yesterday morning."

How simple it must have been, I thought.

"George and I came in at nine o'clock," the boy continued. "George is the cook. We—we found him crumpled up there at the bottom of the stairs. His neck was like

rubber, his head all twisted——" He shuddered, remembering. "George phoned Constable Clark right away. Dr.
Matthews came over with him. They said it was an accident, a terrible, terrible accident——"

Oh no, I thought, there was no accident. It was
cleverly planned to look that way. They did it, and I have
no proof, no proof whatsoever. I have nothing to go on
now, nothing but my own suspicion. I'll never know what
it was Charlie meant to tell me. That's wrong. I already
know what he meant to tell, but there's no one to verify
it now. I have nothing to go on, nothing. . . .

Moving past the boy as though in a trance, I stepped
outside. I had to lean against the wall for a moment,
sunshine pouring down, warming my face. I closed my
eyes, trying to blot out the images that flashed in my
mind. I could see the body hurtling down the stairs, see it
fall in a crumpled heap at the bottom of the stairs. I
could see the rubbery neck, the head at a curious angle,
as though it had been fastened on wrong, and I could see
the dark form hovering at the head of the staircase,
triumphant. It was all as vivid in my mind as it would
have been had I actually seen the crime committed. But
it had been an accident, pure and simple. Poor Charlie
had tripped and fallen. I had no proof to the contrary,
and no one would believe me . . . unless I could find
other evidence of what was going on.

I walked down the street toward the square, still moving as though in a trance. How was I going to get that
evidence? How was I going to find the proof I needed to
convince the authorities of what was happening? I was
certain in my own mind, but others would think I was
imagining things unless I could show them something concrete. It was only after I had crossed the square and
opened the door of my aunt's car that I saw the bright
red XKE Jaguar turning down one of the side streets. It
had been parked in the garage next to the Bentley. Craig
Stanton was behind the wheel now. I wondered if he was
going to be late to his appointment.

CHAPTER EIGHT

I had been gone for little less than two hours. Craig Stanton, of course, had gone into Gordonville "to the stationer's," and my aunt was still up in her room taking her afternoon nap. Mary informed me of this and asked me if I would like her to bring me one of the sandwiches Cook had made for lunch. I shook my head. Mary went on back to her work, and I walked down the hall to where the ancient black and gold telephone stood on a mahogany table. I was rather dubious about the instrument, but after a moment of crackling, jangling static I heard the operator's smooth male voice.

"Number please?" he said.

"I'd like to make a long distance call to London."

"Smashin', ducks. Your number?"

"I'm afraid I don't know. I'm calling from Gordonwood."

"That would be——" He gave me the number.

"Thank you," I said. Our charming male telephone operators were a wonder in this highly mechanized world.

"Hold on, please. I'll give you the London operator."

I waited impatiently, listening to the static and the voices of other operators in the distance. There were various tiny pops and screeches, and once I even heard snatches of conversation about a serious ailment a woman named Tessie had come down with. It was over five minutes before I got the London operator, another two or three before he finally connected me with Scotland Yard. I asked for Sergeant Jacobs' office and had to answer a lot of questions before they agreed to connect me with him. I had to wait again while they rang his office.

Sergeant Peter Jacobs was a very good friend. He was short and stocky with graying brown hair, lively blue eyes, lined, leathery face, and a magnificent sense of humor. Not only was he one of Scotland Yard's best men, he was also an authority on criminology, holding several degrees. It was in that capacity that I had first met him. One of my books had been based on a real turn-of-the-century crime in Soho, and Peter had helped me with my research. I had dedicated the book to him, and we had remained friends. He liked to sit back in a big leather chair with a glass of port, watching flames dance in the fireplace while he expounded at length on some of the horrendous crimes he had studied. I was always an appreciative audience, often taking notes on what he said.

Peter found it amusing that anyone of my age and sex should be so fascinated by such gruesome things. Crime was an important reality to him. He studied it, he encountered it every day in his work, whereas I used it merely as a pepper to flavor books that were essentially romantic. Peter loved to tease me about this, and I knew he didn't take me seriously, even though we were very fond of each other.

"At last," I said when he finally picked up the phone.

"Susan?" he said. "I thought you were in Majorca. My secretary said you were calling from——"

"I'm visiting my aunt," I replied. "Peter, I—I need some help. I think I've uncovered——"

"Things are rather tight at the moment," he said, interrupting me. "A series of robberies in Chelsea, and just this morning a body was found in the Thames, female, well dressed, unidentified. I'm up to my ears in paper work as well, but—this isn't imperative, is it? I mean, you're not in any great hurry for your research?"

"It's very imperative," I told him. "Peter, something is——"

"What is it this time? A whopping bloody axe murder, or just a simple case of arsenic poison?"

"This isn't for one of my books," I said irritably. "Would you please stop interrupting me? Peter, something is going on here at Gordonwood. I think there's been a murder——"

"At your aunt's house?" he inquired pleasantly.

"At the local inn. But my aunt's involved. I—I have nothing to go on but my suspicions, but——"

"Have you been drinking by any chance?"

"Peter, I'm *serious.*"

"Of course," he said dryly. "Want to tell me about it?"

"Not yet. I don't want you to laugh at me. That's exactly what you'd do. The local constable said it was an accident, pure and simple, but I *know* it wasn't——"

Mildred came shuffling down the hall. I laughed merrily into the phone and said I couldn't possibly get back to London for the party, even though it *was* in my honor. Mildred moved past me, pulling her sweater around her, and then she turned down the narrow corridor leading to the kitchen.

"What the *hell?*" Peter barked.

"Someone was in the room. Peter, I want you to check on some people for me. Could you do that? I'd just like to know if they're all they pretend to be. You've got all the resources of Scotland Yard behind you, and it wouldn't take more than a couple of hours——"

He sighed heavily. I could hear the sound quite clearly over the wire. I knew he thought I had gone off the deep end. That's why I didn't give him any details. It was all too improbable to be believed without some kind of concrete evidence, and I didn't have that evidence yet. I intended to look for it, and in the meantime I needed to know all I could about Craig Stanton, Stephen Kirk, and Vanessa Shaw.

"Give me the names," Peter said wearily.

I did so. "By the way," he added, "who was the fellow who died?"

"His name was Charlie Grayson. He owned the inn. He had been having an affair with Vanessa Shaw, and I think she helped murder him——"

"Ho hum," Peter said. "You're a delightful girl, Susan, but you've got an incredible imagination. I don't mind getting the information, but if you knew how busy we are——"

"Thank you, Peter," I said abruptly. "When will you be able to call me back?"

"That depends. Tonight, perhaps, but more likely sometime tomorrow. Give me your number."

I stood in the hall for a moment after I had hung up. Peter's reaction had been all I had expected, and he was a close friend. Any other police officer would have laughed outright if I had gone to him with my story, and the mere fact that I wrote mystery novels for a living would make anything I said even more suspect. No one had paid any attention to Althea when she talked about what she had seen, and no one would pay any attention to me. Althea locked herself up in Dower House and found solace in her gin, but I couldn't sit back and ignore what was going on.

I had to play it very cool, and I had to be extremely cautious. There might be great danger involved in what I planned to do, but I would simply have to risk it. No one knew that I had learned so much. That was a great advantage. I would go about my business as normally as possible, apparently nonchalant, but I would be alert every minute. Contemplating what I was going to do and the possible consequences, I trembled, frightened, but I quickly controlled myself. There was no time for fear, no time for weakness of any sort. It would take great strength, courage even, and I felt sure I had both.

My first concern was for Aunt Agatha. I walked slowly up the stairs, running my hand along the smooth polished mahogany bannister. Aunt Agatha had been firm about her refusal to sell the manuscripts should they eventually be found, and I was certain that Stephen Kirk would not purchase stolen material. The sale would have to be a legitimate one. That meant that my aunt would have to be persuaded to sell, or . . . I refused to contemplate the alternative. She was an obstacle. Obstacles were removed. Charlie had known too much, and he had been removed.

I felt I was in the middle of some horrible nightmare, everything fuzzy, everything vague. Surely I would wake up soon to find that none of this was really happening. Everything had been so utterly normal just two days ago. I had been on the train, listening to the screech of metal on metal, watching the lovely scenery flit past my window, surrounded by normal people with normal faces, hearing them gripe and complain because the train was behind schedule. Babies had whined and a group of soldiers up front had conducted a noisy poker game in

the aisle. I had been content, on holiday, looking forward
to seeing my aunt again. I had stepped off the train, into
the sheets of pouring rain, and the nightmare had begun,
slowly at first, building up to this moment of total un-
reality.

I was a young woman in slacks and sweater, walking
down the hall in an old house. There was nothing unusual in that. I was on my way to visit my aunt who had
taken an afternoon nap. What could be more normal? It
was impossible to believe that my aunt might be in grave
danger, that the house itself posed a threat with its
gloomy halls and dark corners, its winding staircases and
countless closed rooms. I couldn't believe it, and yet I
knew it was real. I hurried towards my aunt's room,
wondering how I would ever find the nerve to go through
with this.

I opened the door quietly, without knocking. Aunt
Agatha was sitting up in bed, wearing a light blue bed
jacket embroidered with green and gold and dark blue
designs. She held a heavy book in her lap, a pair of
green horn-rimmed glasses perched on her nose. The bedside table was cluttered with books and magazines and
papers, a deck of Tarot cards, a box of chocolates, a
glass, a bottle of pills, and on the bed beside her were
more books, pencils, a newspaper, an orange, and a box
of crackers. She nibbled a cracker as she read, her long
plain face screwed up in concentration. I stood just inside
the room, watching her. I wanted to burst into tears, and
I wanted to scream. Instead, I coughed discreetly.

"My word, Susan!" she cried, slamming the book
shut. "You're as bad as Mildred! I was just reading about
a coven of witches in Rumania, and I heard you—come
over here and *sit!* You look like a ghost standing there in
the shadows."

I sat down on the edge of the bed. Aunt Agatha removed her glasses and yawned. She looked different here
in bed. Relaxed, that remarkable vitality not charging
full blast, she seemed older, and I thought she looked
tired. Her face seemed to sag a bit, and there were tiny
mauve bags under her blue eyes. She looked old, vulnerable, and when I took her hand to squeeze it I realized
how fragile the fingers were. I had noticed none of this

before, but before she had been suffused with that electric
quality that gave her every appearance of robust health.

"Why are you *looking* at me like that?" she asked
peevishly.

"No reason. You—you just look tired."

"Fiddlesticks!"

"You *are* tired," I said, peering at her closely.

"I am," she snapped, turning her mouth down irritably. "I suppose I may as well admit it! Paul fusses
over me so—I hate to let him think he's right. I *have*
been overdoing it, Susan. I do get tired, but I loathe not
being up and about. This afternoon—well, I've decided to
stay in bed for the rest of the day."

"Should I phone Paul?" I asked, worried.

"If you start clucking over me I'll throw back my
head and scream! I simply got carried away in the basement this morning. I overdid things. I have enough sense
to realize I'm sixty-two years old and require a dab more
rest than I did at sixteen, so I decided to rest up for tomorrow. We plan to start on the attics then. We've
searched them once, but we didn't really take things
apart and give them the thorough going-over they require, just looked through the trunks. I don't think the
papers will be in a trunk. I think they'll be tucked away
somewhere, in a secret compartment, maybe, or maybe
behind some loose bricks."

"Did you take your pill?" I asked, ignoring her transparent attempts to divert the conversation from her
health.

"Yes, I did," she replied, wrinkling her brow. "You
should have seen Mildred simper. Great triumph for
her. I wanted to slap her face! I took my pill and I took
my nap and now I've decided to stay in bed. That's all
there is to it."

"If you don't feel better tomorrow——"

"I'll feel splendid tomorrow!"

"Aunt Agatha——" I said impulsively, "let's—let's go
to Majorca. I planned to go two weeks from now, but—
let's leave tomorrow. I'll buy your ticket and pay all
your expenses. The change of scene will be wonderful."
I saw the look of astonishment on her face, but some-

thing prompted me to go on. "I know it's spur of the
moment, but spur-of-the-moment things are such fun and
—and I think you should get away from Gordonwood
for a while. The trip would be marvelous for you."

"Have you taken leave of your senses?" she asked
calmly.

I stared down at the dark green carpet, realizing my
outburst had been prompted by cowardice.

"I couldn't possibly leave Gordonwood now," she said,
"just when we're on the brink of something so exciting. I
appreciate the invitation, dear, but you know it's out of
the question."

"Of course," I replied, my voice lethargic.

"Whatever made you make such a suggestion?" she
asked, peering up at me with shrewd blue eyes. "You just
arrived yesterday, and already—is something *worrying*
you, Susan?"

"Nothing whatsoever," I said lightly. I gave her a reassuring smile, but I wasn't at all sure it was a convincing
one. She continued to peer at me, those blue eyes so
sharp, so wise. I couldn't tell her about what I had
learned, of course. My job was to protect her, not to
make her worry. She tapped her fingernails on the cover
of the book she had been reading, a sly expression on her
face.

"I think *I* know what's wrong," she said. "I think it's
Craig. You're falling in love with him, aren't you?"

"Don't be absurd."

"Oh, I notice things, dear. I notice the way he looks
at you, and I notice the way you act around him—tense,
self-conscious. Two healthy, attractive people—it was
bound to happen. He's a slippery one, but you can pull
him in if you use the right tactics. Forget all this foolishness about dashing off to Majorca, dear. You can't run
away from it—a trite statement but true nevertheless."

"I can't run away from it," I said in a flat voice. "I
realize that. For a moment I thought I could."

"Craig's an exceptional young man."

"Quite," I said, looking away from her. "Aunt Agatha—Craig stayed at the inn for a while, didn't he?"

"Indeed he did, until I asked him to come stay at

Gordonwood. It made no sense for him to spend all that money for a room when I had so many here going to waste."

"He would have been at the inn during the time Charlie was carrying on with that woman," I said. "Isn't that right?"

"That's right, but I shouldn't let it bother me. From all accounts she was a common little thing, hardly the type to have interested a man like Craig."

"But he would have met her there."

"I don't see how he could have avoided meeting her. Anyway, she disappeared shortly after Craig came to Gordonwood. Probably met a traveling salesman and took out for parts unknown. It must have been *something* like that. No one saw her leave, and she would have been noticed if she'd been at the station. The man probably had a private car."

"That's probably it," I said.

"You don't need to worry about any mysterious woman, Susan. Just worry about wearing the right sort of perfume."

I stood up, not wanting to tax her any longer. She needed to rest, and as long as I was in the room she would continue to chat and exert herself. She leaned back against the fluffy pillows, watching me.

"What are you going to do for the rest of the day?" she asked.

"I don't know. I think I'll go down to the library for a while."

"Would you take this chapter, dear?" She rummaged among the papers on the nightstand, pulling out a sheaf of long yellow pages fastened together with a paper clip. "I forgot to take it down this morning, and Craig will want to work on it later on. You might read some of it. Fascinating material."

I took the pages from her and leaned down to kiss her cheek. She told me to pay her another visit later on tonight, and I promised to do so. I started out of the room, pausing at the door. I turned to face her, realizing there was something I had forgotten.

"Aunt Agatha—do you lock your bedroom door at night?"

"Of course not! What a preposterous idea."

"Would you start locking it?" I asked, trying to keep my voice as airy as possible. "I know it's foolishness on my part, but—all that talk at the table last night. I— I'd just feel better if I knew your bedroom door was locked."

"I've never heard anything so foolish! It's absolutely neurotic. We have the dogs, and———"

"Will you promise to lock your door, Aunt Agatha?"

"I suppose so, if it will make you *feel* better."

"It will make me feel much better."

"Really, Susan, you're acting most peculiar! The first thing you do is dash off to Gordonville as though it were a matter of life or death that you get a silly shoe repaired, and now———" She gave an exasperated sigh, throwing her hands up. "This whole family has always been madly eccentric. I guess I'll just have to indulge you."

"Indulge me," I said, smiling.

Aunt Agatha patted her short, sandy hair and pulled the beautifully embroidered bed jacket around her. She gave me a disgruntled look, picking up the heavy book and slipping the comical green glasses back on. Reaching for another cracker, she ignored me and started reading about the coven of witches in Rumania. I felt much better as I closed her bedroom door behind me and started back downstairs.

The library was a lovely high-ceilinged room with Persian carpets of orange and gold and green spread over the dark, gleaming parquet floor. Long green velvet draperies hung at the windows, parted to let in the afternoon sun, and the furniture was perfect: a sofa and chairs of dark gray leather, tables of dark mahogany holding large, ornate lamps. There was a huge old leather-topped desk in one corner, littered with books and papers, a gold and bronze globe on a mahogany stand beside it. The bookshelves rose from floor to ceiling, filled with books: musty old volumes with limp, battered bindings, sets gorgeously bound in brown and dark orange and gold leather, modern novels with bright jackets, paperback thrillers stuck helter-skelter next to weighty, impressive tomes.

The fireplace was gray-green marble, smoothly polished, and a portrait of Sir Robert Gordon hung over the mantel. Framed in dark brown wormwood, the portrait dominated the room, that powerful, magnetic figure seemingly standing watch over everything in sight. Posed against a backdrop of stark desert, blazing yellow sand, and flat brown hills, Sir Robert wore a native burnoose of green and white striped linen, immense folds of cloth cloaking his body, the hood pulled up to frame the cruel, sinister face. He was as dark as an Arab, with wide, thin mouth, hawklike nose and eyebrows that arched like dark wings. The eyes were coal black, piercing, peering out with savage ferocity.

I stared at the portrait, fascinated. Here was the man who was responsible for all this. He had lived with fierce abandon and fantastic courage, streaking across the drab Victorian era like a mighty comet, one of the most daring, intelligent, and colorful men in the history of that or any other age. He had explored Africa when it was still the Dark Continent, following the Nile to its source, discovering lakes and waterfalls and lost cities in the dense jungles, dwelling among the cannibals and returning to write books that shed light for future explorers. Disguised as an Arab, he had penetrated the holy city of Mecca when discovery would have meant immediate execution. His exploits in Arabia had been no less spectacular, and in the United States he had gone to Salt Lake City and written a definitive book about the Mormons. I found it incredible that one man could have done all those things, even more incredible that he was able to write over forty books. His own works were crammed with exotic lore, and his translations had brought the classics of the East to Western civilization.

Lady Arabella's bonfire had caused a great loss to the world, and it was exciting to think that some of the papers had escaped the flames. I had been unreceptive to the idea before, not at all impressed by Craig's evidence or my aunt's enthusiasm. It had seemed too improbable that the manuscripts might still be in existence, but things seemed different now. If there were not a strong possibility that the manuscripts existed, the plot would be pointless. No one would take such risks without a near certainty of reward. Staring at the portrait of Sir Robert Gordon, I began to feel some of that excitement Aunt Agatha had displayed when she spoke of the papers. It was almost like a fever, spurring me on to search and discover. The pioneer miners must have felt this way when they went panning for gold.

I knew, then, that I was going to spend the rest of the day searching for the Gordon manuscripts. Aunt Agatha had mentioned the attics. I would start there. I felt foolishly excited at the prospect, and, too, the search would help take my mind off other things. I could really do nothing until I heard from Peter. Perhaps the information he provided would give me some kind of direction.

I was still holding the sheaf of long yellow paper in my hand. Taking it over to the desk, I sat down in the modern swivel chair and started to read. The pages were tightly packed with firm handwriting, several words and sentences crossed out, many blots where the black ink had splattered. I read casually at first, turning the pages with little interest, but gradually the vivid scenes captured my complete attention. This chapter described Gordon's mission to Dahomey, the forbidden West African kingdom where human sacrifice and cannibalism were rampant. Craig described the courtyard littered with bones, poles topped with human skulls, the bloody rites of these treacherous savages. Finishing the last page, I pushed the chapter away, shaken by what I had just read. Craig Stanton was an accomplished writer, a master of graphic prose carefully documented. I had no doubts whatsoever that the book would be a raging best seller.

"You look upset," he said. "Was it that bad?"

I jumped out of the chair, startled. He was lounging in the doorway, watching me with a wry smile on his lips. I had no idea how long he might have been there, spying on me. I felt a blush starting to burn my cheeks. Craig Stanton chuckled.

"You looked so absorbed, I hated to disturb you. You actually cringed once. You must have been reading the passage about——"

"Aunt Agatha asked me to bring the chapter down,"

I said hastily, interrupting him. "I—I thought I'd read a few pages."

"I'm flattered. What do you think of it?"

"It's awful," I replied.

"Oh? Remind me to keep the rest of the manuscript away from you. I don't know if my ego can stand such frank evaluation."

"I didn't mean it that way. It—it's brilliantly written. It's just so—vivid. All those details—were they really necessary?"

"Certainly," he replied. "Gordon believed the Foreign Office wanted to get rid of him and assumed that was why he was sent to Dahomey. I had to show the blood and bones in order to justify his suspicions to my readers. Fortunately, he got along famously with King Akhosu Gelele and was able to leave with his head still on his shoulders, foiling his rivals at the Foreign Office and adding another episode to his legend."

Craig strolled over to the desk, carrying two reams of paper and a box of pencils he had obviously purchased in town. He was still wearing tennis shoes and the loose sweat shirt, although he had changed into khaki pants. We stood facing each other, the desk between us. Craig smiled at me, his eyes filled with amusement.

"You look terrified," he said.

"What—what makes you say that?" I asked, trying to control the tremor in my voice.

"Your expression, luv. You look like a tiny bird paralyzed by a cobra. Tell me, am I really that offensive?"

"You're imagining things," I replied, tossing my head and pretending to be totally unconcerned. I was supposed to play it cool. I was supposed to be the intrepid girl detective, undaunted, and yet he had sensed my attitude at once. I would have to try and repair the damage.

"It—it's just the chapter," I said. "I really was shaken by it. I don't know when I've read anything so— totally real. I was impressed. I had no idea you were such a wonderful writer."

"That's more like it," he replied. "Maybe I'll let you read the rest of the manuscript after all. I may even let you help me with the chapters that deal with romance.

There's a good love story there, Lady Arabella so prim and proper yet so devoted to her lord and master. I'm not sure I can do as good a job with the sentiment as I've done with the savagery."

"I'm sure you'll do an excellent job."

"Ah, now you're really after my heart."

"Hardly that," I retorted.

I mustn't overdo it, I realized. I couldn't do a sudden about-face. I couldn't be too friendly, too responsive. That would surely arouse his suspicions as much as my fear had just a few minutes ago. I walked over to one of the shelves and pretended to examine the titles. I could feel him watching me. His very presence seemed to permeate the air, leaving an indelible impression as real as smell and yet just as intangible. I had never known anyone with such a forceful personality, nor had I known anyone who caused me to react in such a strange way.

"You've got some explaining to do," he said in a stern voice.

"Oh?" I continued to examine the book titles.

"This morning. Why did you go off like that?"

"To have my shoes repaired. I thought I mentioned that."

"Is that the only reason you went into town?"

"Why should I answer these——"

"Is that the only reason?" he asked sharply.

"Of course."

"Then why was it so important that you leave immediately? I told you I had to go to the stationer's to pick up some items. Why couldn't you wait and go with me?"

"I don't know if your ego can stand such frank evaluation."

"Don't get smart, Susan."

"I didn't want to go into town with you, Mr. Stanton. I don't want to have anything to do with you. I made myself quite clear last night."

"You made yourself clear, all right," he replied, "but not by anything you said. You didn't want me to leave your room last night, Susan. That was the only thing you made clear."

"I take back what I said earlier. Your ego could stand anything. It's incapable of———"

"Christ!" he muttered. "You're impossible!"

I was pleased with myself. I had convinced him that I had left in the Bentley merely because I had wanted to avoid him. My performance had been almost as good as the one I had given for Stephen Kirk.

Stepping over to the window, I looked outside, one hand holding back the long green velvet draperies. The sunshine was weaker now, and the sky was turning gray, clouds forming. It looked like we were going to have one of those abrupt changes of weather. It might storm before nightfall. When I turned around, Craig was standing in the middle of the room, looking at me with a bewildered expression.

"What's bothering you?" he asked quietly.

"Nothing is bothering me."

"You're quite sure of that?"

"Of course I am."

"You're acting strangely."

"Because I don't hurl myself into your arms?" I said acidly.

"It's not that. There's something else. I can sense it."

"Whatever are you talking about?"

"Last night at the lake, when I first came up to you, I had the impression you were trying to hide something from me, and then you acted so enigmatically this morning. I have the feeling something's going on."

"What could possibly be going on?" I inquired.

"I don't know," he said, shaking his head slowly.

He moved closer to me, knees dipping foward a little as he walked. He was incredibly appealing in his khakis and sweat shirt, exuding an animal vitality, but I was immune to his magic now. He stopped a few feet away, folding his arms across his chest. I felt the same icy calm I had felt at the inn.

"What are you hiding from me, Susan?" he asked.

"Nothing at all."

"I wish I could be sure of that."

"I suppose you'll just have to take my word for it."

"I suppose I will—for now. I've got work to do. I don't have time to get to the bottom of this now, but I will. I can assure you of that. If you're meeting some man——"

"Is *that* what you think? You think I'm—oh, how absurd. How gloriously absurd!"

I couldn't restrain my laughter. It pealed merrily, but it wasn't an expression of mirth, it was the laughter of relief. He thought I was meeting a man! He had failed in his attempts to woo me and his strong male ego couldn't stand the thought that someone else may have succeeded. I laughed, and he glared at me angrily and finally went back over to the desk, turning his back to me and straightening the books and papers with furious energy. I stood in front of the window, feeling quite superior.

"I don't know what you plan to do for the rest of the afternoon," he said irritably, glancing over his shoulder, "but I suggest you find a good book and stay in your room. I'm going to be immersed in revising this chapter, and I won't have time to look after you. Don't go wandering off by yourself. I won't be there to get you out if you——"

"Oh, don't worry about me, Mr. Stanton," I said in honeyed tones. "I'm quite capable of looking after myself."

"I strongly doubt that!" he snapped.

I gave another short laugh and left the library, a smile on my lips. I felt strangely elated. I had won the first round hands down, and he had proved himself a very vulnerable opponent. Craig Stanton was a clever man, but he was not as clever as he thought. Not quite. Sooner or later he would give himself away, and when he did I would be there, waiting. I climbed the stairs, flushed with my success. It was not going to be so difficult after all, I thought, and what I had said to Craig was undoubtedly true. I was quite capable of looking after myself.

CHAPTER NINE

The stairs across the hall from my bedroom were dark and narrow, one flight leading down to the kitchen area, another leading up to the attics. They had once been bright golden oak, but the wood had darkened with age and the varnish had started to peel. Hesitating only a second, I started up, putting all thoughts of Craig Stanton out of my mind and thinking now only of the Gordon papers which I might be fortunate enough to discover. It was not very likely, I admitted, but as I moved up the stairs I felt that curious fever I had felt earlier, a combination of excitement and expectation. The stairs were steep, and there was little light, but surely I wouldn't need an oil lamp in broad daylight.

The door at the top of the stairs creaked on rusty hinges as I pushed it open, stepping into a small, narrow room with low beamed ceiling, empty of everything but dust and cobwebs. Dust stirred as I crossed to a doorway and stepped down three shallow steps leading to a second room, as narrow as the first, cluttered with ancient furniture and old lampshades and piles of yellowing magazines. The room didn't look very promising, so I passed on through another doorway, down five steps, and walked down a hallway barely four feet wide, one wall solid, the other with tiny windows set high up under the eaves. Beams of weak sunlight slanted down, swirling with motes of dust.

I remembered the attics only vaguely from my first visit. Aunt Agatha had brought me up here to hunt for an old China doll she wanted to give me. The doll had had a beautiful painted face and painted black hair and had worn a red muslin dress and tiny gold slippers. I still had it, a treasured keepsake. It had taken us some time to find it, and we had gone through several of the attic rooms before eventually locating it, covered with dust, tucked in the corner of a shelf. I had been amazed then at the number of rooms up here, at various levels, connected by narrow halls and wooden steps leading up and down from level to level. There were twelve rooms, some large, filled with fascinating relics, others mere cubbyholes.

Leaving the narrow hall, I stepped into a large, dusty room with ceiling high in the center and sloping down sharply on one side in conformity to the roof. Three small windows permitted the weak sunlight to filter in, pale rays shimmering with dust motes affording just enough light to permit me to search. The room was an antique dealer's dream. Old tables and chairs were piled high in one corner, and there were cupboards and cribs and teakwood boxes, all layered with dust. I saw an old spinning wheel, a dressmaker's dummy with the stuffing coming out, a big chandelier dumped on the floor, crystal pendants yellow from neglect. Cleaned and repaired, most of these items would bring an impressive price in some chic shop. I began to search and was immediately lost to the world of the past.

One of the cupboards contained old clothes, limp, worn, smelling of camphor and moth crystals. I examined a white lace dress trimmed with velvet rosebuds and black ribbons, an elegant ballgown that must have caused sighs of admiration at some party over a hundred years ago, and there was a dark green velvet traveling suit trimmed with brown fur, a purple silk tea gown, a brown and green plaid skirt, and a white blouse with leg-of-mutton sleeves. Lady Arabella must have worn these garments, I thought, looking at the plump dressmaker's dummy that must have been used to fit them. I could visualize some prim, underpaid seamstress working diligently to finish the ballgown while her employer entertained friends downstairs in the big drawing room.

A small teakwood box held a withered rose and a dance program, Robert Gordon's name in violet ink after each dance listed. The rose disintegrated into dust as I lifted it to take out the stack of letters neatly tied with a faded blue ribbon. They were love letters, written by Arabella Radcliff to Lieutenant Gordon, the stiff, yellowed pages covered with the same violet ink as on the dance card. I sat on a footstool beneath one of the windows, reading the letters, handling them very carefully. They were frightfully intimate, hardly the sort of letters a prim Victorian maiden should have written to a proper suitor. I could sense the passion and impatience of the young Arabella, stifled by the society she lived in and eager to join her lover in a life of adventure.

I realized that these letters were extremely valuable, shedding much light on the character of the young Arabella. Aunt Agatha had given Craig access to all the family papers, but for some reason or other this little teakwood box had not been among those other trunks and boxes that contained the diaries and letters and documents the family had preserved. The letters I was reading hadn't been touched in all these years, or else the rose sitting on top of them would have been destroyed. I had happened upon them by accident, and it was an exciting discovery.

The light gradually faded as I read, turning the priceless pages with great care. The love story that unfolded was thrilling, charged with drama and conflict. They had met at a fashionable French watering place where the whole Radcliff clan had come for the waters. Arabella chanced to be walking along the embankment by the sea at the same time Lieutenant Gordon strolled in his dashing uniform. He was already world weary and disillusioned by his experiences in India, cynical and brooding, and she was a healthy eighteen year old, just blooming into womanhood. It would have been hard to find two such dissimilar individuals, yet they had fallen in love on sight with typical Victorian fervor, and Arabella's parents had been horrified that such a rake would dare pay court to their treasured daughter. They had forbidden her to see him, but she had slipped out to meet him by the sea, even after they locked her in her room. Robert had gone to Paris to make arrangements for his next trip into Africa, and it was while he was there that she had written these impassioned letters. They planned to elope, and Arabella outlined the arrangements she was making with the aid of a sympathetic housemaid.

I finished the last letter, holding it in my lap and thinking about the elopement as I had read of it in books. Sir Robert had come back to the watering place under the cover of night, bidding the coachman wait for him while he collected the young girl who had flung her bags out of her bedroom window and climbed down a drainpipe to grab them up and flee into the darkness, meeting her lover by the embankment while great waves crashed on the ancient sea wall. They had hurried to the waiting coach which carried them back to Paris, and there a priest married them in a shabby old church just as the first rays of morning sun stained the bricks with rose-colored light and woke the pigeons roosting under the eaves.

How bold they had been, how daring and unconventional, even more so when one considered the age they had lived in. Arabella had made her decision and cast everything else aside, rushing into the arms of the man who would love her and torment her, making her life a hell at times, at times a heaven few women could hope for. She had been as flamboyant as he, yet in middle age she had turned to religion and charity, assembling about her all those staid Victorian conventions she had defied in youth, going as far as to destroy priceless manuscripts that might have offended a straightlaced Queen and her more pious subjects.

I put the letters back in the teakwood box, closing it and setting it aside. I would tell Aunt Agatha about the letters and let her decide what to do with them. The letters had distracted me from the business at hand, and I continued the search with renewed vigor, going through all the boxes and cupboards, finding countless interesting objects but nothing of any real importance. Through the windows I could see that the sky had turned a dark, brooding gray, hanging low, swollen with rain, and the wind soared about the rooftops with a sharp, whistling sound.

I really should have gone down then, but it wasn't late, and there was still enough light to search by, even though everything seemed to be tinged with gray and shadows were beginning to form. Leaving the large room, I passed down another hall, going down four steps, turning a corner, following the narrow hall to where three steps led up to another room. The attics were like a labyrinth, I thought, rooms stuck here and there with no apparent rhyme or reason. The next room I entered was filled with old statues that must once have stood in the gardens, white marble gods and goddesses covered with dust. I pitied the poor workmen who must have lugged the heavy figures up here. The statues seemed to stare at me accusingly as I passed through, as though I were to blame for their banishment.

A short passageway led to another room that looked more promising. One side of the room was filled with tattered Persian carpets tied up in rolls, and heavy chests stood across from them. Overhead was a skylight of murky glass panes that gave me all the light I needed. I pulled out the drawer of one of the chests and saw a coconut and took it out, wondering why on earth anyone should keep such an item. I held it up to the light and then let out a bloodcurdling scream, hurling the object away.

It rolled across the floor and stared up at me. It wasn't a coconut at all. It was a shrunken head, lank black hair hanging down, lips sewn together, eye sockets vacant. I shuddered, wiping my hand across my slacks vigorously. The drawer was filled with shrunken heads, one of them with long blond hair. I slammed it shut, wondering if I dared open another. I finally summoned enough courage to do so and found a drawerful of brightly colored African masks, exquisitely painted but hideous nevertheless. These chests obviously contained curios from Sir Robert's travels, I assumed, and further examination proved that assumption to be correct. I found no more shrunken heads, but there were knives and feathered pouches and grotesque little idols carved in wood and ivory, some graphic in detail. All belonged in a museum.

I forgot all about the ugly black and gray head on the floor behind me and was soon immersed in my task. I found maps on heavy parchment, crudely stained with red and black and green dyes, and there was a necklace made of bones, the kind a witch doctor would wear in a jungle movie. Such items were fairly common in museums all over the world, and none of these things was particulary valuable in itself, but the collection as a whole was most unusual. I could see Sir Robert trekking through the jungles, picking these pieces up as he searched for lost cities and recorded the customs of pygmy tribes along the way.

I was examining the contents of the final chest when the rain began to patter on the skylight, gently at first, gathering momentum until at last great drops pounded on the glass like showers of pebbles, making a furious racket. The light was almost gone, and I realized that I should leave the attics immediately if I didn't want to be caught in the dark. It would only take me a few more minutes to finish searching the chest, and then I would leave. The last drawer held beautiful silk prayer mats, sadly faded with age, smelling of mildew. No manuscripts here, but there were several more attic rooms, and perhaps I could search them tomorrow.

Retracing my steps, I moved back down the short passageway and stepped into the roomful of statues. It hadn't been a fruitless search, I reasoned. I had discovered the letters, and that in itself was quite important. Aunt Agatha was sure to be elated when I told her about them. I paused to look at the statue of Diana, rubbing some of the dust from her cheeks and touching her chipped nose. The rain was making a dreadful racket overhead, clattering angrily, and the wind was raging. It was hard to realize that this morning had been so gloriously bright and sunny. Leaving the forlorn marble statues behind, I walked down the narrow hall to the corner where the hall branched off and led to the room with the letters. I was lost in thought, and I didn't hear the footsteps at first. It was not until I was almost to the other room that I distinctly heard someone moving around.

I stopped, peering through the open doorway into the dim room. I could see the dressmaker's dummy leaning against the wall and the furniture piled up in the corner. I heard a board creak, then another, the sounds clear and distinct even with the elements raging outside. At first I was merely curious, wondering if someone had come up to find me, and it took me a moment to realize what that might imply. Icy fingers seemed to grip me, holding me rooted to the spot, unable to move. Another board creaked, and then there was a shuffling sound as though someone had pushed something out of the way. I saw a long shadow stirring, thrown against the wall by someone who was out of my range of vision.

This can't be happening, I told myself, almost cheerfully. Such things don't happen, not in real life, not to real people. . . . I almost laughed aloud, hysteria welling up inside of me.

Another board creaked. The shadow moved stealthily.

Black wings seems to close in on me, fluttering, blotting out everything else, and there was a ringing in my head. I threw my hand out to support myself, steeling every nerve in my body and willing myself not to pass out. I stumbled against the wall and my head seemed to spin, but I didn't faint. I leaned against the wall, limp. I felt as though all the blood had been drained from my body, and I had to close my eyes, catch my breath, and summon strength that had to be there.

My throat was dry, but I managed to call out.

"Who is it?" The words were a raspy croak.

There was no response. The shadow was still against the wall, long and black, leaning forward. Someone was waiting for me to step into the room. It wasn't a figment of my imagination. There was an aura of evil in the air as strong and real as it had been in the east wing yesterday morning. Someone was waiting, and I had been a fool, a fool, a bloody fool to have come up here alone. I had been so sure of myself, so confident, and now . . . I realized I couldn't panic. I had to pull myself together. I couldn't give in to the hysteria that was like another being inside, fighting to break out and overcome me.

Somehow I was able to move. I backed slowly down the hall, keeping my eyes on that dark doorway, expecting someone to come tearing out after me at any moment. It seemed like hours before I reached the corner, and then I fled down the hall, stumbling up the steps and through the room filled with statues, racing through the passageway and into the room that held the African collection. I leaned against one of the chests, panting, trying to catch my breath. Thunder rumbled and rain pounded, but there were no sounds of pursuit. I stared back the way I had come. The passageway was empty, the statues still standing stiffly in the room beyond, casting long shadows on the floor. There was another shadow, moving slowly, ever so slowly, and I caught a quick glimpse of something dark before I dashed out of the room, fleeing down yet another hall that twisted and turned, leading me through a series of dark, cluttered rooms.

I stumbled against a wall and stood there panting. It was almost totally dark here, everything solid black, a faint gray light barely penetrating the gloom. Somewhere behind me a dark form was moving steadily foward, looking for me, and I realized it would be impossible to escape. I couldn't go back the way I had come, and I had no idea where I was now. I was at the mercy of the darkness and the evil that stirred in the air. Tears slid down my cheeks, and the corners of my mouth quivered. I had no hope, no hope whatsoever. For one long terrifying moment I was resigned to whatever might happen, and then I rallied.

I don't know where the calm came from, but it was suddenly there, coming over me with cold deliberation and driving away the panic. Behind me, in one of those rooms I had stumbled through in haste, someone was moving. The sound of the rain was muted, a monotorous drumming, but the sound of footsteps moving stealthily was loud, boards creaking. Whoever it was was in no hurry, confident in the knowledge that I couldn't possibly escape. I leaned against the wall, my breathing even now, that icy calm gripping me like a live thing, forcing me to think.

I was trapped in the attics, surrounded by darkness and dust and cobwebs, unfamiliar with the rooms and passages, and I hadn't a prayer of retracing my steps and slipping past my pursuer and getting back downstairs. But I could hide. I realized that that was my only chance. I could hide in the darkness and be very still and quiet and hope for the best. I inched my way along the wall, sliding my back against the wood, and finally I came to a corner and turned and sped silently down the hall.

I found a tiny room no larger than eight feet square, one small window set high up making a wet gray square on the outside wall. There was a door opening onto the hall, but I didn't dare pull it shut behind me, afraid the noise would give me away. The room was a nest of dark-

ness, and I crept into a corner and leaned against a pile
of boxes and waited, peering into the hall.

Long minutes passed. The rain stopped pounding.
There was a dripping sound now as wet rivulets slid off
the eaves of various levels and splashed on other levels of
rooftop. Inside there was only the souṅd of my breathing.
I strained to listen, but there was no sound in the hall
outside the room where I stood huddled. Not at first.
Then I heard the slow, careful shuffle of stealthy footsteps echoing softly. It was distant and subdued at first,
growing louder, drawing nearer. I clasped my hands together and bit my lower lip, every nerve tensed.

The footsteps were only a few feet away from the
open doorway now, and then they stopped. A floorboard
creaked as weight was shifted. Someone was standing just
outside, listening. I was screaming inside, and had the
sound been audible it would have split the silence with
shattering impact. I had to gnaw my lower lip to keep
the scream from escaping. Someone hovered out there,
and I could hear heavy breathing, and then a noise that
sounded like a giggle. It was the most horrifying sound
I had ever heard. It rose up and then stopped abruptly
and there was a loud creaking and a bang and I realized
that the door had been slammed shut, closing me up in
the room. There was a loud click as a heavy bolt was
jammed into place, then only the sound of my own panic.

I flew to the door. I pulled the knob. I tried to turn
it. I pounded on the heavy oak with my fists and screamed
and pleaded and knocked and cried and finally fell back,
realizing that it was futile. This was far more terrifying
than anything else could have been. I had a horror of
tight closed places, and now I was locked in and the walls
would crush me and I felt sheer animal panic. There was
no way out. The door was solid oak, three inches thick,
and the bolt was iron and I could throw my whole weight
against the door and it wouldn't budge even the tiniest
fraction of an inch.

The terror I had felt in the maze yesterday was as
nothing compared to what I felt now. It swept over me
like a gale, blotting out all reason, all sanity. I trembled
violently, and my knees were weak, unable to support
me. Sitting down on one of the boxes, I let the panic

sweep over me until it reached a crescendo and crashed and left me weak and empty of everything but the knowledge that I was going to die. I could scream until my lungs burst and no one downstairs could possibly hear me. If I didn't suffocate I would die of thirst and starvation. Whoever had locked me in here had no intention of letting me out. The others wouldn't miss me until morning and then they would assume I had gone exploring and wouldn't grow alarmed until late afternoon and they would start a search but they might not come up to the attics and . . . I closed my eyes and leaned against the wall, smelling the sour smell of dust and mildew and listening to rainwater splashing off eaves.

This would have every appearance of being an accident, too, just as Charlie's death had. They would assume I had stepped into the room and the door had swung to behind me and the bolt accidentally clicked into place. It wouldn't look like murder, but . . . Peter would guess. He would remember my call and he would guess what had happened. That was very little comfort to me at the moment.

Perhaps an hour passed. Perhaps it was only a few minutes. I stared about me, my eyes accustomed to the darkness now. There were boxes and an old broken chair and a coil of rope and a huge old discarded mirror here in the room. The mirror was tilted against the opposite wall, and I could see a dim reflection of myself huddled on the box, my arms wrapped around me, my face a pale oval. Through the tiny square of window I could see a bleak gray sky. The air was fetid, and it was growing more and more difficult to breathe. I had to break the window if I didn't want to suffocate within a few hours. The window was so small, perhaps a foot and a half square, surely no more than that. . . . I stood up and stared at that tiny opening.

I pushed two heavy boxes over beneath the window and then climbed up on them, the window level with my shoulders. I could climb through it. It would be a tight squeeze, but I could wriggle through. Pulling off one of my shoes, I smashed the glass. There was a shattering explosion of sound, and pieces of glass clattered to the floor and onto the roof outside. Cold air blew in through the opening, caressing my cheeks as I carefully removed the jagged pieces still stuck in the window frame. I peered out. The roof sloped down steeply, the eaves overhanging another larger expanse of rooftop gleaming with wetness. I might slip and go crashing to the ground three stories below, but anything would be preferable to staying closed up inside this prison.

The sky was wet and gray, and somewhere behind that gloom the moon had just come out, its weak silvery light seeping through and gilding the dark wet rooftops directly beneath the window. As I leaned forward to look out, the boxes I was standing on tilted back and shifted beneath me, and I fell tumbling to the floor, the boxes dumping down beside me. I was stunned by the impact of the fall, and I blinked, shaking my head to clear it. In the thin rays of moonlight now streaming through the window I saw something flat and dark on the floor beside me. It was the same shape and size as an envelope and seemed to be made of some kind of thin leather. It must have fallen out of one of the boxes, I thought, picking it up.

I opened the flap and pulled out a piece of stiff paper with some sort of geometrical design in violet ink. There was not enough light to really examine it properly, and I wondered what it could possibly be. I folded the paper back up and put it into the pouch again and slipped the pouch into my hip pocket, promptly forgetting it in my eagerness to get out of the room. Climbing to my feet, I stared at the window, a little dizzy from my fall. The opening was so small, so very small.

I was still wearing only one shoe, and I took it off, standing in my bare feet. The roofs would be treacherously slippery, and I would have a much better footing with my bare feet than with the leather-soled shoes. I shoved the boxes back into place under the window, lifting one on top of the other, and then I remembered the coil of rope and picked it up, tossing it out the opening. It might come in very handy a little later on, and I fully realized how fortunate I was to have had it in the room.

Climbing back up on the boxes, I gripped the windowsill and tried to pull myself up. It wasn't easy. Sitting in front of a typewriter for hours on end isn't the best kind of physical exercise, and I was in sad shape. I strained and heaved, finally managing to get my head and arms out the window. The cold breeze stung my cheeks, and drops of rainwater dripped down on my upturned face.

I was stuck. I twisted and turned, finally wedging my shoulders out, my waist resting on the windowsill, hips and legs dangling in the room behind me. I was utterly calm now, concentrating on the job at hand, all traces of panic gone. The fresh air revived me, and freedom was at hand. Twisting around until I was facing the sky, I stretched my arms out, placing my palms flat on the wall on either side of the window and shoving. I had been able to stretch and contort and get my shoulders through, but hips were another matter all together. I tugged and pushed and pulled, wincing with pain as the wooden window frame scraped against flesh.

Squeezing my hips tightly together, I gave a mighty shove against the wall with my hands, pulling my body at the same time. Flesh scraped wood, straining, sticking, but I managed to pull my hips free, falling back on the sharply sloping roof, completely free now. I lay there for a moment, my cheek against the wet slate, breathing in great gulps of fresh air and savoring the wide open spaces around me. I finally sat up and peered down at the slope. I didn't dare stand. I had a phobia about closed, confined places, true, but great heights weren't among my favorite things. I admired Sir Edmund Hillary but thought he was slightly insane to go clambering over those mountain peaks. The rooftops of Gordonwood were not as high as Mount Everest, needless to say, but they might as well have been, judging from my state of nerves.

I had no earthly idea how I was going to get down. There were thick strands of ivy growing along one side of the house, but I wasn't about to try climbing down them. I had the rope, but I didn't know what to do with it. I peered at the multiple levels of rooftops, dark and gleaming in the night, gilded with silver and spread with shadows from the many chimneys and stout black smokestacks. The level I was sitting on was the highest point, sloping at a much steeper angle than any of the others.

I took a deep breath and said a silent prayer, thankful to be out of the attic room but realizing my peril was, if anything, greater than ever. The wind whistled and soared, blowing locks of hair across my face, and I felt sure it would sweep me off the roof and out into space at any moment. From this vantage point I could see the lake, a huge expanse of inky black water, bordered by trees, the mists just beginning to form.

I couldn't sit here all night.

Reaching for the coil of rope and holding it securely, I began to move down the slope in a sitting position, scooting hands and hips over the wet slates in an undignified but highly successful manner. The drop from eaves to the next level was little more than five feet, and I managed to get down by twisting around and sliding my body over feet first, holding on to the rim of wood to keep from falling, rope looped over my shoulder. This level wasn't nearly so steep. I was able to walk easily enough, although my knees shook and I didn't dare look out toward the edge.

I reached a tall orange brick chimney and leaned against it, catching my breath. I stared at the slanting, sloping, sprawling roofs and remembered those movies I had seen as a child in which Douglas Fairbanks, Jr., and Errol Flynn had gone dashing and leaping from rooftop to rooftop with great aplomb and remarkable agility. Frauds, both of them. I stood trembling, my back against the bricks, the wind tearing about and blowing up gusts of water. I finally had enough nerve to study the terrain and try and orient myself in respect to the rooms below.

The chimney I was leaning against would service the fireplace in the library, I decided, and the main staircase would be approximately twenty yards to the right of it, while my bedroom would be a hundred yards or so to the left. For a while this information did me no good whatsoever. Then I remembered the balcony outside my bedroom windows. It would be less than a fifteen-foot drop from the outside edge of the roof to the floor of the balcony. If I could fasten the rope around a smokestack and drop over the edge. . . . I shuddered at the thought, but I realized it was the most logical plan. There would be great risk involved, naturally, and I wasn't made of the same stuff as those movie heroes, but I could do it.

I had to do it.

Leaving the chimney behind, I moved slowly toward the left, hunching down, my bare feet slipping on the wet slate. I leaped down from one level to the next, although the drop was only three feet or so, and finally arrived at a point that must be somewhere near the vicinity of my bedroom. I was twenty feet from the outside edge of the roof, and I had to make sure where I was before I could do anything further. I edged slowly towards the drop, knees shaking, body trembling, finally getting down on my hands and knees and crawling to the edge.

I gripped the wood and slid my head over, lying flat on the slates. I peered down, and down, and down. The balcony was nowhere in sight, but I could see the ground below, a pool of light coming from one of the windows and making a yellow glow on that distant drop. I had miscalculated. Turning my head slightly to the left, I saw nothing but dark wall, but when I looked to the right I could see the railing of the balcony gilded with silver moonlight. It was approximately five yards to the right of where I was stretched out. I backed away from the edge, turning around and crawling on up to where I had left the rope.

I would like to have been brave and dauntless, ready to attempt the feat with unshakable courage, but in truth I was absolutely terrified. I looped the rope around a smokestack, securing the knot and tugging to make sure it was sturdily tied, and all the while my hands were trembling and I was trying not to think of what I was about to do. The rope was old. It had probably been in the attic room for years. What if it broke? I examined it carefully. It looked sound enough, but I stood up and pulled with all my might to see if it was going to hold. It did. The smokestack creaked loudly from the strain. That was hardly reassuring.

Holding onto the rope, I walked back to the edge of the roof and stood peering down. The balcony was directly beneath me, not more than fifteen feet down, but it looked frightfully far from this angle. I sat down and dangled my legs over the edge of the roof and knew that I couldn't possibly do it. Not this girl. Not tonight. I called myself every kind of coward, but this self-admonishment only increased my resolve. The heartiest marine would think twice before taking such a risk, and I was a mere girl. . . . There was a crash of thunder. Lightning streaked like jagged white fingers tearing at the sky. The rain began to pour again.

It was just too much. I gripped the rope tightly and slid off the edge of the roof and dangled in space, hanging there over the balcony and swaying to and fro. I folded my knees around the rope just like they did in the movies and let myself slide down. It was surprisingly easy. I dropped onto the floor of the balcony and let go of the rope and struggled to my feet as the rain splashed and spewed. I could hardly believe I had actually done it. I could hardly believe the nightmare was over. I pushed open the French windows and stepped into my bedroom, feeling that I deserved a medal for my valor but willing to settle for a good, strong, very stiff drink.

I bathed and brushed my hair and changed into fresh clothes, and I was surprised to see that it was just after eight o'clock. I felt remarkably fit, strangely stimulated by my adventure. I had no way of knowing for sure who had locked me in the room, but I knew I must go about my business as though nothing had happened, closely watching for any reactions that my appearance might cause. Standing before the mirror, three oil lamps burning brightly in the room, I examined myself. My experiences in the attics and on the rooftops had left no marks whatsoever. I looked alarmingly healthy. If anything, my color was a bit more vivid, cheeks pinker, eyes brighter, and my hair gleamed with rich chestnut highlights after the brisk brushing.

I went downstairs and stepped into the library. Mildred was sitting with a book in her hand. Craig was behind his desk, scribbling away. They both looked up as I came in. Mildred seemed very nervous and Craig seemed mildly surprised, one eyebrow slightly higher than the other. The elements raged outside, rain lashing against the windows, thunder rumbling fiercely. The candles flickered, throwing golden-yellow light over the room.

"Long time no see," Craig said glibly. "What have you been doing with yourself?"

"You'd be surprised," I replied.

"I came up to your room," Mildred said breathlessly. "I wanted to tell you Cook left sandwiches for us. You weren't there—I couldn't find you. Mr. Craig said not to worry——"

"Have there been any calls for me?" I asked.

"I don't think so," Mildred whined. "Mary would have told me."

"Where were you?" Craig inquired.

"Around," I said.

"Cryptic, aren't we?"

"Did you take a tray up to my aunt, Mildred?"

She nodded, huddling in the big chair. "I gave her her pill, and she took it without any argument. I—I was frightened of the thunder and worried about you and—and came down here where Mr. Craig was."

"Charming company," Craig muttered.

"Did you finish revising your chapter?" I asked him.

"Not quite. I've been working for hours. Why don't you be a sport and tell us where you were? Mildred was quite worried, and if you hadn't shown up when you did——"

"You would have come dashing to the rescue," I said.

"*After* I finished the chapter," he replied. "Where were you?"

I left the room without answering. Prince and Earl were in the main hall, agitated by the storm outside. Prince cowered under a table, growling. Earl dashed around in circles, giving leaps of joy when he saw me. I let him kiss my cheek all he wanted.

"You don't know what glue is, sweetie," I said, "but that's what you and I are going to be like. We're going to stick together from now on. Come along, let's go see Aunt Agatha."

He followed me up the stairs, elated. I knocked on Aunt Agatha's door and tried the doorknob. It was locked. That, at least, was reassuring. I heard her shuffling around inside, and in a moment she threw open the door, muttering angrily. Earl pounced up and slurped his tongue across her cheek, and Aunt Agatha screamed at him with such scathing fury that he ran across the room and scurried under the bed, whining.

"You look like you just stepped out of a bandbox,"

she said grumpily. "That yellow dress is quite becoming, and your hair——"

"I just bathed and changed," I replied. "I've been up in the attics, looking for the manuscripts."

"Good show! I knew you'd come 'round. Well, come on *in*, Susan! Don't just stand there in the doorway! I was beginning to worry. You promised to pay me another visit, and when Mildred came in she was sniffling something about your not being in your room. She'd gone up to tell you Cook left some sandwiches, and—oh well, have you eaten anything, dear?"

I shook my head. "I'm not hungry, but I could use a drink. Surely you keep a bottle."

"Althea is the one who *drinks*, pet. Why should I have a bottle under my pillow?"

"Is it under your pillow?"

She nodded, smiling coyly. "For *medicinal* purposes only. Sometimes I wake up in the middle of the night, and a slug or two puts me right back to sleep. I have to *hide* it or Mildred would snitch and Paul would be livid. Come on, I'll pour you a snort."

"A strong snort," I said.

"I must say, Susan, you're *full* of surprises."

Aunt Agatha handed me the drink and climbed back in bed. She was looking better than she had earlier, although there were still signs of fatigue around the eyes. I drank the whisky and told her about finding Arabella's letters, making no mention of anything else that had happened. She was very excited about the discovery. They would be marvelous for Craig's book, and what a stroke of luck it had been, she claimed, plying me with questions. I finished the whisky and listened to her chatter. I felt much better now. I could hardly believe that only a short while ago I had been in grave danger. No doubt I would have a delayed reaction and be paralyzed with shock, but at the moment I felt perfectly normal, as though it had all happened to someone else.

"——we'll have to *organize*," Aunt Agatha was saying. "Now that you're eager to help us I'm sure we'll find them soon. After all, you found those letters, just by accident. We'll probably stumble upon the manuscripts in similar fashion."

Earl peeked out from under the bed. I snapped my fingers and told him to come on out and told Aunt Agatha that she needed to sleep. She grumbled a bit but finally admitted that she was weary. I walked to the door, Earl at my heels.

"Tell me, dear," Aunt Agatha said wryly, "have you been thinking any more about Craig?"

"I've been thinking about him all day," I replied.

"Super! Isn't it *exciting*, Susan?"

"I suppose you could say that," I said dryly. "Be sure you lock your door behind me. Good night, Aunt Agatha."

I was glad to have Earl's company on the long walk back to my bedroom. I hadn't brought a lamp with me, but Mildred had left lamps burning at various intervals along the dark hallways. Earl scampered on ahead, his paws making loud thumps on the carpets. He paused at the east wing, disturbed by the cold, clammy air. Once inside my bedroom, I locked the door securely and told Earl to behave. He was sniffing the peacock feathers in the green, black, and gold Chinese vase in the corner.

I knew I couldn't sleep, yet I didn't intend to brood about what had happened. I could do nothing till morning. I would call Peter immediately. Surely after he learned that someone had tried to kill me he would take me more seriously. For the moment, I was quite safe with Earl locked in the room with me.

The lamps burned brightly, shedding tremulous golden light over the faded Chinese silk wallpaper. I piled the pillows up against the headboard and sat down on top of the covers, still wearing my yellow dress. Picking up the historical novel, I tried to read. It was difficult to concentrate, but I was finally caught up in the flamboyant melodrama. Earl leaped up on the bed, snuggling his great silver body over my feet and looking deplorably contented.

I finished the book and set it aside, drowsy now, too tired to change into my pajamas. I dropped off to sleep, still on top of the covers, lamps still flickering, and it was three in the morning before I woke up with a start. Earl had leaped off the bed, his sudden movement jerking me out of my sleep with rude abruptness. He was standing at the door, hair bristling, emitting a long, low growl that caused my flesh to creep.

"Earl," I whispered.

He gave one furious, ear-splitting bark and then leaped back up on the bed, licking my face with abandon. I pushed him aside and got up, moving over to the door. It was several seconds before I had the nerve to open it. There was no one there. The hallway was empty. Earl must have been having a nightmare, I decided, relieved.

I was closing the door when I saw the shoes I had left up in the attic room. I gasped, my whole body going limp. The shoes were sitting primly side by side right in front of the doorway. The shrunken head I had hurled away from me was resting grotesquely in one of the insteps.

CHAPTER TEN

It was macabre, a master touch deliberately planned to reduce me to a mass of quivering terror. It had the exact opposite effect. After the first shock subsided I felt only calm, icy anger. After all I'd been through, a prank like this wasn't going to defeat me. It only strengthened my resolution to get to the bottom of things as soon as possible. Wrapping the shoes and the grisly shrunken head up in newspaper, I dumped them into the wastebasket. I would certainly never be able to wear the shoes again, not after this.

Making sure the door was locked, I changed into my pajamas and blew out the lamps and climbed into bed, Earl draped over my feet, and the next thing I knew it was after ten and sunshine shimmered into the room and Earl was whining to be let out. I opened the door for him, yawning, amazed at my own commendable calm. Someone expected me to be pale and terrified, but I was filled with energy. In the mirror, my cheeks were quite pink, my violet-blue eyes bright and shining.

It was a lovely morning, the sky like wet blue-gray silk, the sunlight thin and silvery. The dark green shrubs in back dripped with moisture, and there was a very fine drizzle in the air. I changed into a pair of black and white checked slacks and a navy blue sweater, sitting down at the mirror to brush my hair, sadly tangled during the night. It finally gleamed darkly, framing my face with soft waves.

Mary knocked on the door with distressing loudness, but I was ready for her this morning. I opened the door for her, disappointed that she had no tray. She tossed her short blonde curls and started chattering about the accident at the inn which she had heard about in town last night. Yesterday afternoon seemed a long time ago to me.

"Poor Charlie," Mary babbled. "Always so peculiar. Just like him to have such a wretched accident—I'm ever so sad, actually. He was sweet, a real sweet chap. Charlie may have been a bit dense at times, reckon he *was* rather tetched, but he knew how to make a girl feel all shivery inside, all warm and nice all over——"

"You knew Charlie well?" I inquired.

"I went with him, ma'am. I'll tell you this—he knew how to kiss a girl so she stayed kissed. Charlie wasn't at *all* slow in that department. I know for a fact. Lots of people wondered why that actress woman would take up with him—her bein' so sophisticated, him bein' such a hick. I know the answer to that one. He was terrific in the——" She caught herself just in time, a vivid pink blush coloring her round cheeks.

"When did you go with Charlie?"

"It was over a year ago. Went with 'im for over a month. I've got a new fellow now, Bertie Clemmons. He's dumb, too, drives a lorry, but he has these gorgeous muscles——"

"I suppose people in town are distressed over Charlie," I said, cutting short her paean on Bertie's attractions.

"Everyone's distressed," she retorted. "Charlie was a character and some poked fun at him, but we'll all miss him. These things happen."

She shook her head, looking quite philosophical as she smoothed down her frilly white apron over the tight black dress.

"No breakfast tray this morning, Mary?" I asked.

"The old la— Lady Agatha, I mean, she wants you should have breakfast with her in her room. Cook's sending up a tremendous tray——"

"Aunt Agatha isn't up yet?"

Mary shook her head. "Shockin', isn't it? She's usually up and tearin' things apart by six, at least. The creepy one—Mildred, I mean—she said Lady Agatha should stay in bed today, and the old lady is throwin' all kinds of fits——"

"Thank you, Mary," I said. "I'll go to her room at once. Oh, by the way, has there been a call for me?"

"No, ma'am."

"I'm expecting one. It's very important. If I'm not downstairs when it comes, be sure to send for me."

"Certainly," Mary replied saucily.

I met Mildred on my way to Aunt Agatha's room. The nurse looked properly cowed after the reign of terror my aunt had no doubt instigated on her behalf. Sniffling and shuffling at a dreary pace, Mildred seemed to be on the verge of tears, her dark brown eyes glistening damply.

"I can't take much more of it," she whined. "I just try to do my job, and she treats me like—like I'm some kind of insect. I'll quit. That's what I'll do. Dr. Matthews was so kind, getting me this position. I hate to disappoint such a fine man, but——"

"Please, Mildred," I said, impatient with her. "Stop sniveling. My aunt means well—you know that. Is she—is she ill? Mary said that you insisted she stay in bed. Is something——"

"She looks a little pale and drawn. She needs another day of rest, and if she goes galloping about I'm not going to be responsible." She gave me a defiant look. "No one seems to realize I'm a *nurse*. I can't help it if I'm not sparkling and brilliant like everyone else around here."

"Of course not," I said, forcing back a smile.

"I'll quit. Dr. Matthews can find someone else."

Still sniveling, she crept on down the hall. I wouldn't have been at all surprised to see her vanish into the woodwork.

I expected to find Aunt Agatha in a rage, but instead she was sitting up in bed with a pleasant smile on her lips, short sandy hair disheveled. She looked weary, I thought, the plain face sagging, lined with fatigue. Wearing an apricot-colored robe with froths of beige lace, the blue bedcovers pulled up over her legs, she was pouring coffee from a stout silver pot and eyeing the lavish breakfast tray on the bedside table. Newspapers were scattered over the bed, and there was the inevitable pile of old books.

"I've been doing the crossword puzzle," she said gaily. "I need a four-letter word—leader of a religious sect. Priest, parson, rabbi—none of them fit."

"Guru?" I suggested.

"Marvelous! That's it. Why didn't I think of it? Come sit, Susan. Let me pour you some coffee. Cook's baked some heavenly sweet rolls—my favorite kind. My, you're looking chipper this morning."

"You're not," I said.

"What an outrageous thing to say!"

"I met Mildred in the hall, and——"

"Horrid creature! I took her pill, but that didn't satisfy her. She had to keep hovering! I wasn't very *nice* to her, I'll readily admit, but she's so dreary!"

"She said you need to stay in bed for another day."

"I fully intend to," she replied, surprisingly agreeable, "but not because *she* said so. I feel rather—lazy today. I've decided to stay in bed and read. I have these old Dorothy Sayers novels—I adore Lord Peter Wimsey, don't you?—and besides, dear, I should think it would be more fun for you and Craig to be alone. That's really why I'm staying in bed. I'm playing matchmaker in my own sly way."

"I think we should phone Paul," I said firmly.

"Nonsense! Let an old lady indulge herself. Gracious, Susan, if I'd known you were going to carry on this way I'd have popped out of bed at the crack of dawn and joined you for a game of tennis! I plan to reread *Gaudy Night* and *The Nine Tailors*."

"You're certain you're feeling all right?"

"Darling, I feel glorious. What do I have to do to *convince* you, jump up and do the Charleston? I just feel like being lazy today, and it's been so long since I've read any Sayers. I can't think of a more delicious way to spend the day."

She looked up at me with twinkling blue eyes. She had too much vitality to be really ill, I thought, deciding not to worry about it just yet. I would certainly phone Paul if she wasn't her old self tomorrow, but perhaps she really was merely tired from all the recent excitement. At least she was taking her pills, and that in itself was reassuring. She poured a cup of coffee for me and passed the tray of flaky, warm cinnamon rolls.

Aunt Agatha talked merrily as we had breakfast. I was preoccupied and paid little attention to her chatter.

Half an hour later I left her snuggled up with her copy of *Gaudy Night* and started downstairs. Mary met me at the corner of the upstairs hall.

"There you are," she sighed. "I was just on my way to get you."

"Has my call come?" I asked eagerly.

"No, it's the old woman—the one who tipples! She came bursting into the kitchen and said for me to come get you. Everyone giving orders, as though I had two pair of legs! She said for you to come over to Dower House as soon as you could."

Wondering what Althea wanted, I walked on down the hall. Rays of sunlight gilded the dark wainscoting, burnishing it a soft silver, and the garnet carpets looked rich in this light. Had Althea seen something else? I wondered. It must be something important, or she wouldn't have unlocked her door and come over to Gordonwood.

Craig Stanton was talking on the telephone in the main hall as I came downstairs. I paused at the foot of the stairs, my hand resting on the bannister. He was wearing jeans and the bulky white sweater he had worn day before yesterday when he had let me into the house. Gripping the instrument angrily, he scowled, eyebrows lowered. He was immersed in the conversation and unaware of my presence.

"You learned what? Yes, yes, I see."

He stood listening, his shoulders hunched forward, locks of rich brown hair spilling over his forehead. His large hand gripped the telephone with such fierceness that I felt sure it would snap.

"What? When?" he barked. "But, damnit, this is—I know, I know. I understand, but——" He frowned, glaring at the wall. "You can't get here any sooner? We have to 'act *now*, while—sure, I can handle things, but the girl——"

He looked up and saw me standing at the foot of the stairs and hung up the phone abruptly without even finishing his sentence. I tilted my chin at a haughty angle. Craig sauntered over, and when I started to move past him he seized my arm.

"Eavesdropping another of your habits?" he growled.

"As a matter of fact it is," I said airily. "I've over-heard some very interesting things these past few days."

"What do you mean by that? How long were you standing there? How much did you——" His blue eyes were dark with suspicion, his jaw thrust out. His fingers were gripping my arm savagely.

"I didn't overhear anything," I said innocently. "I just this minute came downstairs. Was there something I should have heard?"

"I don't believe you."

"You seem terribly upset, Mr. Stanton. I wonder why."

"You heard nothing?"

"Nothing at all," I retorted lightly, looking at him with a cool and level gaze. He stood directly in front of me, blocking my way. The sleeves of his white sweater were pushed up over his forearms, and the bulky knit clung loosely to his chest.

"You're hurting me," I said.

He released my arm. For a long moment we stood staring at each other, his long body very close. I wore an expression of bland innocence, not at all intimidated by him. Craig finally lifted his shoulders in a shrug and seemed to relax. He stepped back, hooking his thumbs in the corners of his pockets and tilting his head to one side.

"Sorry," he said in a smooth voice. "I didn't mean to be brutal. I'm rather tense. That was—uh—my publisher. He wants to come down and look over the chapters I've done. We had an argument about it. Insistent chap. Told him I'd bring the chapters to London in a few days, but he wouldn't be put off."

He told the lie with great aplomb. He looked very satisfied with himself, convinced I believed him.

"You understand how these things are," he continued. "We authors get riled up easily, particularly when it's something pertaining to our work."

"I understand perfectly," I replied, charming. "Now, if you'll excuse me."

"Where are you going?" There was a slight edge to his voice.

"For a stroll. It's a beautiful day."

"It's drizzling. You might catch cold."

"I'll risk it."

"I thought we might spend the day together," he said pleasantly. "We could look for the manuscripts, perhaps. Your aunt and I intended to start in the attics today. Perhaps you and I could go up together—I'd like you to be with me so I could—uh—keep an eye on you. You disappeared yesterday afternoon. I was worried."

"Were you?"

"You seem prone to—be where you shouldn't be," he said. "First the maze, then down by the lake at midnight. When Mildred said you weren't in your room I imagined all sorts of things. You stick close by me today, and my mind will be at ease. I'll watch after you."

"I don't need anyone to watch after me," I replied.

"Don't you?" he said quietly. He lifted one eyebrow, his blue eyes suddenly hard.

"Of course not," I said.

"I think you may," Craig told me. His voice was no longer pleasant. "You're entirely too inquisitive."

I moved past him toward the door without replying, and Craig made no attempt to stop me. Once outside, I breathed a sigh of relief. The encounter had upset me far more than I cared to admit. His words had contained a subtle, veiled threat, and I knew I couldn't carry on alone. Not anymore. It had been foolhardy of me to think I could play girl detective. I had to do something, find help. Peter hadn't called, and, besides, he was far away in London. I stood in the gardens for a moment, the fine, silvery drizzle stinging my cheeks. I was afraid.

Althea unlocked the door for me. She was wearing a loose purple robe, and her blazing red curls were wrapped around large tin curlers, giving her a crazily comic appearance. Her face was very grave, and for once there was no odor of gin. She was completely sober, though highly agitated, fluttering about like a plump, nervous bird. Seizing my hand, she led me into the littered room. Her gray-green eyes were full of apprehension.

"I saw them again last night," she began abruptly.

"He was wearing the raincoat, walking towards the house from the lake. She stepped out of the shadows to meet him. They went into the house together."

"What time was this?"

"Around six thirty," she said breathlessly. "If it hadn't been pouring down rain I could have gotten a good look at 'em. Everything was blurry and gray. They went into the house through the back door, and I didn't see 'em again for ever so long—until——"

She paused dramatically and stood looking at me with her hands on her hips. "You're not going to believe this," she said, "but there was someone on the *roof*tops! I couldn't tell if it was him or her or whoever, but I saw someone moving around up there."

"I believe you," I said in a flat voice.

"What are we going to do?" she asked. "This has gone too far. Something terrible is going on."

"You're right, Althea. I—do you have a telephone?"

"Over there on the desk, behind those papers. Who are you going to call? The police? Aggie will have six fits, but—yes, you've got to. I should have called them myself a long time ago——"

I placed a long distance call to London. Althea hovered about nervously as I waited for Scotland Yard to answer. I intended to tell Peter everything and insist that he come down immediately. He would know what to do. He wouldn't be quite so cavalier about my suspicions when he found out what was going on. It seemed an eternity before I finally got his secretary on the line. She calmly informed me that he was out of the office and wouldn't be back in today. I hung up, bitterly disappointed.

"That was Scotland Yard," Althea whispered, her eyes wide.

I nodded. Peter had failed me. He had probably forgotten all about my call. Althea looked incredulous, and I found it highly ironic that my one ally should be this ludicrous old woman in purple robe and hair curlers.

"Scotland Yard," she said. "I never dreamed—do you think it's *that* serious, Susan? I suppose so. I suppose—yes, of course. If Aggie had only listened to me——"

I stood looking out the window, oblivious to Althea's

clucking. There was no one I could turn to, and I knew I couldn't face Craig Stanton again without giving myself away. Someone had tried to kill me. Someone had left a grotesque warning at the door of my bedroom. I couldn't be calm and casual. The full realization of all that had happened struck me, perhaps for the first time. The delayed reaction I had been expecting hit me with full force, leaving me weak. This was real. A murder had been committed. Another had been attempted. I had been so blithe, so foolish. I couldn't keep this to myself any longer. But there was no one to turn to. . . .

"What are we going to do?" Althea asked shakily.

"I don't know———" I began, and then I suddenly realized that there was someone I could turn to after all. I wondered why I hadn't thought of him from the very first.

"I'm going to see Dr. Matthews," I said. "He'll help us."

"Oh, dear—I don't know. He wouldn't believe what *I* said."

"He'll believe me."

"Do you think it's wise? I mean, maybe we're jumping to conclusions. Perhaps we should just wait and see."

"Althea, someone tried to kill me yesterday."

"What!"

"Someone locked me up in the attic, in a tiny room, leaving me to die. If I hadn't broken a window and climbed out———"

"It was *you* on the roofs," she said, her face pasty white.

"It was," I replied. "You see now why I have to tell someone else."

Althea didn't bother to answer. She dashed over to the table, grabbed a bottle of gin, and poured a drink with trembling hands. She gulped it down in one mighty swallow and busily poured another. "To think I was plannin' to stay sober," she muttered, plump cheeks beginning to flush. "Not now I'm not!" She was tossing down the second drink as I left her.

It started to rain as I drove into Gordonville. I had to pull over to the side of the road and put the top up on the

Bentley. Fortunately, I had left the keys in it yesterday and hadn't had to return to Gordonwood after leaving Althea. The rain came down in torrents as I drove down one of the side streets. Paul's office was located in a small pink brick building shaded by an immense oak. I parked the car in front and dashed inside, slamming the door and startling the lanky receptionist who sat behind a small gray desk. She asked if I had an appointment while I rubbed water off my hair. When I said no she looked highly disapproving and told me to sit down.

I had to wait quite a while. There were two brown leather sofas and a coffee table littered with back issues of *Punch* and medical magazines, all of them battered. A plump, worried-looking woman in a printed crepe dress sat across from me, limp strands of auburn hair slipping over her temples. A very fat little boy sat beside her, licking a lollipop and casting nasty looks at me.

A buzzer sounded on the receptionist's desk and she told the boy to go on in. He clutched his lollipop and waddled to the door of the inner office and opened it, turning to give me a final sneer. The woman in crepe wrung her hands for the next twenty minutes while I listened to the rain pounding on the roof and tried to contain my impatience. The door of the inner office finally opened and Paul came out, one large hand grasping the boy by the scruff of his neck, the other holding a solemn-looking paper. The woman in crepe jumped up, expecting the worst.

"Johnny!" she exclaimed fervently.

"He took my lollipop away from me!" Johnny cried. "He said I was too *fat!*"

"Much too fat," Paul said jovially. "He's perfectly all right, Bessie. Nothing wrong with him a strict diet won't cure. I have one here. I want you to put him on it immediately."

He handed her the paper and turned to speak to the receptionist. Johnny and his mother left, and I stood up. The receptionist said something to Paul and he turned around, seeing me for the first time.

"Susan," he said, his handsome, craggy face registering surprise. "What brings you here in this weather?"

"I need to talk to you," I said. "It—it's rather important. Can you spare the time?"

"Surely," he replied. "Johnny was my last patient for the day. Come on in."

He led me down a hall and into a small sitting room in back, offering me a chair. I shook my head, nervous now, wondering how I was going to begin. Paul looked solid and impressive in his crisp white smock, a stethoscope hanging around his neck. His golden-bronze hair was thick and untidy, his dark brown eyes full of concern. He sensed my uneasiness and gave me a reassuring smile, the wide, sensual mouth turning up at the corners. I felt safe with him, secure, and just looking into those solemn eyes made me feel much better.

"Now what's this all about?" he inquired, his voice friendly but firm. "You look like you're about to fly apart. What's bothering you?"

"You—you're going to find this hard to believe," I said.

"Suppose you let me be the judge of that."

"I hardly know where to begin."

Paul folded his arms across his chest and leaned against the wall, his face stern and professional-looking. I fumbled around for words and finally started talking. I told him everything that had happened, beginning at the beginning, ending with the episode at Dower House not more than an hour ago. Paul nodded once or twice, looking very grave, but he didn't interrupt me. When I finished he shook his head slowly from side to side, heaving his chest.

"Who else have you told this to?" he asked.

"No one. I didn't give Peter any details—he would have laughed. He doesn't take me seriously."

"It's hard to take this seriously," Paul said solemnly. "It's a pretty fantastic story. You'll have to admit that."

"I know it is," I said calmly.

"Still——" He frowned, furrowing his brow. "I examined Charlie myself. It had every appearance of being an accidental death. There was no argument as far as Constable Clark was concerned. Just the same, something bothered me. I didn't pay too much attention to it at the time, but—there were no lights burning upstairs. I wondered why Charlie would have started downstairs in the dark. It seemed logical that he would have turned on the hall lights when he left his room. That's an irrelevant point, of course, but someone *could* have broken his neck and tossed him downstairs, putting the slipper on the stair——"

"I'm sure that's what happened. I *know* it is."

Paul reached up to brush a golden-bronze lock from his forehead. His crisp white smock rustled. He toyed with the stethoscope, looking strong and solid, inspiring confidence. I felt much better after talking to Paul, as though a great burden had been lifted from my shoulders. He would help, and I felt sure he was quite capable of dealing with matters. He looked at me, one corner of his mouth turned down.

"Let's not be too hasty about things, Susan. We have to consider this from every angle."

"Even if Charlie's death was an accident, there was nothing accidental about what happened to me in the attics."

"The door could have slammed shut, the bolt could have accidentally fallen into place. You say you heard someone, but it was pouring down rain. You say you saw someone, but it was dark, and the attics must have been a nest of shadows. You could have imagined it."

"Paul, someone was there. I didn't imagine any of it. If I hadn't climbed out that window——" I paused, staring at him. "And what about the shrunken head? I didn't imagine *that.*"

Paul shook his head again, his brow still furrowed. He was finding it hard to accept my story. I could see that. His craggy face wore an expression of deep concentration, the brown eyes dark. He seemed to be pondering everything I had told him, examining every detail in his mind with a cold, unemotional analysis. Several minutes passed, and he finally straightened up and looked at me, his mouth a severe line.

"All right," he said. "I'll buy it. It's improbable. I've never put much stock in those damned manuscripts, but if they exist, and if someone thought——" His face grew angry. "I've never liked that Stanton fellow. He took advantage of Agatha from the start, sucking up to her, using her. I distrusted him from the first."

"What are we going to do, Paul?"

"I don't know," he said. "The first thing I've got to do is go have a long talk with Constable Clark. I should think he'll find all this highly interesting. I don't know what kind of action he'll take, but—we'll do something, Susan. Don't worry. We'll get to the bottom of this."

"You don't know how relieved I am."

Paul patted my shoulder and looked down into my eyes. He was so big, so sturdy. I could sense the strength in him, and those deep brown eyes were warm, full of understanding. Everything would be all right now. Paul would see to it.

"I suppose I'd better be getting back to Gordonwood," I said.

"I hate like hell to see you go back there, but—I suppose it's best. We don't want to arouse any suspicion. I imagine Clark and I will drive out to Gordonwood tonight to pay Mr. Stanton a visit, but if anything at all out of the ordinary happens before we get there, you call me. Call me right away. If I'm not at home, my landlady will know where to reach me."

Paul walked to the front door with me. The receptionist was gone. The office was dim. It had stopped raining, but the sky still hung low, dark gray, filled with threatening clouds. Paul and I stood on the front steps for a moment, water pouring off the eaves with a monotonous patter. Out in front the Bentley glistened, dark and shining.

"You're sure you've told me everything?" he asked.

"I—I don't think I've left anything out," I replied. Something was nagging me, some small, minor detail I seemed to have forgotten. Oh well, I thought, it can't be very important.

"You be careful," he said gravely.

"I will be."

"And—don't mention this visit to anyone, Susan, not even your aunt. I don't want her to be alarmed."

"I won't, Paul. I—I'll see you later on?"

He nodded. "You can count on it."

Paul opened the door of the Bentley for me. I drove away, confident that everything would soon be resolved. The country road was muddy, and the rain had denuded the dogwood trees of their blooms, pink and white blossoms scattered on the wet ground like shreds of silk. It was only after I turned through the graystone portals and onto the crushed-shell drive that I remembered what I had left out in my account to Paul. I hadn't told him about the small leather pouch I had found in the attic room and the curious paper it contained. I had forgotten all about it.

CHAPTER ELEVEN

Cook was leaving a lavish buffet in the dining room, Mary informed me, and everyone could help themselves. Cook was in a bad mood what with preparing all those trays and if a buffet wasn't satisfactory that was tough luck all around, servants were human beings. Pulling on her raincoat and wrapping a bright pink scarf around her hair, Mary said that the old lady was still in the room readin', and Mr. Craig was locked up in the library scribblin' away furiously, and the creep, Mildred, that is, was prowlin' around lookin' pitiful. Mildred would take a tray up to my aunt later on, Mary said, buckling the belt of her sleek black vinyl raincoat.

"And Cook 'n I are leaving now, if it's all the same with you, ma'am. It's been rainin' something awful and we want to get back to town before it starts again."

"I'm sure that will be satisfactory, Mary," I replied.

"Incidentally, them dogs looked pitifully sad out in the rain. I brought 'em in and let 'em stretch out in front of the fire in the kitchen, though Cook like to bust a gut. Fed and brushed 'em myself, though it ain't really my job. They're roamin' around the house somewhere now."

"Fine, Mary."

"Well, ta ta, then. We'll be off."

It was shortly after four when I got back up to my room. Earl was sitting in front of the door, waiting for me. He gave yips of joy when he saw me coming down the hall. Through the French windows I could see the bleak soggy gray sky and the dark green dripping shrubs and, further away, the black trees that seemed to huddle together around the lake. Thunder rumbled in the distance, like drums rolling, and there were occasional flashes of lightning, brief streaks of silver. I closed the windows and drew the draperies shut and lit three oil lamps. The room was soon brilliant with cozy yellow-gold light.

"I wonder why I forgot about the pouch," I said. Earl tilted his head to one side, looking very wise. "I suppose it's understandable. So much happened after I put it in my hip pocket that it just slipped my mind. Oh, stop looking so smart. You can't understand a word I'm saying."

Earl looked offended and crawled under the bed, head and front paws sticking out, eyes alert with interest as I pulled the pouch out of the hip pocket of the slacks I had worn yesterday. Pushing the brushes and bottles to one side, I spread the piece of paper out on the dressing table and sat down to examine it. It seemed to be some kind of intricate geometrical design, with letters dotting it here and there. The paper was old and stiff, and the ink was violet. Arabella Gordon had had a fondness for violet ink, and there was no doubt in my mind that she had drawn this curious pattern. What was it, and why had it been so carefully preserved in its own leather pouch?

At the bottom of the page were nine words: PART OF HIS LIFE, WITH US BOTH IN DEATH. They made no sense whatsoever. I pulled the oil lamp nearer and peered down at the paper, my brow creased in puzzlement. I had a feeling that this was something very important, but its significance eluded me. The Victorians had been very fond of anagrams and word games, but this was neither. Dotting the squares and slanting lines of the pattern were several single letters: E, S, W, A, R, R, X, P, I, N, W, G, G. I made individual words from them: SWING, WING, RING, SWAN, SWEAR, RIP, GRIP, and so on, but that only confused me more. Ignoring the letters, I concentrated on the design itself. There was a central square, smaller oblong squares to the left, the whole crisscrossed with diagonal lines that made inverted v's. I was totally bewildered.

I must have studied the paper for an hour and a half, utterly frustrated. All the while my excitement mounted. This was important. It was a key. If only I could unravel it. . . . At first I had the wild idea that it was a map that would lead me to the Gordon manuscripts, but I

finally had to discard it. This was no map. It was . . . it
was almost like a blueprint, I thought, but if so, what
did those words and letters mean? Thunder rumbled, and
rain dripped from the eaves, plopping on the floor of the
balcony. Earl crawled out from under the bed and rested
his head on my feet, wanting attention. I bent down to
scratch his ears, my mind filled with confusion. I had a
feeling I was overlooking something obvious, something
that should have been perfectly clear the minute I looked
at the paper.

I stared at it again, and suddenly a fog seemed to lift
in my mind. I had been so dense! It *was* perfectly clear.
To the left of the large square were two oblong squares:
A. G. in one of them, R. G. R. I. P. in the other. Arabella
Gordon, Robert Gordon Rest In Peace. S. W., N. W.—
south wall, north wall, E.—entrance. In one corner, an
X. I was staring at a hand-drawn blueprint of the mausoleum. The diagonal lines were meant to indicate the sloping roof of the tent, and the x . . . I was weak with excitement. I had discovered the hiding place of the Gordon manuscripts.

Sir Robert had designed the mausoleum himself. It
had been completed a few months before his death, and
he had rested there alone for twelve years before his wife
joined him. She had burned his papers in a burst of Victorian prudery, but two of the manuscripts had been too
personal, too meaningful, too much a part of the man
who had composed them. PART OF HIS LIFE, she had written at the bottom of the page, WITH US BOTH IN DEATH.

Arabella had destroyed the other papers, yet she
couldn't bring herself to destroy these particular manuscripts. She had realized their value, had realized, too,
that the world wasn't ready for them, not the world of
crinoline petticoats and stuffy parlors and repressed emotions. She had put them in the mausoleum, leaving behind this clue to their whereabouts, perhaps visualizing
some future age in which they would be found and given
the fair evaluation they deserved. She had died with her
secret, and it had taken all this time for that secret to be
discovered.

It was overwhelming. I could hardly contain my excitement. Reason told me to keep calm, be sensible, but I

wasn't in a sensible mood. I knew I should stay in my room and wait for Paul to come with Constable Clark. The secret would keep a while longer. After everything was resolved, I could go down to the mausoleum and fetch the papers, in daylight, in safety. It was the only reasonable thing to do, but I couldn't be reasonable at a time like this, I had to see the papers. I couldn't just sit here and wait, not when I knew the papers were there in the mausoleum, waiting to be found. I would take Earl with me, and I would be very cautious. . . .

Slipping the paper back into the pouch, I slid the pouch in my pocket and told Earl to come along quietly. The manuscripts were probably in a secret cache, bricked-in. I would need tools, I thought, remembering the tool-box I had seen in the garage. It was bound to contain a hammer, and I could use a screwdriver for a chisel. I crept quietly down the hall. Earl sensed my mood, and he crept along beside me, down on his haunches, finding this a jolly good game. I passed the door of Mildred's room. An edge of yellow light shone under the door. She was probably inside, reading or brooding about Aunt Agatha's treatment of her.

Turning the corner, I moved silently down the main upstairs hall. The windows were wet gray squares, dripping with slippery cobwebs of water and admitting little light. It would soon be night, but there had been a flash-light hanging on a peg in the garage, and I could use that. I moved down the staircase, Earl scooting along ahead, turning to give me conspiratorial glances. The library door was closed. I hesitated in front of it, finally stooping down to peek through the keyhole.

Craig Stanton was working at his desk, his face lined with concentration, hair tumbling over his forehead. He looked up, almost as if he could sense me watching. He stared at the door with a vacant look and then gave a heavy sigh, frowned and went back to work, a candelabra spilling wavering yellow light over his broad shoulders. Cautioning Earl to be silent, I went to the front door and opened it, shooing him outside, stepping out myself and pulling the door shut behind me.

Earl barked gleefully and capered around under the portico. I glared at him, and he hastily resumed his stealthy crouching position, deciding the game wasn't over yet. We moved toward the garage. The air was chilly, laced with dampness, and there were puddles of water. Earl paused by one of the shrubs to perform a most undignified function, looking up guiltily as he joined me in front of the garage. I caught hold of the handle, lifting the heavy door. It swung up with a loud, grating noise. Surely no one could have heard, I thought, stepping into the garage.

There was an odor of grease and rust and gasoline, and my shoes clattered on the concrete floor as I stepped between the Bentley and the bright red XKE Jaguar. It was very dark, but I could see the toolbox standing in front of the cars, the flashlight hanging over it. I took the flashlight down and switched it on. The battery was weak, and there was only a thin, feeble ray of yellow light, but it was enough. Taking a hammer and a large screwdriver out of the toolbox, I left the garage, pulling the door down, holding the bottom rim to keep it from squeaking so loudly.

There was no holding Earl back now. He danced and darted about, elated at the freedom to romp and splash in the puddles of water. He dashed on in back of the house, but I moved a bit more cautiously. It wasn't likely that anyone could see me, but if Craig Stanton chanced to get up and stroll to the library windows he would be certain to spot me. I kept close to the side of the house, passing the drawing room windows, hesitating, passing the library windows with one quick glance. Craig was still at his desk, intently working with his shoulders hunched over the papers. I hurried on to the lawns in back, relieved now, no longer worried.

I walked rapidly down the sloping lawns towards the trees. The ground was muddy and my shoes were soon caked with mud. They would be ruined but that was a trivial thing. This whole business had been hell on shoes, I reflected: one pair broken, one pair discarded, this pair turning soggy and limp. Earl scampered around in circles ahead of me, tearing up turfs of wet grass. The sky was so low that it seemed I could reach up and touch it. Thunder made a quiet rumble in the distance, and brief streaks of lightning made occasional silver flashes.

A soft violet haze hung in the air as dusk approached and shadows thickened.

The excitement I had felt earlier hadn't abated one jot. I still felt it surging through me, urging me on. I was actually on my way to find the Gordon manuscripts. In a short while I would hold them in my hands. It was a staggering thought. Walking along the edge of the trees, I hunted for the path leading down to the lake, finally locating it and moving quickly into the densely shadowed woods. Earl scurried about in the bushes nearby, and a bird cried out shrilly. Limbs made a thick canopy over the path, protecting it from rain, and the ground was hard packed, only slightly damp. On either side the trees were tall dark sentinels, gleaming black and wet in the faint light. I could barely see my way, but I didn't want to switch on the flashlight just yet. I would need it inside the mausoleum, and the battery was so weak I feared it might give out.

I could see the lake ahead now. Mists hung low, swirling over the wet black surface of the water, moving like ghosts engaged in a lilting waltz. Water lapped at the shore, wind whistled over the surface, and the sound of whispers filled the air, accompanied by the drip-drip of rain pattering off limbs. I called Earl, but he was nowhere near. I wondered where he had gone. I called again, and there was an answering bark from far away. I heard him crashing through the woods, and suddenly there was silence. He had stopped abruptly. There was one loud bark, then a growl, then silence sharply underlined by the whispers. I heard the growl again, followed by a feeble yip.

I wasn't afraid, only bewildered. Nevertheless, I would have felt much better had Earl been beside me instead of roaming through the woods. He had probably seen a rabbit, I thought. Yes, a rabbit, or perhaps a bird. The bark had not alarmed me, but the growl . . . . I called him a third time, my voice shrill. Night noises rustled in the trees, but there was no sound from the dog. He might have vanished. That curious yip . . . I couldn't let my imagination run away with me. There was a perfectly logical explanation for his conduct, yet I was unnerved.

I peered through the trees. I could see glistening black

trunks and a multitude of limbs, the faintest light penetrating. Far away there was movement, a glimmer, something barely visible. My heart was pounding now. I couldn't prevent it. I squinted, peering through the trees at that movement. It was slick, dark, like . . . like a black raincoat, like a man in a raincoat moving slowly through the woods. I closed my eyes and opened them again. The moving black glimmer was gone, and I realized that it had been a trick of light and shadow, augmented by an overactive imagination. Earl came prancing nonchalantly down the path. I scolded him harshly, telling him in no uncertain terms that he was to stay by my side and ignore all rabbits. He licked my hand, abject.

The brief moment of fear had shaken me, shattering my confidence, and I moved on toward the lake with much less assurance than I had felt before. Stepping out of the woods, I walked along the shoreline toward the mausoleum. The mists had already spread damp, wavering tendrils of white over the ground, a thin, shifting veil of white that made it impossible to see five feet ahead of me. A frog croaked. Earl barked, leaping off into the mist, rejoining me a moment later with a frisky swagger.

I could see the mausoleum ahead now. By some curious accident of wind and atmosphere the mists had parted, leaving a small clearing free of the drifting veils, and the mausoleum stood out, black silk shimmering in the faint light, sides billowing softly, so real, not marble at all. I stood several yards away, strangely hesitant. The tent pole seemed to sway, the black marble ropes growing taut. I shivered for no apparent reason. Earl stood beside me, his silver body rigid, all playfulness gone now. It was almost as though he could sense that this was a place for the dead.

"There's nothing to be afraid of," I told him, realizing that I was speaking more to reassure myself than for Earl's benefit.

I stood just inside the clearing, the mists making a constantly moving white wall on three sides, the trees forming the other wall, dark trunks solid. Charlie had stood over there, I remembered and wished I hadn't. He had been watching me. I could almost feel those eyes on me now, and the sensation was upsetting. Charlie was dead . . . but someone was watching me. One of the tree trunks moved slightly, gleaming, and there was a white oval, a face with a hat brim pulled down over the forehead. The man in the raincoat was watching me . . . absurd, of course. Earl would have barked had there been anyone nearby. I shook my head, frowning. This wouldn't do at all. I was too attuned to the atmosphere and far too imaginative for my own good. I stepped over to the mausoleum, putting all sinister fancies aside. Earl hung back, not wanting to come any closer.

I didn't blame him. I didn't particularly relish the idea of entering that bizarre black tent, but I knew I had to. There were dead people inside, but they were dead, moldering in their crypts, and . . . this line of thought was hardly encouraging. Switching on the flashlight, I directed the weak beam on the entrance. One flap of the tent was lifted slightly and held in place by a black marble rope. The opening was barely two feet wide and not more than five feet high. I could get inside easily enough, but I still hesitated. Tight closed places, particularly tight closed places with dead people inside . . . was it worth it?

I admonished myself severely and stepped through the opening, bumping my head on the edge. I muttered something more descriptive than dignified and rubbed my head, directing the feeble beam of light over the walls. The interior was smooth polished brick painted in red and white stripes, carrying out the tent effect, but the paint had peeled and faded and the walls were festooned with large brown moisture stains. To my left were two bronze plaques indicating the resting places of Sir Robert and Arabella, and directly across from them was a small black marble bench. The stench of mildew and moisture and decay was overwhelming, a sharp sour smell that assailed the nostrils with potent force.

Cobwebs hung from the ceiling and stretched across the corners, swaying in and out as the air stirred, and dust was everywhere. I heard a tiny squeak and a rustling noise and, switching the beam of light in the direction of the sound, saw a fat gray rat scurrying across the floor. I tried not to shudder. The sound of whispers from the lake penetrated inside, and the noise echoed, as though the place were full of invisible beings urgently warning me to leave, to leave, to leave right now. It took great will power not to obey those ghostly instructions. I controlled myself, bracing my shoulders and pressing my mouth in a resolute line. I had come this far. I certainly didn't intend to give up now.

Taking out the pouch and removing the paper, I sat down on the bench and studied the intricate blueprint, holding the flashlight over it so that all the light spilled directly down. Arabella had marked everything clearly and distinctly, and the X indicated that the papers would be on the same side as the crypts, in the far corner. I took the flashlight and studied the spot, running my hands over the brick. I coughed as clouds of ancient dust flurried in the air. The bricks were neatly mortared together, and the wall looked quite solid, but as I leaned forward to study it I noticed that there was a section about four feet up from the floor where the mortar was a slightly different color, more yellow than gray. That was where I would start prying the bricks loose.

I rested the flashlight on the edge of the bench, the flickering beam directed toward the corner, and, with hammer and screwdriver, started to chip away the mortar. It was hard work. The mortar was old and as hard as rock, cracking away in small particles. The noise of my efforts echoed in the small chamber, sounding frightfully loud. The screwdriver slipped and scratched, the hammer clanged, chips of mortar fell to the floor, and dust swirled in the air. I coughed, squinting my eyes. The thin beam of light seemed to grow weaker and weaker, now no more than a faint suggestion of yellow illumination. After what seemed hours I finally managed to wedge one brick out of place.

I stuck my hand in the opening. There was nothing but space behind it, and I knew my calculation had been correct. I worked all the more eagerly, scraping away the mortar, prying the bricks loose. A second brick was removed, a third. I had to pause for a moment to catch my breath. Dust was thick in the air. A gust of wind flurried into the chamber through the entrance, blowing a cobweb into my face. I gasped, wiping the sticky strands away with repugnance. The whispers seemed to rise and swell, growing more urgent. I could hear Earl whimpering outside. After a moment I went back to work, forgetting everything else in my zeal. I banged against the wall with the hammer, impatient now, not even bothering to use the screwdriver. Bricks crumbled into pieces and fell to the floor with loud thumps and soon I had knocked away all of them not mortared against solid wall.

Bringing the flashlight over, I beamed it into the opening. There was a cache three feet deep, two feet high, and the pale yellow light shone on a rusty metal box the size of an overnight case. I caught my breath, so excited I could only stand and stare, speculating on the contents of that box. The Gordon manuscripts, I thought, awed by the sight. I knew now what the people at Malahide Castle had felt when they first discovered the Boswell papers. I took the box out reverently and set it on the marble bench. A small padlock held the lid securely fastened. I was examining this lock when the flashlight gave a final violent flicker and went out, casting the chamber into absolute darkness.

The walls seemed to loom closer, closing in, while the whispers grew louder, taunting. I was stunned, terrified by the sudden black darkness, the sound, the smell. I was painfully aware of Sir Robert and Arabella in their crypts, and it seemed I could hear them breathing, stirring, protesting my intrusion. Earl barked outside, and I could hear him running around in circles. The fetid atmosphere inside the chamber seemed to swirl angrily. I clutched the box and stumbled toward the entrance, my flesh icy cold. Bumping my head again, I stepped outside, panting heavily, and the fresh air was like ambrosia. Earl gave joyous leaps, licking my face with reckless abandon.

"There, there," I said. "Everything's fine. The light just went out—have you been missing me? Down! That's quite enough for now, fellow. What were you barking at?"

I stood in front of the mausoleum for a moment, catching my breath. I had felt a moment of sheer panic there in the darkness, but it was gone now and I felt only relief. The mists had closed in, wavering white tendrils floating a few inches from the ground, creating a sur-

realistic effect. The mausoleum seemed to vanish, black
sides billowing as the mists closed over them. The camel's
bell tinkled, a ghostly sound, but I knew it was merely a
trick of the wind.

I started back along the shoreline, Earl moving se-
dately beside me. The water lapped at the shore and
several frogs croaked, but the whispers weren't nearly
as loud as they had been inside the chamber. It was raining quietly, gentle drops pattering down from a sky gray-
black now, the moon a prisoner behind swollen clouds.
Holding the box tightly I located the pathway and turned
into the woods, wet dark trees on either side.

I felt someone watching me, but I knew now that that
was caused by my own nervous fancy. Footsteps sounded
in the bushes, quite loud, very near, but they were merely the echo of my own footsteps. Nevertheless, I was relieved to get out of the woods and start up the lawns toward the house. I could see Dower House far away, shel-
tered by the oak trees, a light burning downstairs. I
wondered if Althea was using her binoculars tonight. If
so, she was bound to see me. Earl ran on ahead of me,
leaping up on the back porch and shaking raindrops from
his body.

The back door was unlocked. Careless of Mary, I
thought, but lucky for me. It would save me a trip around
the house. I let Earl in and followed him into the kitch-
en, closing the door and shoving the bolt in place. The
remnants of a fire burned in the kitchen fireplace, hot
golden-orange coals crackling behind the screen and
shedding enough light to reveal large oak cabinets and a
drainboard cluttered with dishes. Down the hall from the
kitchen the narrow staircase led upstairs, and I hurried
up, reaching the hallway just outside my bedroom door.
Minutes later I was in my room, drying Earl off with a
fluffy bath towel.

The box was sitting on my dressing table. I could
hardly wait to open it, but I realized that Aunt Agatha
should have that privilege. I would take it to her as soon
as I could dry off myself and change into some fresh
clothes. A loud clap of thunder crashed nearby. The
whole house seemed to shake. It began to rain harder,
heavy drops pouring down like pellets. I took off my

damp clothes and dried my face, rubbing the towel over
my hair. Earl was curled up lazily at the foot of the
bed, watching me change into a leaf-brown dress and a
pair of dark gold slippers.

"Ready for another walk?" I inquired.

Earl looked dubious, but he followed me out of the
room nevertheless. Lights were burning in the hall, but
they were spaced at intervals and the walls danced with
velvety black shadows. I held the box in my arms, thinking of Aunt Agatha's excitement when I presented it to
her. Another clap of thunder crashed, causing the windows to rattle violently. Rain pounded on the roof. Earl
seemed nervous, cowering beside me as we moved slowly
down the hall. At the east wing he paused, bristling suddenly. I felt the clammy air eddying out into the hall.

"What's wrong?" I said. "Why are you——"

Someone whistled. Earl looked up at me questioningly
and then darted down the dark wing, disappearing into
the shadows. My pulses leaped, and I was paralyzed with
fright, so stunned I could hardly breathe. I heard a door
opening, closing, a loud click as the door was locked. Earl
barked furiously, the sound muffled. Someone had lured
him into a room and locked him in. I peered down the
shadowy hallway, and I saw the dark form moving in a
doorway, just as I had seen it my first morning at Gordonwood. Pitch-black shadows stirred, scurrying along
the walls of the east wing. I felt my throat go dry. My
heart started pounding. The form moved, walking down
the hall toward me. For several seconds I was unable to
move, held there by sheer, icy panic, and then I turned.

I ran towards Mildred's room. The door was standing
partially open, a wedge of light spilling out into the hall.
I darted inside, slamming the door behind me, leaning
against it, panting. It was half a minute before I had the
presence of mind to lock it.

"Mildred," I cried, "someone is——"

The room was empty. Mildred had probably gone to
carry a dinner tray to my aunt. Two oil lamps burned
brightly, shedding a golden glow over the flocked tan
wallpaper and the cocoa brown carpet. I caught my
breath, still leaning against the door, the box clutched in
my arms. The door was securely locked, and no one could

get in without breaking it down. I was safe, at least for a while. There was a telephone sitting on the dressing table, and I hurried toward it. I would call Paul. . . .

I didn't lift the receiver. I stared at the curious assortment of objects spread out on the dressing table. There was a pot of pancake makeup, several dark eyebrow pencils, a mousy brown wig, a tiny plastic tray containing two thin brown discs. Contact lenses, I realized, and I knew then just how clever they had been.

There was the sound of a key turning in the lock, and the door swung slowly open. Vanessa Shaw stepped inside. There was a satisfied smile on her sultry mouth, and she was pointing a stubby black gun at my heart.

CHAPTER TWELVE

She was incredibly beautiful, the personification of chic in a light green sheath printed with emerald green leaves, stockings sheer, shoes dark tan. She wore a dull gold bracelet, and emerald pendants dangled from her ears. Her short-clipped hair was like a tight ebony cap, and her deep blue eyes were surrounded by long, thick sooty-black lashes, the lids etched with a subtle blue-green shadow, brows curving in graceful arcs. The mouth was a little too large, a shade too red, but this defect only made an interesting contrast. I hated her. I would have hated her even if she hadn't been pointing a gun at me.

"You're quite an accomplished actress," I said calmly. All fear was gone. I had been afraid of a mysterious dark form lurking in the hallway. I couldn't take this woman or her stage-prop gun seriously.

"Yes," she replied, "though perhaps I overdid it just a trifle."

"Mildred *was* rather outlandish," I agreed, "but then acting is a magnification of life. A good actress knows how to exaggerate basic characteristics to set them off properly. Your makeup was fantastic. I suppose you used rubber pads to give the jowly effect?"

She nodded. "Tiresome, getting into character. I could hardly wait to get that gook off my face every night."

"And every night the two of you searched for the papers, roaming about the house while everyone else was asleep."

"Right. Of course I searched during the day, too, when I wasn't playing the part. Mildred was so obnoxious that no one wanted her around, so I had plenty of time to go through the vacant rooms. I was searching in the east wing the morning you arrived. You almost saw me. Wouldn't do to have you find me prowling about— I slipped into the shadows and went into one of the rooms."

"You were up in the attics yesterday, too, weren't you?"

The red mouth curled into a wry smile. "Clever of you to climb out of that window. I thought the room was a storage closet, didn't realize there was a window. I planned to tell them I saw you wandering down by the lake. They would have assumed you'd fallen in, and by the time they drug the lake you would have suffocated."

"You're really quite nasty," I said.

"Just determined, dear."

She lifted the gun a bit, getting a firmer grip on the butt. It wasn't a stage prop at all, and Vanessa Shaw quite obviously knew how to use it. I had never touched a gun in my life, but she handled the stubby black revolver as though it were a natural appendage. I realized I had to keep her talking. I had to play upon her vanity, distract her. Paul would be here soon. Something would happen. This was far too melodramtic to be real, like something out of a poor movie. I held the rusty box cradled in my arms and stared at her, marveling at my own calm.

"I can't understand how a woman with your talent could get involved in anything so—so unscrupulous," I said.

"Lucked into it actually," she replied. "Had a bit of misfortune in London. The police were looking for me— not that they could have pinned anything on me, mind you, but I found it convenient to skip town. I took a train and got off at Gordonville. No one in their right mind would *dream* of looking for a woman like me in a place like this. I went to the inn, and Charlie was a delightful host. He was absolutely in awe of me, and I found him rather amusing—you wouldn't believe it, dear, but he could be frightfully sexy under the right circumstances."

"But you got tired of him," I said, "and you met someone else."

"Right. Charlie was getting too possessive. He wanted

to marry me. Can you believe it? Anyway, I met someone else, as you say, and he told me all about the Gordon papers and we planned this whole thing. I thought it was an absurd idea at first, but when I realized how valuable the papers would be—well, it was too good a thing to pass up. Of course, there was a possibility that it would all be in vain, that the papers might not exist at all, but we decided to gamble."

"So Vanessa Shaw disappeared, and Mildred materialized."

"Right again. You seem to know an awful lot about it—how did you happen to know my name?"

"Your shoes. You left them at the cobbler's. I saw them there. There was a tag with your name on it."

"Careless of me to have given him my real name, but it had been several weeks since the affair in London and I was beginning to grow lax."

"Charlie knew everything," I said. "He—"

"He didn't know everything, but he was growing very suspicious. I had to pacify him—he was the only one who knew I hadn't left town. I went to see him every now and then. He actually believed I'd come back to him, and I felt sure I could keep him from talking. Unfortunately, he started putting two and two together——"

"So you killed him."

"Gracious no, *I* didn't, dear. Much too strenuous a job for a person with my build. I did, however, furnish a key to the inn—Charlie had given me one—and my friend slipped in and broke his neck and arranged the 'accident,' very convincingly, I might add."

She described the murder as someone else might have described a Sunday social. Her beautiful face was composed, her deep blue eyes serene as she spoke of the crime. She was no more bothered by Charlie's death than she would have been bothered by the death of a fly. Vanessa Shaw was completely amoral. Right and wrong simply didn't exist so far as she was concerned. I found it almost unbelievable that such a lovely facade could conceal such total corruptness. Lucrezia Borgia must have been like this, I thought, all beauty on the outside, all evil within.

"Your coming to Gordonwood rather messed things up," she said. "Everything was going beautifully until you came blundering in. Your aunt is such a trusting soul—she didn't suspect anything."

"Althea did," I retorted. "She knows what's going on. She has a pair of binoculars. She's seen you both——"

"Who would believe anything an old drunk like her said? Of course, we may have to arrange an accident for her, too, but first things first."

Those last words had a sinister ring. I stared at Vanessa Shaw, knowing full well that she would think nothing of shooting me. She couldn't do it now, of course. She couldn't risk it. I would have an "accident," just like Charlie. Bullet holes would cause far too much trouble for them. That was definitely to my advantage. It amazed me that I could be so calm about something so grisly. If only I could keep her talking. Paul would surely be here soon with Constable Clark. . . .

"You've really been much too meddlesome for your own good," Vanessa Shaw continued. "Shame. You'll have to be eliminated."

"Do you actually think you'll get away with it?"

"Naturally."

"You won't. I phoned the police in London yesterday——"

"I know. I overheard part of the conversation—rather, Mildred did. But you didn't tell your friend anything really conclusive, dear. You just babbled about something going on and asked him to check on some people. I didn't catch the names you gave him, but I'm sure they'll lead him nowhere. He won't have anything whatsoever to go on—your accident will look very convincing. We'll see to that."

"I told Paul Matthews everything this afternoon. He's on his way——"

"You really are a little fool, aren't you?" she said, curling up the corners of her mouth. "What's in that box? Why are you clutching it so intensely?"

"You mean—you don't *know* what's in the box?"

"I haven't the foggiest notion and really not much interest. It's irrelevant."

I managed to laugh. Vanessa Shaw looked startled, then angry, gripping the gun tighter and coming a few steps nearer.

"What *is* in the box?"

"The Gordon manuscripts," I said nonchalantly. "I found them tonight, hidden in the mausoleum."

"You're lying," she said coldly.

"Not at all. You were really quite instrumental in their discovery, Miss Shaw. If you hadn't locked me in the attic room I wouldn't have found the blueprint that led me to them."

"You found them? You—actually found them? After we've been searching all this—I don't believe it. You're bluffing. Give me that box. If you're lying——"

She was flustered, but only slightly. She glared at me with blue eyes as hard as agates, her dark red mouth an angry line. I held the box out, examining it closely as though reluctant to part with it, taunting her. She grew very impatient, waving the gun angrily.

"Give it to me!" she cried.

"Certainly," I said sweetly.

I hurled the box with all my might. It caught her in the stomach. She gasped and fell back, dropping the gun. It took her only a second to recover, and she leaped for the gun. I gave it a mighty kick, sending it flying under the bed. Vanessa gave a little cry and hesitated, her eyes wide as the ugly black weapon skidded across the carpet and disappeared, then she flew at me in fury, grabbing my hair. I shoved her away violently, and she fell crashing against the wall.

"You bitch!" she cried. "I'll——"

"Very unladylike language," I retorted.

I doubled up my fist and drew my arm back, and as she ran towards me I swung, my fist exploding into her jaw. Vanessa Shaw screamed, and then she crumpled to the floor, out cold. I was as startled as she must have been. I rubbed my stinging knuckles, staring down at her in amazement. Emma Peel couldn't have done a better job of it, I thought.

"Bravo," Paul said.

I whirled around, startled. He was standing in the doorway, a lock of golden-bronze hair plastered across his wet forehead. There was a look of amusement in his dark brown eyes. He wore a long black raincoat dripping with water, and a black hat rested on his head.

"Vanessa didn't make a very good showing," he said quietly, "but then she's a delicate thing, and you're remarkably healthy——"

"Paul!" I whispered.

"Yes," he said, smiling vaguely. "You had everything figured out perfectly, my dear, but you had the wrong man. Stanton has no idea what's been going on right under his nose. He's responsible for all this, you know. He told me about the manuscripts one night over whisky, working hard to convince me they existed. He showed me the diary entry, brought out the page he'd found in an old trunk. I brooded about it for a long time before deciding just what I'd do."

He paused, heaving his enormous shoulders. Rivulets of water slid off the raincoat, making dark spots on the carpet. "Then I went to London one week to pick up some office equipment," he continued. "I met Stephen Kirk purely by chance, in a bar. He was rather plastered, bragging about the money he planned to spend on some Shelley papers. He wanted to start some kind of collection for a library he'd built—things fell into place, and I saw how easy it would be to make a fortune."

"You had an appointment with him yesterday," I said in a flat voice. "Craig really *did* just go to the stationer's."

He nodded grimly. "Kirk's getting impatient—quite eager to buy the papers and get back to Texas. I couldn't have stalled him off much longer, but now I won't have to stall. It was jolly nice of you to have found the manuscripts for us—I was beginning to believe they'd been destroyed after all."

"It won't work," I said. "How do you intend—Stephen Kirk may be naive, but he's not dishonest. He wouldn't touch those papers if he thought there was anything——"

"I'm way ahead of you," Paul said, growing impatient. "You see, your aunt trusts me completely. She made out her will—you're to inherit everything, incidentally—and named me as her executor. When she dies I'll have every legal right to dispose of the papers any way I see fit. The sale will be quite legitimate."

"You—you plan to kill Aunt Agatha," I whispered.

"Naturally. It will be quite painless and relatively simple. I'll give her a single injection that will cause complete muscular paralysis as soon as it's introduced into the bloodstream. Nothing clumsy like poison, mind you. Curare, if you want the technical name for it. It's the same substance natives in the Amazon jungles used to dip their arrows in. She'll die with all the symptoms of heart failure, and, of course, as I'll sign the death certificate myself——"

"The pills she's been taking——"

"Harmless," he said. "Cause fatigue, slow down the blood a bit. I thought it would look better for her to drag around for a week or so before the fatal stroke."

"You intended to kill me, too."

"But of course, Susan. What other recourse do I have? You must die. Actually, it'll fit together beautifully. You'll have an accident, and the shock of your death will bring on Agatha's stroke. I like things neat."

He spoke in a lazy matter-of-fact voice, and his nonchalant manner was far more terrifying than menace would have been. He was calm, relaxed, his handsome, craggy face composed, a thoughtful look in his dark brown eyes. He took his hat off and flung it on the dressing table, running his fingers through the damp golden-bronze locks. The long, loose black raincoat made him seem even larger. He glanced at me as though I were a bothersome insect, and I realized he was as amoral as Vanessa.

"Why?" I whispered. "Why are you doing this? You've got everything, a good practice, respect——"

"You think I like being a general practitioner in a town like this? I used to have an elaborate practice in London, very plush, very profitable, but there was an unfortunate incident—a Peer's daughter hemorrhaged after an abortion I performed. She recovered, fortunately, and everything was hushed up. Must avoid scandal, the tabloids, that sort of thing, but I had to leave London, under a cloud. No one knew any of the details, luckily, and I was able to keep my license. I came to Gordonville. It was like being buried alive after what I was accustomed to."

"You took everyone in," I said. "The people in this town worship you. My aunt——"

"Agatha is a fool, just like all the others. People believe what they want to believe. They wanted to believe I was some kind of benevolent humanitarian, solid and trustworthy, giving up a rich practice to serve where I was needed. I hated it, from the first."

He smiled bitterly, the big mouth stretching wide. "I've built up an impeccable reputation. No one would believe me capable of anything as heinous as murder. I've been what they wanted—I'm a damn good doctor, by the way, and I've done a lot of good here. The local folks will be sorry to see me leave."

"You can't possibly get away with this, Paul. You must see that."

"On the contrary, I have every reason to believe I will get away with it. You'll have an accident, the shock will kill your aunt—no one would think of connecting Charlie's death with any of this. Three murders, and I'll go scot free. I imagine Vanessa and I will go to South America," he said reflectively, nodding his head gently. "Yes, that's where we'll go, and there'll be a million dollars to tide us over."

I was in a trance, stunned. I seemed to be standing a long way off, watching all this through the wrong end of a telescope. It was happening to someone else, a girl in a leaf-brown dress and dark gold shoes who was so terrified she could feel nothing, an emotionless shell. This man intended to kill me, and I merely stared at him, unbelieving. I didn't scream. I didn't try to escape. I knew that he was insane, with the same cold, methodical madness that had possessed the Nazi doctors who had performed terrible experiments in the concentration camps. Human life meant nothing to Paul Matthews.

The room was cozy and warm, snug and comfortable with the fire burning in a gray marble fireplace and the oil lamps shedding golden light over the cocoa-brown carpets. A girl in a chic green dress was crumpled up on the floor, and a man in a dripping black raincoat stood rubbing the water from his hair and calmly contemplating a murder. I was numb, and I closed my eyes, willing the nightmare to end and reality to return. This couldn't be happening.

"Are you ready?" Paul asked. He was actually smiling.

My skin prickled. Blood seemed to rush to my head. I stepped back, the numbness gone now, animal panic in its place.

"You—you can't do this," I stammered. "You can't just go around killing people."

"Can't I?" he asked reasonably, lifting one eyebrow slightly.

"You're insane!"

"Is that what you choose to think? You're mistaken, my dear. I'm not insane, I'm strong. The strong have an obligation to overcome the weak, to dominate. But we've talked long enough. The time has come to settle things. You're going to have an accident, Susan. You can fight and struggle, or you can make it easy for yourself. Either way, you die."

He spoke wearily, as though trying to reason with a stubborn child. He stood a few feet away from me, his powerful bulk blocking the way. I knew I couldn't possibly elude him. I backed away slowly, looking around frantically for some sort of weapon. The gun . . . the gun was under the bed. If I could get around to the other side of the bed and crouch down, perhaps I could reach it before . . . .

"The gun wasn't loaded," Paul said, impatient. He seemed to be reading my mind. "There's no escape, Susan."

I dashed toward the door. He seized my arm, jerking it out and twisting it behind my back with one savage motion. He clamped his free hand over my mouth, pulling me up against him. I struggled violently. He gave my arm a brutal thrust. I almost passed out from the pain. Paul forced me out the door, into the hall, towards the east wing, holding me securely and pushing me ahead of him.

"I should have killed you this afternoon," he said amiably, conversationally. "I wanted to. You don't know how near death you were as you sat there with that trusting look on your face. It took a great deal of control not to kill you then and there, but that would have been far too risky. I had to comfort myself with the knowledge that you would die later on."

We were in the east wing now. Flurries of cold, clammy air stirred in the dark hallway, and the sour smell of dust and decay was heavy. I could hear Earl whining in one of the rooms further down the hall. Paul relaxed his grip on my arm and cautiously moved his hand away from my mouth, curling his arm around my throat in a firm but painless stranglehold.

"There—that's better," he said. "If you try to scream, Susan, I'll break your neck now. You understand? Good. I thought you might like to chat a while before the end."

"Where are you taking me?" I whispered hoarsely.

"This wing has been closed up for a long time," he replied. "Everything has gone to ruin, I'm afraid, including a staircase at the end of the hall. The bannister's broken, the steps themselves rotten. You're going to tumble down them——"

"Just like Charlie," I said.

He chuckled quietly. "Right. It was a pleasure killing Charlie. He was such a meddlesome fool. No great loss to the world, Charlie. He seemed to have somewhat different views—struggled violently until I finally broke his neck and tossed him down the stairs. I found the struggle rather stimulating."

We passed the room where Earl was locked up. He barked viciously, and I could hear his paws thudding against the door. It was almost as though he could sense what was happening. He barked and snarled, throwing himself against the heavy oak door. Paul pushed me on down the hall, through the black and gray shadows that cascaded down walls covered with torn, tattered beige wallpaper. Our footsteps echoed loudly, reverberating against the walls and sounding like a whole troop of people marching down the hall, and from outside came the sounds of the storm: thunder rumbling, rain lashing, wind blowing against the windows and making them rattle.

"Clever of me to send the dogs over," Paul commented. "They would keep out genuine intruders, and at the same time they wouldn't bother me when I came to the house every night to join Vanessa."

"Althea has seen you down by the lake."

"She couldn't possibly have known it was me. She saw an intruder, but no one listens to her. Althea will be easy to handle. I'll simply commit her to an institution where she can babble all she likes. You wonder why I was by the lake? Simple. I can't very well drive up in front of the house, so I take a side road that winds through the woods down near the other side of the lake. I park under the trees, then walk along the lake to the path and on up to the back door. Vanessa leaves it unlocked for me every night."

"You—you were down there tonight, weren't you?"

"True. I wondered what on earth you were doing. When you came out of the mausoleum with the box, I knew, but I couldn't do anything about it. There was Earl, you see. He's a fickle beast—seems to have developed an inordinate fondness for you. He was quite overjoyed to see me in the woods, but he would have torn me to shreds if I'd laid a hand on you."

"You followed me."

"Quite true. Thoughtless of you to lock the door behind you when you came in. I had to force the lock with a penknife—well, my dear, here we are."

There was a wide foyer at the end of the hall. Heavy draperies were pulled across three windows but flashes of brilliant silver-blue light came in through the cracks, illuminating the scene with bizarre light. In back of us was a solid wall, the windows on our left, and directly in front was a narrow, rickety staircase, the railing splintered, several of the steps completely broken away.

Paul released me. I turned around quickly, facing him, my back to the staircase. In the weird flickering light I could see his face: heavy, ponderous, dark eyes flat, the mouth twisted down at one corner. My heart was pounding violently, my throat dry, my body paralyzed with fear. Paul held his hands up, examining them as he might examine them before an operation. I watched with horrified fascination, edging back step by step.

"You understand," he said quietly, "I must break your neck first. I will try to do it neatly, quickly. You'll have just one moment of exquisite pain, and then it will all be over."

"No," I whispered. "You can't."

He raised his hands, fingers cupped in air, and I screamed. I kept on screaming, and I saw the look of surprise on Paul's face. Then there was another noise, horrible, horrible, and I saw him grimace with pain, and then Paul was screaming, too. I stumbled against the windows, half enveloped by the mothy draperies, watching in sheer terror as Earl attacked his master, tearing clothes, tearing muscle, blood spurting, screams splitting the air. Paul broke loose. He backed away from the animal. Earl leaped forward, and Paul disappeared down the staircase. There was an explosion of sound as wood collapsed, and one last scream that seemed to hang in the air long afterwards.

Earl whined, looking up at me with mournful eyes. I could hardly see through the haze of tears. Two men were standing across from me. One of them struck a match and lit an oil lamp. The light spluttered and spread, and I saw Craig's face, mouth set, eyes grim. Peter Jacobs stood beside him, his face a study in shock.

"Peter," I whispered. "You came——"

"Righto, old girl. I talked with your fellow this morning."

"It was Peter on the phone."

"That's right," Craig said. "When he found out who Vanessa Shaw was, he didn't waste any time. She was involved in a murder in London. I happened to answer the phone this morning. He told me to keep everything as normal as possible, not to alarm anyone, not to arouse suspicion."

"I got here an hour ago," Peter said. "We've been looking all over the place for you, upstairs and down. We just finished searching the basement and decided to come up to the attics. We found the woman unconscious, heard the dog barking."

"I let him out of the room," Craig said.

Peter stepped over to the staircase and peered down.

He shuddered. I knew that Paul was dead. Craig stared at me, and I straightened up, wanting desperately to feel his arms around me.

"I found the papers," I said. "They were in the mausoleum."

"And you went down there all by yourself."

"Of course. I wanted to——"

He shook his head in disgust. I tried another approach.

"I—I think I'm going to faint," I said.

"I doubt seriously that you'll faint," Craig said, "and if you think I'm going to put my arms around you after what that dog just did you're out of your bloody mind."

CHAPTER THIRTEEN

Stephen Kirk grinned a sheepish grin, his very blue eyes full of amusement, his short sandy blond hair tousled by the breeze. He wore hand-tooled brown boots, an elegantly tailored beige raw silk suit, and a wide brown tie. Tall and lanky, boyish charm turned on full blast, he lowered his lids and gave me a look that would have melted the strongest feminine heart. We had just left Aunt Agatha on the terrace and were standing on the drive. Stephen's gleaming white Cadillac was parked in front of the house.

"That was some trick you played on me, Susan," he said, "or should I call you Winnie? You know what? You oughta be spanked. I reckon I'll let it pass this time, but next time I see you———"

"Is there going to be a next time?" I inquired.

"I reckon so. I sure do. I'll be in London awhile before flyin' back to Texas, and I'll make a point of roundin' you up—even if I have to use a lasso and spurs. I've got your address—your *real* address—and I 'spect you'll be hearin' from me mighty soon."

His eyes were appreciative and not a little mischievous as he studied me. I wore green high heels and a green and white striped dress with short, full skirt, tight waist, and low-cut bodice. I smiled, pleased with his appraisal. I felt very feminine, and very susceptible. Stephen Kirk was not only one of the most charming men I had ever met, he was by far the richest. A girl would have to think twice before turning down a chance to snare a man like this.

"By the way," he drawled, "do you think a healthy English girl like you could get used to a rowdy place like Texas?"

"Why, what makes you ask that, Mr. Kirk?"

"Just wondered. Now that I've got the Gordon papers, thought I might start a new project—somethin' a bit more personal. Would it be worth my time?"

"It might," I replied. "It just might be."

"I'm mighty glad to hear that. You hurry on back to London, hear? I'm gonna be gettin' restless."

He laid his hands on my shoulders and looked down at me, and I felt a delicious expectation. Stephen Kirk didn't kiss me. He was far too modest for that. He just clicked his tongue and shook his head, giving my shoulders a tight squeeze. I watched him climb into the Cadillac and drive away, and then I started back around to the terrace.

Aunt Agatha had finally consented to see Stephen a week ago. She had been completely disarmed the moment she laid eyes on him. She refused outright to sell the papers, but she decided to give them to him. In return, Stephen agreed to distribute a million dollars among various charities Aunt Agatha subscribed to: a home for unwed mothers, an orphanage, the S.P.C.A., and a rather radical group of etymologists who were striving to establish a universal language. Duplicate copies of the papers had been made for Craig to use, and Stephen's alma mater would keep the originals. He was planning to finance a university press so the college could publish the manuscripts. Everyone was happy except Craig. Craig had loathed Stephen Kirk on sight, and for reasons that I found enchanting.

Aunt Agatha was sitting on the green chaise longue, a stack of books and a pot of tea on the table beside her. Silvery rays of sunlight bathed the cracked white tiles, and the oak trees spread soft violet shadows. The blue delphiniums added vivid color. The gardens beyond were in full bloom. There was a fragrance of roses, underlined by the pungent odor of fertilizer and soil, and there were distant barks as Prince and Earl romped on the back lawns. Aunt Agatha had adopted them. She was the picture of robust health in her tan tweed suit and sturdy brown shoes, the chunky coral beads around her neck. She looked up as I stepped onto the terrace.

"Well, Susan, did you say goodbye to Mr. Kirk?"

"Ummm . . . he's very nice, don't you think?"

"He's maddeningly attractive, and such charm! They sure can grow 'em in Texas."

"Yes," I replied vaguely.

"I'm so *pleased* at the way things have worked out. I rather fancy Sir Robert would have approved of having the papers in Texas—much more colorful than letting them gather dust at Oxford, and Lady Arabella would have been glad to know that she was responsible for so much charity, however indirectly. Yes, I do believe she would have liked that."

A robin scolded from a nearby tree. I looked at the gardens, beautiful in the sunlight, the sky a blue-white canopy overhead. Far away, near the maze, I could see a man stalking around with hands thrust in the pockets of his tight, faded jeans. He wore a bulky beige sweater, the sleeves pushed up over his forearms, and the sunlight burnished his rich brown hair. He glanced up towards the terrace and then moved angrily on around a clump of greenery and out of sight.

"Wicked of you, Susan," Aunt Agatha said abruptly.

"What are you talking about?"

"Leading that poor Texan on like that, putting on that dress. It's cut much too low in front, dear, as you very well know—and all just to make Craig jealous."

"Why, I never——"

"Humph! Didn't fool me for a minute."

"I *like* Stephen Kirk. I may even——"

"Nonsense! He'd be a marvelous catch, no doubt about it. If I were twenty years younger—well, let's say thirty—I'd be chasing him around the square myself. He was looking at you like he wanted to gobble you up, poor soul, and with a little careful maneuvering you could land him, but you're not even about to try. You and Craig have hardly exchanged a decent word since that dreadful night—I *refuse* to dwell on that ugliness, it's over, it never happened as far as I'm concerned—and, furthermore——"

"Your syntax is getting frightfully garbled," I said pleasantly.

"Never you mind!" she snapped. "Craig's been brooding about like a regular Heathcliff, all surly and dark looks, and you've been quite skittish every time he walks into a room. You're not fooling anyone, either of you. And as for this foolishness about your leaving for Majorca tomorrow——"

"I've already set back the date of departure once——"

"It's not every day a girl has the chance to trap a genuine, bona fide millionaire, granted, but Craig's the man for you and you know it. He's going to be very important after his book comes out, and——"

"Don't fret so," I interrupted. "I *know* all that."

Aunt Agatha gave a lusty cackle. "Your tactics are rather transparent, Susan, but still quite effective. You're your mother's daughter, all right! But don't keep him dangling too long, dear. He's about to explode. If you don't give him an answer soon he's liable to go berserk."

"He hasn't asked," I said.

"Oh? Then I suggest you get a *move* on."

Mary came bustling out onto the terrace. There was a black bow in her short blonde curls, and she wore a fresh organdy apron over the tight black dress she so bountifully filled. Her brow was creased, and she looked quite put out with all and sundry.

"It's the old lush—it's Miss Althea, ma'am. She says you're to get your tai—she says you should come over right away or she'll never get the portrait finished in time. Right hateful, she was. Said for me to *hustle,* just like I didn't have a million things to do."

"Very well, Mary," Aunt Agatha replied. "And, by the way, be sure you tell Cook to bring a bottle of good wine up for dinner tonight."

"Surely," Mary said, put upon and pouting as she marched back into the house.

"I'm sure all this is wonderful for Althea," Aunt Agatha said as she got up, "but sometimes I wish she'd go back to gin. Wicked of me, I know, but she was much easier to deal with when she was drinking."

There had been a harrowing invasion of newsmen and cameramen and magazine reporters and police officials after Paul's death. Gordonwood had been like a three ring circus for several days afterwards, and somehow or other Althea had managed to make herself the center of attention, posing for photographs with out-

rageous abandon, collaring every newsman in sight and
assailing him with stories of her sleuthing. They had been
delighted by her, and, to the surprise of no one, Althea
had been the heroine of the case as far as the newspapers
were concerned. FORMER ARTIST CATCHES KILLER WITH
THE AID OF BINOCULARS, the headlines blazed, and a pub-
licity-conscious gallery in London sent a man down to in-
quire if Althea would consider giving an exhibition of her
paintings. Althea would be delighted. She had been impossible to live with ever since.

"I'm off," Aunt Agatha said peevishly. "I do hope she
finishes that bloody portrait soon. I'm quite eager to
start my new project."

"Oh?"

"Didn't I tell you, dear? I plan to start merchandising
my herbs. I mean, I have to do *some*thing. You write
books, and Althea's gone back to her painting, and there's
this divine man in London who's been begging me for
years to put my special remedy on the market. He's eager
to finance, but I'll give you all the details later."

Aunt Agatha hurried off, indomitable. Now that the
Gordon manuscripts had been found, she had to have
something else to occupy her mind and keep her perk-
ing, and I could visualize her in a smock, supervising a
crew of workers, sticking labels on boxes, going over lists
of sales figures. If she employed half her vitality, the
new project was sure to be a huge success, and I knew it
would be great fun for her. Aunt Agatha was incapable
of being bored, and she suffused everything she went into
with an electric excitement that affected all around her.

I thought about the Gordon manuscripts. There were
two of them: Sir Robert's autobiography and an anthropological study of mating customs among certain African
tribes. The books would create a sensation when they
came out, and they were sure to boost the sale of Craig's
biography, which would be published at about the same
time. It was all over. The papers had been found, Paul
was dead, Vanessa Shaw was in prison awaiting trial for
murder. Althea was going to give an exhibition, Aunt
Agatha was going into a new business . . . only one thing
remained unsettled, but I felt sure that would be resolved
soon.

I was lost in thought and didn't hear Craig walking up the steps. He was standing a few feet away when I turned, and his face was angry, mouth sullen, blue eyes very dark. I smiled pleasantly, but he merely scowled. He was really quite irresistible with those rich brown locks tumbling over his forehead and his eyebrows lowered so severely.

"That cowboy gone?" he asked in a rumbling voice.

"Why yes, he has as a matter of fact. Everything's settled. The papers are in a safe in London, and he's distributed checks to all Aunt Agatha's charities. Stephen was kind enough to bring the thermafax copies of the manuscripts with him today. They're on your desk."

" 'Stephen' is it? He doesn't waste much time, does he? I suppose I should be *grateful*. Did he make a pass?"

"In a manner of speaking, yes. He asked me how I'd like Texas."

"And what did you say?"

"Really, Craig, I don't see that it's any of your business. I don't have to answer all these questions."

"You'd damned well better," he said menacingly.

"How dare you speak to me in that tone of voice?"

"I'm getting sick and tired of this bloody cat and mouse game, Susan. It's time we got down to essentials."

"I don't know what you're talking about."

"Oh yes you do. Don't try to be coy, Susan. It's not your style. You know exactly what I'm talking about. Night before last when I came to your room——"

"And made an absolute ass of yourself," I reminded him.

"I thought you *wanted* me to come," he protested.

"Whatever gave you that idea?"

"You did. There was an invitation in your eyes."

"What a quaint phrase. I can assure you there was *nothing* in my eyes but disdain. I'm sure you've had raging success in the past with your masterful onslaughts, and I'm sure some women *adore* being grabbed passionately, but I'm not one of them."

"You're lying."

"Am I?" Maybe I was.

"What do you want me to do? You want me to woo you with tender sentiments and flowers? You want me to act like one of those guys in your silly books and pledge eternal devotion and all that rot———"

"My books aren't silly! I'll have you know the last one sold———"

"I'm a man, flesh and blood, not a gallant cavalier, and you're a woman, even if your head *is* filled with romantic nonsense."

"I don't think we need to discuss it any further."

"Oh yes we do. That bloody cowboy comes driving up in his vulgar car—it makes me furious! I think we'd better settle things once and for all. You're not leaving for Majorca tomorrow. You're staying right here. You're helping me finish my book. Later on. . . ."

"Yes?" I prompted.

"First things first," he retorted, "and if you've got any ideas about seeing Mr. Stephen Kirk again you can just put them out of your mind. Where are you going? You can't just walk away from me when I'm talking to you. I say, Susan———"

I left him standing there on the terrace with a look of utter bewilderment on his handsome face. I went upstairs to my room and put away the suitcases I had laid out earlier. I wouldn't be going to Majorca after all, but the sun and the sand held no attraction for me now. Smiling thoughtfully, I took down the sexy violet-blue silk cocktail dress. I planned to wear it tonight. Tonight Craig Stanton was going to get an answer to the question he had no idea he was going to ask.